6/7
11/22/09

Hello
GOODBYE

RANDOM HOUSE | NEW YORK

Hello
GOODBYE

A Novel

Emily Chenoweth

Copyright © 2009 by Emily Chenoweth

Published in the United States by Random House, an imprint of The Random House Publishing Group, a division of Random House, Inc., New York.

RANDOM HOUSE and colophon are registered trademarks of Random House, Inc.

LIBRARY OF CONGRESS CATALOGING-IN-PUBLICATION DATA
Chenoweth, Emily.
Hello goodbye : a novel / Emily Chenoweth.
p.   cm.
ISBN 978–1–4000–6517–2
1. Mothers—Death—Fiction. 2. Mothers and daughters—Fiction.
3. Family vacations—New Hampshire—Fiction.
4. Self-realization—Fiction. I. Title.
PS3603.H465H45 2009
813'.6—dc22   2008038496

Printed in the United States of America on acid-free paper

www.atrandom.com

1 2 3 4 5 6 7 8 9

FIRST EDITION

Book design by Dana Leigh Blanchette

*For my father, my brother,
and my mother*

. . . into light all things
must fall, glad at last to have fallen.

—JANE KENYON

Hello
GOODBYE

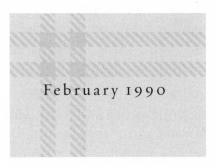

February 1990

By the time Helen comes in from her run, the first sparks of dawn, pale orange and chilly, are reaching through the bare trees in the backyard. On the other side of the fence, across a gully cut by a thin creek, the neighboring hospital puffs steam into the morning. From its vents and chimneys and pipes, clouds rise, catching light in their curling forms, turning pink and then fading to white.

She slides a filter into the coffeemaker, pours in the last of the dark grounds, and leans against the counter. She's been dizzy since her last mile, and sometimes when she turns her head quickly, her vision takes a moment to catch up: the breakfast table seems to wobble in the corner, and a silver blob resolves itself belatedly into the refrigerator. *Call eye doctor,* she scribbles on the grocery list, then adds *Folgers* below *milk* and *carrots.*

When her daughter came home for winter break, Helen brewed endless pots of coffee; four months of college had turned Abby into a proper addict. She'd become a vegetarian, too, and a quasi-environmentalist, and an earnest proponent of domestic equity. She'd lectured Helen about the necessity of composting and talked at length about "the second shift," which had something to do with how Helen, like most American women, had to work outside the home as well as make the dinners and do the laundry.

When Helen went to college, there was Mass every day in the chapel and a dress code; one studied European history, geography, and psychology. Two decades later, her daughter is going to classes with names like "Literature of Conscience" and "Gender, Power, and Identity," in jeans with sagging knees and sloppy, fraying cuffs. She reads books about poverty and oppression, which she discusses in classrooms with the children of the privileged. Abby considers Helen oppressed, though she will admit that, on the scale of cosmic injustices, her mother doesn't have all that much to complain about.

Helen yearns for her daughter when she's gone, and she knows that Abby misses her, too. If Helen could, she'd go back to college with Abby—not to learn about poststructuralism or semiology, whatever those are, but just to watch her daughter's life unfolding. She'd live in a different dorm, of course, or even off campus. But she'd be nearby, for support, and maybe sometimes they could meet for tofu burgers at the student-run café. She knows this is ludicrous, but there is no schooling the heart.

She presses the start button on the coffeemaker, and it begins to make its comforting, burbling noises. The cat stitches itself around her ankles as she stands watching the first drops of coffee fall. Helen nudges her with her toe, but the cat comes back, purring, insistent. "Oh, Pig," Helen says. "Get a life."

She rubs her temples—*Honestly,* she thinks, *maybe I should go lie down again*—and then her thoughts turn to Regina McNamara, one of her favorite and most incorrigible kids, busted yesterday for underage drinking in the city park right next to the police station. Helen has been a counselor at the county juvenile court for almost a decade. She knows all the bad kids and all the formerly bad kids, and every time she pumps her gas or goes to the grocery store she runs into one of the reformed; helping them find jobs is one of her specialties.

The coffeemaker hisses and bubbles. She stares at it, willing it to work faster, and in the corner of her eye there is a strange flash, like that of a lightbulb that has popped and burned out. A second later, there is another flare, a jagged red spark. Her headache intensifies. She puts one hand on the counter and with the other touches her brow. She is alert, wary, and her pulse quickens. She blinks and blinks again, holding on to the old avocado Formica counter that she has meant, for years, to have replaced. The light grows brighter.

There is so much to do—she has to find out Regina's court date and get Bill Gordon's transcript and see if she'll be able to beg him in to Kenyon despite his two turns in juvie (his SAT scores are excellent), and she has to defrost the ground beef for dinner, and she hasn't called Abby in a whole week—

Wait, she thinks. *Wait.*

But the light doesn't wait. The light explodes from a star that suddenly rises up from the kitchen sink. It shines in all the colors she has ever seen and in colors that don't exist on this earth—colors of nebulae or comets, colors of time and gravity. There is a glow that contains an afterglow; there is a light that eats itself and grows brighter. There is a candle burning in the center of a supernova. The light has arms, fingers, wings. The light is splendid, but there is no word for splendid anymore.

A great wonder of anguish washes over her. Her hand slips from the counter and she falls down. The sun climbs the trunks of the trees, and the clouds from the hospital billow and pulse and pull themselves apart in the sky. On the counter in the chilly morning, the coffeemaker fills with weak coffee. There is a prism in the window, and soon it will fling rainbows about the room.

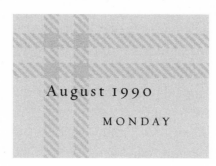

August 1990

MONDAY

Cupped in its summer valley, ringed by humped blue mountains, the Presidential Hotel rose up like a marooned ocean liner—massive, ornate, and radiantly white. It was five stories tall and, according to the brochure Abby had read, nine hundred feet long, capped with a turreted roof of scarlet tile. It was so spectacular and sudden a vision that Abby, though dulled by hours of dim tree-lined highway, very nearly gasped from the backseat.

"Voilà," her father said, winking at her in the rearview mirror. "The best hotel in New Hampshire."

Elliott had been calling it that for months—not, Abby thought, because he knew it to be true but because it drove her crazy, and this amused him. He turned in at the ornate iron gates, and they rumbled up a narrow road beneath vine-wrapped lampposts whose globes flickered with gaslight, past a pond edged by daylilies and tall, whispering grasses to the left, and then a smooth green plane of golf course to the right. The driveway curved alongside manicured lawns and flower beds and big granite boulders positioned as deliberately and artfully as sculptures.

"It looks like that ship—" Abby's mother said.

"What ship?" the other two asked.

"You know," she said, "that one . . ." Helen watched out the window as they approached, the hotel looming larger and larger. A flag at the roof's highest point seemed to pierce the low-lying clouds.

"Actually, we don't know," Abby said.

Through the bars of the headrest, Abby could see the thin, corded column of her mother's neck and the trailing ends of the bandanna that she wore instead of a wig. In March, doctors had found an astrocytoma in her frontal lobe, which had stretched, tentacle-like, into the temporal. That explained the headaches, the blurred vision, the elusiveness of familiar words; that was what caused the seizures, which had been the first undeniable indications that something was wrong.

She'd had high-dose chemotherapy and a course or two of radiation, all while Abby was away at school, and now, during a brief pause in the treatment—time off for good behavior, Elliott joked—they were taking a vacation. Abby, who wanted her mother to rest up for the next therapeutic onslaught, had been against the idea, but she'd discovered that her opinion counted less than it used to.

Elliott brought the Volkswagen to a rest by the front steps, and the valets lingering beside them uncurled from their slouches and readied themselves to be of service. Helen sat with her purse on her knees, waiting until Elliott came around and reached over her to unbuckle her seat belt.

Abby waited, too, enjoying a new and unexpected hopefulness. In a grand place like this, it seemed possible that everything might get a little bit better. She could imagine her father relaxing, her mother feeling stronger, and herself becoming kinder and more attentive. Maybe for a week, she thought, they could all be happy, transformed by the hotel's elegance and order into superior versions of themselves.

"Are you planning on getting out?" Elliott asked Abby. He hadn't shaved that morning, so there was an uncharacteristic shadow of stubble along his jawline.

She plucked peanut shells from her lap, dumped them into the ashtray, and then gathered up her backpack and her copy of *The Mill on the Floss,* a book she'd been assigned last term and hadn't even opened because she'd taken an incomplete for the course. She might have waited still longer—inside the car, inside that moment of lovely anticipation—but her door swung open and a hand presented itself to her, palm up and fingers outstretched. Beyond the hand she could see a maroon coat from waist to neck, with a double row of brass buttons gleaming like coins. She hesitated, and the hand gave a flick of its fingers. Uncertainly, she placed her palm against the other palm. The fingers closed around hers, and she felt herself drawn up into the August afternoon.

The valet had brown hair and large dark eyes, and the faint mustache he was struggling to grow was thin and wispy, like dry moss. His ears stuck out beneath his silly cap—real flappers, her father would say. The valet let go of Abby and shut the door with a smart flourish. "Welcome to the Presidential Hotel," he said. Then he bowed.

Beneath the politeness Abby sensed a fillip of mockery, light and quick as a grace note. It was directed not at her but *to* her, as if the ridiculous uniform, with its stiff epaulets and swoops of gold braid, were a joke they could share. He extracted the Hansens' old Samsonite suitcases and returned to stand quite close to her. "I hope you enjoy your stay," he said, bowing again.

She was embarrassed by his manners and by the cutoffs she was wearing. Peanut skins still clung to her thighs, and when she brushed them off, they fluttered away like ashes.

The pallid gray glow of the sun through the clouds made the Presidential almost luminescent, and the broad sweep of lawn was green and uniform as baize. A wide veranda set with rocking chairs and wicker couches encircled the hotel, and between its columns, hanging pots of scarlet geraniums were suspended like beautiful, disembodied heads.

Another valet took the keys from her father and climbed into their car, which stalled as he attempted to pull away.

"Try second," Elliott directed, "and go heavy on the clutch." To the boy next to Abby, he said, "It's got something against first gear." He peered at the boy's name tag. "Dave."

"He's good with foreign cars, sir," Dave said.

"Expensive ones, maybe," said Elliott. He kept his hand cupped around his wife's elbow.

A breeze blew Abby's hair into her mouth, and though it was not cool, goose bumps prickled up her arms. Her mother smoothed her shirtfront and pulled her bandanna down a little farther on her forehead. A peacock lurched alongside the hotel, dragging his iridescent train through the grass.

"That's the Duke," Dave said, following Abby's gaze. "The hotel has kept a peacock since 1929. He's only our third one. They can live like fifty years or something."

The Duke bobbled toward them on spindly, awkward legs. Occasionally he paused and cocked his head, as if to contemplate the world from a different angle.

"He's a big one, isn't he?" Elliott asked.

"Everyone feeds him," Dave said. "Last week I saw him eat an entire ham sandwich."

"See, Abby? Even peacocks like deli meats," her father said. She refrained from rolling her eyes at him.

Flanked by Dave and another uniformed attendant, the Hansens climbed the wide steps, slowly because of Helen. The double doors gave way to a sumptuous, intimidating lobby whose crystal chandeliers were reflected and redoubled in tall gilt-edged mirrors. There were chairs upholstered in pale silks, oil paintings of rocky, monumental landscapes, and red roses spilling like flames from a giant fireplace. A grandfather clock chimed a quarter past the hour, and it stopped the Hansens in their tracks.

"This way, sir," said Dave. He gestured toward the front desk, a mahogany edifice bookended by tidy potted trees with miniature oranges dangling from their branches.

The lobby was like a period room in a museum, Abby thought, watching a maid in a blue uniform nip a feather duster along a railing. Abby could imagine her literature professor's allergy to such a monument to a dead, moneyed lifestyle; she could picture her friends' revulsion at the liveried servants. ("It's not enough that they're being paid three-thirty-five an hour, they've got to be humiliated with costumes," her roommate, Lizzie, would say with all the indignation of a person who had never held a job herself.) Abby understood that the Presidential ought to inspire disgust or, at the very least, a whiff of class indignation, but instead she ran her hand along the smooth polished arm of a chair and felt the pleasure of fantasy: for a week, she was going to live in a *castle.*

"Helen, your purse," Elliott said to his wife. "I don't think the clasp's shut. Abby, will you help your mother with her purse?"

Abby reached for it, but her mother smiled, shaking her head, and clutched the purse to her hip. On it, an appliquéd red sun set behind purple and blue calico mountains. Helen had made it years ago and had recently begun carrying it again, though it had grown lumpy and faded and was not smart like the purses other women carried. She fumbled with the mother-of-pearl button that fastened it closed. "I've got it, honey," Helen said, but she stopped before she'd worked the shell through the buttonhole. Abby, who did not want to be seen with the purse, did not press the issue.

Elliott loomed above the desk, his big hands resting on the wood. "Hand-carved?" she heard him ask. The woman behind the desk wore a ruffled white shirt and an obliging expression. "Believe so," she said. "It's a beast, isn't it? Now, here, if I can just get your signature—"

A bellhop wheeled some departing guest's luggage outside, and a woman in a black dress wandered out of a doorway and then turned around and went back in. A breeze moved between the open doors at the front and back of the lobby; the gardenias in their hammered gold planters and the orange trees in their dark glossy pots whispered to each other. A phone rang and was quickly answered.

The woman at the front desk handed Elliott a thick envelope. "Enjoy your stay, Mr. Hansen. Everything you need is inside."

"I guess there's a bottle of Tanqueray in there," Abby heard her father say, and inwardly she cringed: his impulse to joke with clerks and valets and customer service representatives horrified her.

But the woman laughed; she could be charmed. "There's a copy of the *Eagle,*" she offered. "That's the hotel paper."

The maid had finished dusting the railing and had moved on to a marble-topped table. Abby could imagine women in moiré silks swishing through the lobby, and servants bringing letters stamped with wax seals, but there were only her parents, in their cotton pants and tennis shoes.

Elliott turned to the bellhops lingering near the Hansen luggage. "I think we can take it from here, fellas," he said. "You can go back to making trouble." He turned to Abby and frowned. "Where's your mother?"

She looked around; somehow Helen had disappeared from the lobby. Abby sighed and put down her backpack—she knew what to do. She checked the women's bathroom and then jogged down the hallway toward the ballroom, and when she didn't see her mother there, she turned around and hurried down the other hallway, past the shut doors of the hotel managerial staff. Her father stood by their suitcases with his arms crossed.

Helen couldn't have gone far, but that didn't mean she could be trusted to find her way back to them. The doctors had said the brain cancer would affect her behavior—how could it not? But no one really warned a person, Abby thought, peering into the empty dining room. No one ever said: *Someday you'll have to babysit your own mother.*

Abby went to the rear of the lobby, past a small bar tucked into the corner where a man was polishing wineglasses, and stepped out onto the back veranda. Its pillars and potted geraniums, an exact mirror of those in the front, framed the distant mountains and the silvery sky. There were Adirondack chairs and wicker couches with chintz cushions, and in them sat tanned people drinking pale wine. The air was warm and soggy as a washcloth.

Abby's mother was halfway down the porch, leaning over the railing with her purse dangling from her arm. A powder compact had fallen out of it, and as Abby neared, she watched a lipstick drop out and roll slowly over the edge.

Abby took a deep breath. It was hard, it was very hard. *Don't worry,* her mother always said, *things are going to get better.* And of course Abby believed her.

"Hey," Abby called, "your purse—"

Her mother turned to her. She looked frail and small, and her sneakers were glaringly white, and her shirt had a stain on it from when she'd drunk juice in the car. She never wore makeup anymore; who knew why she still carried it. She held her hands out to Abby.

"Oh, honey," she said, "it's so beautiful here."

Nine months, the oncologist had said, and so Elliott had brought his wife to the state where they used to live. He had changed the Jetta's oil and packed its trunk and herded his family into its upholstered seats. He'd ordered a TripTik from AAA, with the rest areas marked in red and the towns where they would stay highlighted in blue. He'd set aside two and a half days for the drive, a trip they used to make in one with a cooler full of sandwiches and hardly a pit stop. It wasn't exactly a pilgrimage, but neither was it a simple holiday.

Ten years ago they'd had a house just two hours from here, but they'd never set foot inside the Presidential—had never, in fact, even heard of it. In the summer they were campers, or renters of modest Cape Cod beach houses, whereas the Presidential was a destination resort on two thousand acres in the White Mountains, built in fin de siècle splendor in 1905, after the siècle was fin. But when Helen came home from the hospital, Elliott showed her the brochure and proposed the trip. "For our twentieth anniversary," he'd said. "We'll throw a party and invite all our old friends." This, he hoped, was a little good news to distract from the terrible news of the tumor; it would give her something to look forward to.

"You hate parties," she'd said. This was in March, when she was still more or less herself.

"Only surprise ones," he said. "Only ones I don't control."

And so in the acts of planning and organization, he had found purpose and reassurance. This hotel in the wilderness, this haute bourgeois relic, would offer them daily possibilities for diversion and pleasure. Its history was long and its order well established; it was full of healthy people pursuing leisure. At the Presidential Hotel, long naps were encouraged, cocktails were served on the veranda in the afternoons, and men were expected to wear jackets after six. There was golf and horseback riding, dance lessons and tennis, and if his wife, in her failing health, could no longer enjoy these activities, she could at least watch them being enjoyed as she rested in a chaise longue by a heated blue pool.

So he made the reservations and he put down his credit card number and he invited all their New Hampshire friends to come and stay there, too. The Schmidts and the Callahans would arrive on Wednesday, and owing to a previous engagement, the Wrights (Neil and wife number two, who had since moved to Boston) were coming on Thursday. On Friday, the night of the party, Elliott was expecting Gregory Klein and Lila Schipp and Alice Fellows, wonderful old friends all.

He hadn't told them the exact nature of Helen's diagnosis, but everyone understood the importance of their attendance. Just say the words "brain cancer," and people started paying attention. They wept, even, but they didn't necessarily ask for specifics. Elliott certainly planned to provide them; he just hadn't done so yet.

What was impossible was to share the details with his wife. With Helen, he focused on hope, on positive thinking, on the advances in modern oncology: yes, there was a large malignancy, but brilliant people were doing everything they could to fight it. He read her books about optimism and visualization, he drove her to her appointments, and he prevented anyone from mentioning the prognosis when she was in the room. He knew his wife, and he knew this was the right thing to do.

And as for his daughter? There his certainty faded. Surely she must wonder—surely she must look at her mother and think, *This doesn't look good*—and yet she'd never asked him for the facts. He thought she must grasp them on some level, because what one didn't know was so often a matter of choice, a semiconscious decision about the processing of available information. But standing in the way of Abby's comprehension were grief, anger, and pure adolescent self-absorption, the latter of which surrounded her like a veil, invisible but complex, full of flourishes and textures. It became a kind of unyielding will, and he thought it was, at base, an instinct for self-preservation. Abby didn't want the truth any more than his wife did. So he kept the knowledge for them all.

Elliott understood that in the story of his and Helen's marriage, the end had already been written. But the path to that conclusion was still left to forge—how the days and weeks would go, and what solace and joy would be found in them, were in many ways up to him. It was ironic, he thought, the way a situation that exposed once and for all the essential powerlessness of the human animal in the face of fortune also revealed the importance of good conduct within that powerlessness. There was nothing you could do, and yet you could not do nothing.

So he had summoned their friends to this place where they would eat and drink and reminisce, and when they left, they would say, for the last time, goodbye.

Their room smelled like his mother's house: floral, warm, with an undernote of sweet decay. There was a large four-poster bed, a pair of wing chairs on either side of the east-facing window, and an imposing dark armoire that opened to reveal a television set. Elliott plumped up the pillows and patted the bed, and Helen came to sit down on it. When she was settled in to his satisfaction, he handed her a can of Ensure. He tried to make her drink two a day.

"Did you get the honeymoon suite?" Abby asked, eyeing the bottle of champagne in an ice bucket shiny with condensation.

"It comes with the room," he said.

"Mine too?" She stood on the threshold of her own room, which was connected to theirs and much smaller. There was no champagne. "You gave me the maid's quarters."

Elliott grunted. He held the back of Helen's ankle with one hand and with the other slipped off her new sneakers. She leaned against the pillows, looking sleepy and pleased.

Abby moved to the window. "It's going to rain or something," she said.

Elliott slid the shoes under the bed's dust ruffle. "The weather will be better tomorrow. You can check the forecast in the *Eagle*."

"I believe you," Abby said, opening the paper.

"There's a crossword. Five-letter word for 'vacation accommodations,' if you're up to that kind of challenge."

"It could be 'hotel' *or* 'motel.'" Abby turned the page. "It says there's a nature walk at four, and at six an expert is going to talk about 'indigo buntings, dark-eyed juncos, goldfinches, and the many other songbird species native to the area.'"

Abby slid down the wall so she was sitting on the floor with her long bare legs stretching into the room. Elliott thought she should put those legs inside some pants. She folded up the paper and fanned herself with it. "Birds," she sighed.

"They also have tango lessons," Elliott said. "In the ballroom."

He opened the larger suitcase and, from a felt bag tucked inside it, extracted the loafers he planned to wear to dinner. He hadn't had time to polish them before leaving because he'd been busy packing, vacuuming the house, and watering the plants. Meanwhile Abby had dawdled, complaining that she didn't know what to wear and being no help to him.

"Hand me the *Eagle*, will you," he said, and when she tossed the paper at him, he caught it and spread it out and positioned his shoes on the pages. Next to them he placed the tin of polish, the cloth cut from a soft old T-shirt, and the stiff wood-handled brush. He was conscious of his deliberate movements, the order he sought in everything encapsulated in this ritual. He slipped his left hand inside the cool mouth of the loafer, and with his right he began to rub the polish into the leather in slow, careful circles. Abby watched him, and he sensed a judgment being made.

"I don't like loafers with tassels, but these are Cole Haan and they were on sale."

"They're fine, really," Abby said. She flopped over and rolled onto her back. "It could also be 'lodge' or 'cabin.'"

He was perturbed at himself for feeling the need to justify his shoes to her. And what was she doing on the floor? "'Hostel,'" he offered.

"Six letters."

Elliott experienced another minor spasm of annoyance that he quashed like the first. "I was testing you," he said, then added, "I don't know if I'd lie on the carpet like that."

"'Tents.' 'Sheds.' 'Hovel.'" She crossed her legs and gazed up at the ceiling. "'Resort' is six."

Helen placed the Ensure can on the end table. "I like the vanilla better than the chocolate," she said.

"Well, it's a good thing we brought mostly vanilla," he said. For a moment he felt overwhelmed by these women. He had always taken care of everyone—that was just what he *did*—but Jesus Christ, he could use a little help.

He looked around for an ashtray. He wouldn't smoke in the room, but it would be nice to know that he could if he wanted to, which he did. He wanted also to take a nap, and to pour himself a drink—not Moët & Chandon but something that meant business. In place of the things he wanted to do but could not, he continued to rub the polish into the leather in perfect circles, each the size of a quarter. The motion, repetitive, calming, was a habit of three decades—he'd been schooled by his father, who'd made his wing tips last for decades.

Abby moved her bare arm along the floor. Perhaps she had forgotten his warning, or perhaps she was trying to torture him.

"You'll have to dress appropriately for dinner," he told her.

"God, Dad, I know," Abby said. "I read the hotel brochure." She stood up, flicked her hair at him, and went into her own room, shutting the door gently but firmly behind her.

He set the shoes on the newspaper while the polish soaked in. In five minutes he would buff them with the boar-bristle brush and then with a sponge, and they would gleam as if they'd just come off the shelves.

Helen had taken out her journal. He peered over her shoulder.

Arrivle. It's good to be out of the car it was a very long drive—poore Elliott! The hotel is very nice. It has a peacock.

"The Duke," he said.

"What?"

"The Duke. The peacock's name."

"Don't read over my shoulder, nosy," she said.

He kissed her on the warm top of her head. "Sorry."

In the bathroom, he washed his hands with a pygmy bar of scented soap and took the prescription bottles from the Ziploc bag he'd packed them in and sorted her pills into neat compartments labeled with the day of the week and the time she was supposed to take them.

He the smoker, the drinker; she the runner, the eater of salads—of course he'd thought he'd die first. There were the lungs to go wrong, or the heart. There was the blood pressure and the soft little walnut of the prostate. He had imagined Helen holding his hand on his deathbed—never, ever the other way around, and he had the fantastic life insurance policy to prove it. But Jesus, they weren't even forty-five.

He took up his shoes again and, one by one, gave them the final, gentle buffing. The trees outside the hotel window were green and lush. It was August, month six.

A_{gainst} Helen's back, the pillows are soft and pleasing. Elliott has turned on the television, so they're listening to a documentary about trout. Listening only, Elliott because he is slowly pacing the carpet, and Helen because the TV is on the other side of the room, and with her vision the way it is, the picture seems too dim to bother watching. Elliott stops to adjust her pillows and she waves him away: they're fine where they are. But he is eager to make her comfortable—feeling, as he does, that he knows the way to do it best—so she lets him try, and when he's done, she shifts everything back to where it was.

Her wig sits in a plastic bag on the nightstand, folded like a hibernating animal. Though Elliott bought a Styrofoam head to keep the wig's shape, he hadn't wanted to bring it to the hotel, and that's just as well; she doesn't like looking at the featureless whiteness where a face should be, or that long, inhumanly thin neck. Abby had drawn eyes and a mouth on it, which somehow made it worse. Each curl on the wig looks just like its neighbor, and every hair is the same color as the one next to it. The inside is woven mesh with a bit of stretchiness. If Helen holds it in front of her face, she can see tiny pinpricks of light filtering through. It's called a cranial prosthesis.

Her hair never looked like that. Her hair was like a mane—shiny, coarse, tough. She had it frosted every two months at the salon on Winter Street, blondish streaks to blend in with the gray, which had seemed a more genteel acknowledgment of her age than a cover-up dye job.

When it hadn't fallen out right away, she had allowed herself to think that perhaps it wouldn't. She'd heard of people going through a full run of chemo and keeping it all, hadn't she? Or if she hadn't, mightn't she be the first? But of course it had happened: fistfuls in the shower, circling around the drain, clumping like birds' nests. She sat on the floor of the bathroom and cried, even though she'd promised herself a hundred times that she would not.

Goodbye, vanity, she thought—*goodbye, what kept me looking like the rest of you people.*

Now that her hair's all gone, she doesn't mourn it. It's just another thing that is. She doesn't want to be sad. She knows a positive attitude is key to recovery.

It's too bad about her eyebrows, though. They said that she'd keep them, and yet they are thinning, lightening, blowing away.

Elliott is done hanging up his jackets and polishing his shoes, and now he stands in front of her, wanting to make sure she's all right. "What was that ship you were talking about?" he asks.

For a minute Helen closes her eyes to remember, forming a circle with her thumb and forefinger because someone once told her that helped concentration. She was talking about how the hotel reminds her of the sternwheeler she used to watch when she was little. It, too, was vast and white, with a gleaming red roof, and it rose from the silty brown waters of the Mississippi as perfect and incongruous as this venerable hotel in the middle of the New Hampshire woods.

She and her sister used to stand on the bluff above the river and watch for the ship on picnics with their parents, their father with his whiskey in a thermos and their mother hardly eating, smoking Pall Malls. For the girls there was chicken salad and carrot sticks, and, for dessert, ice cream tucked away in the bottom of the cooler, half melted by the time Helen and Susan got to it.

That ship at nighttime is her earliest memory: the majestic dark shape of it, like a shadow strung with lights, sliding through the black water between Iowa and Illinois. Helen was two, wrapped in a blanket in her mother's arms. Susan was five and too big to be held. The windows of the ship were gold, and silhouettes moved across them. The mammoth stern wheel turned and water slid off it in white-edged sheets; the wake slipped away on either side. Blinking lights on the ship's prow and stern were echoed by fireflies flickering on and off along the shore. On windless evenings, before it passed beyond the point and disappeared, the voices, the laughter, and the tinkling percussion of forks and knives that floated back to them were the very sounds of glee.

"The *River Queen,*" Helen says finally. "My father's wake was on it."

There was that, too. For a moment she'd forgotten about that.

After almost three days of breathing the same seventy cubic feet of air as her parents, sitting in the Jetta's backseat and staring at the backs of their heads, Abby was now, with every step she took down the hall, coming out from under them, sloughing them off like old clothes. She waited in the fourth-floor lobby for the elevator, and when it came she directed the small red-faced man who operated it to take her to the main floor. He bowed, cranked his gleaming brass lever, and they descended.

To appease her father, she had changed into a cotton dress in forget-me-not blue scattered with yellow, pink, and green flowers. It was meant to please her mother, too, who had sewn it especially for Abby's high school graduation. The dress had a low scooped neck, a fitted bodice, and a slightly flared skirt that hit just below the knee. It called, demurely, for a rope of pearls; it wanted cucumber sandwiches, champagne cock-tails, tulips in a pink glass vase.

In the lobby the same maid was dusting the mantel, and Abby wondered if she was doing it for show, the way the Ohio Historical Society's pioneer village employed women to card wool that would never be made into blankets or sweaters. The maid was very pretty, and her efforts gave the room a special, almost fragile gentility, as if it required constant and dedicated attention. After a few more moments of photogenic labor in the fireplace area, the maid tucked the feather duster into the pocket of her apron and went outside to the back veranda. Abby followed her.

In the gray distance, the mountains pushed their shoulders into the sky. Below the porch railing lay a rectangular stone patio on which two small boys were marching in a circle. To the right was a lawn dotted with lilies, and then another, larger patio with white wrought-iron tables, and then more well-tended flower beds. Toward the south end of the hotel, the pool was a sliver of blue.

The maid walked purposefully down the length of the porch. Curious, Abby continued to trail her. The girl couldn't have been over sixteen, but away from the direct gaze of her employers, she had a jaunty, swinging walk that sent the ties of her apron swaying and caught the eye of a man reading a book in a wicker chair. At the far end of the veranda, the girl met up with the valet who had driven away in the Hansens' car; he gave her a tap on the ass and a cigarette that she tucked behind her ear. The pair of them descended a set of stairs, saying things Abby couldn't hear. The girl had a high, clear giggle that the valet coaxed from her easily. He was older, in his twenties, maybe, and the girl seemed familiar with his flattering attentions.

On the ground level, they lingered by a heavy double door that the valet kicked idly with his heel. After a moment the door swung in, and a plump girl in a white uniform poked her head out and said, "How many times do I have to tell you not to smoke outside the spa?"

The valet said, "Back off, sis," and leaned against the wall. "I'm on break."

She said, "You're a bastard, Jamie," and shut the door again.

In the shade of the overhanging porch, the maid and the valet smoked, squinting out over the lawn. Abby thought about asking them for a cigarette, but then they would figure out that she didn't really know how to smoke it.

They didn't see her lingering by the trail bike rentals, but she began to feel self-conscious, there in her homemade dress. She smoothed its soft folds, remembering how she'd planned to wear it to spring parties at college, to soirees with boys in seersucker and sport jackets. But as it had turned out, she'd allowed herself to be misled by stories of her mother's alma mater, a Catholic school where women earned, as the joke went, their MRS's. There were no garden parties at Abby's college, and girls did not wear tea dresses. Girls wore vintage skirts and combat boots and called themselves womyn.

These girls lent Abby their ripped jeans, and Lizzie gave her all the sweaters she didn't like anymore, and someone else gave her a pair of Doc Martens that were too small. So Abby became a wearer of items discarded by other people, and no one ever saw the dress her mother had made for her, that lovely thing designed for the person Abby once thought she wanted to be. She was sorry she had put it on now—it had been only for her parents, and they were napping and couldn't see it. She should have worn something that made her look like a person with eccentric opinions and bohemian glamour. She should have put on something of Lizzie's.

When the valet and his girl were done with their cigarettes, they walked back the way they had come, passing Abby without acknowledging her. She waited for a while, in case the spa girl poked her head out again, and when she didn't, Abby resigned herself to solitude and walked north along the hotel's lower story.

In the small garden patio she'd seen from the porch, the little boys were still stomping in a circle, brandishing sticks and shouting rhythmically. Fountains stood at each corner like sentries: thin streams of water poured from the mouths of a dolphin, a lion, an eagle, and a stag, splashing into shallow copper basins. The boys lifted their knees in a sturdy march as butterflies turned fluttering somersaults in the air above them.

They were probably the same age as the twins she had been babysitting since July; Abby thought of them with a twinge of hatred. They had sharp, shrill voices and an aversion to books, television, and anything else that would keep them quiet and immobile. Their mother, Tracey, was writing her master's thesis on masculinity in midcentury American novels; she was near Helen's age yet seemed so much less of an adult. She didn't understand that her children lacked tenderness or conscience, didn't know that her darlings screamed and kicked and threw tantrums on the way to the pool, and that when they fought, they did so mercilessly, biting fingers and pinching each other's tender genitals.

But Tracey's house was big and air-conditioned, and Abby liked being there—or was glad, at least, to be away from her own house, where the kitchen counters displayed rows of orange pill bottles and the refrigerator and cupboards were now stocked with convenience foods: tuna in single-serving cans, little bags of pretzels, storebought trail mix, preshredded cheeses and deli meats in slim plastic envelopes. Her mother never would have bought these things—her mother had made her own *yogurt*.

When Abby had arrived home for the summer, the house was without clutter, and the furniture in the den had been rearranged. The floor gleamed, slick and honey-colored (she used to slip around in her socks, pretending she was ice-skating), and the staghorn fern cast long fingers of shadow across the hall. Pig seemed not to know who Abby was and meowed at her from underneath the dining room table.

Abby had plucked a banana from the fruit bowl and, peeling it, wandered outside. Her parents were by the backyard fence, down near the place they'd buried Licorice, Pig's predecessor, six summers before. Her mother and father, in old clothes and gardening gloves, were kneeling on the grass, their heads bent together, planting begonias in the shade of the redbud tree.

They didn't notice her standing by the back porch, but a robin, perched a few feet away in a dogwood, gave a sharp call and winged himself up toward a more solitary perch in one of the buckeyes. The peonies had browned and dropped; it was unseasonably hot, and there was a hazy moisture, a kind of slime in the air.

"Hello?" Abby had called. "Doesn't anyone want to welcome me home?"

They had risen then, her father helping her mother up. Her mother's face, thin and shadowed beneath a big straw hat, was beaming but unfamiliar.

"Welcome home! Is your hair pink?" That was the first thing her father had said, after she'd driven all the way from Connecticut, 150 miles on I-84 and then God knew how many across the deadly dullness of Pennsylvania, one long end to the other—begged, even, a ride from someone in Cincinnati so that Elliott wouldn't have to come get her. "It looks pink."

He was smiling at her, but she was furious at him for asking. Her hair *was* pink, though she had been trying for weeks to wash it out and thought she had nearly succeeded. The Manic Panic had been such a perfect color in its jar—a rich, bold magenta. Abby had bought it after her mother's biopsy, on one of those days when defiance felt like the only response to fear and despair, one of those days she had put on a black bra under a white shirt and borrowed a tall pair of boots but it hadn't seemed like enough. It had been a stupid idea, and she had been encouraged, she now believed, by girls who did not have her best interests at heart. For what did she have but her looks, her wholesome, rather vague prettiness? Everyone at college was smart—it was one of those places.

Pink-haired Abby had reached for her mother and held her thin shoulder blades cupped beneath her palms. "Oh, Abby," Helen had whispered, "I'm so glad to see you. I wanted to get the begonias in before you came."

Then Abby had gone into her room with its cheerful yellow walls and ratty old stuffed animals and stepped in a puddle of Pig's vomit.

"Pig's having a hard time with things," her father had said.

Pig? Abby had thought. *Pig?*

A shriek came from the patio. It seemed that one of the boys had accidentally hit the other with his stick. But after a momentary pause, they resumed their marching with even greater fervor, around and around, as the butterflies rose and dipped alongside them.

As Abby turned away, she caught her reflection in a window. She looked just like her mother—everyone said so.

At the entrance to the dining room, the maître d' stood patient and attentive, hunched like a turkey vulture inside a voluminous black tailcoat. He bade them a good evening and, upon learning their name, drew a careful X next to the line that read *Hansen, 5:00 P.M.* Elliott, who had called five minutes before to say that they were on their way down, admired the careful adherence to codes of decorum.

The room was octagonal and rosy pink, with diners scattered throughout. Elliott supposed the maître d' had placed them that way to give the illusion of greater numbers, but each table seemed a solitary outpost beneath the vast, domed ceiling. On a small stage along the south wall, a three-piece ensemble played some lively, syncopated number over the low conversation and the scrape of silver against good china.

The maître d' led them to a table by a window overlooking the distant mountains and pulled out two of the dark finial-topped chairs for Helen and Abby. There was a kind of vulgar splendor to the place, Elliott thought, with its Corinthian columns, its foliated reliefs, its heavy chandeliers and wall sconces. His mother would like it, he was sure, and his daughter was looking impressed. That was it, perhaps—it was a room designed to please women.

He handed Helen her napkin and she placed it in her lap. "I guess we know how some people spend their Social Security checks," he said.

"What?" his wife asked.

"Old people," he whispered. "They're the only ones here."

Helen giggled. "Be nice."

"It's practically the middle of the afternoon," Abby said. "Maybe we could make reservations a little later tomorrow. You know, sort of miss the geriatric time slot?"

"Your mother was hungry," Elliott said.

"Yes," said Helen. "Yes, I am."

"We have snacks in the room," Abby said.

Elliott opened his leather-bound menu. "We'll take that into consideration."

The Hansens had always eaten dinner together, but they were not restaurant people; Elliott knew his wife and daughter would appreciate the good linen and the elaborate arrangements of delicate stemware, light and shiny as soap bubbles.

"Excuse me, I've got some extra forks?" he said, holding one up, pretending to summon the waiter. Helen laughed again, but Abby feigned absorption in her menu. "Left your sense of humor in the trunk, I see," he said to her.

"Ha," his daughter said. She had changed into a white cotton dress edged with lace—sort of Indian-looking, he thought—and she looked innocent and clean and petulant.

He scanned the menu with interest. For an entire week they wouldn't have to eat anything from a cardboard box or a tin can. Nor would they have to sate themselves on the contents of the Hansen freezer, which was stuffed with casseroles, stews, and hashes from everyone they knew: beefy macaroni wedged up against spinach lasagna, chicken cacciatore perched on their neighbor Judy's hamburger pie. Half the women in town had cooked them a freezable dinner.

If the women delivered their dinners while Elliott was at home, he of-

fered them a smile so wide it was nearly painful. He held the door open
with his right hand and accepted the food with his left, gesturing them in
with a welcoming nod. Some were proud of their casseroles, while others
blushed and said, "It's not gour*met*, but it'll get some protein in you."
There were some who indicated that the Pyrex dish was needed for an
upcoming potluck, thereby forcing the Hansens to eat whatever it contained sooner rather than later. There were the ones who came embarrassed, who spoke in a whisper and handed over something in a
bag—once, a family value meal from Kentucky Fried Chicken, complete
with mashed potatoes, biscuits, and a two-liter bottle of Coke. Elliott
hadn't eaten Kentucky Fried Chicken before and was surprised to find
that it was delicious.

A woman from Helen's office, someone he'd never even heard his wife
mention, came on a rainy evening in May. She wore a man's trench coat,
and her hair was wet. She thrust a warm pan wrapped in tinfoil into his
hands. "Isn't there something *else* we can do?" she cried. Elliott was struck
by the way the tears were distinct on her wet face—shinier, somehow,
than the rain that also fell on it. Her mascara was running. He invited her
in, as he did the others, but she shook her head and ducked away toward
the car she'd left idling. "It's beans!" she called over her shoulder. "Rice
and *fucking beans.*"

"I'll bet this is going to be delicious," Helen said now. She held her
menu carefully. Her diamond earrings, pretty little solitaires Elliott had
given her for Christmas, glittered when she turned her head. "Can you
help me decide?"

Elliott scanned the menu for things that were easy to cut and chew.
That had been the first sign, actually—a dinner at the Heartland Café
when she'd asked him to read the menu for her. "I must need new
glasses," she'd said; "I'll have to make an appointment." He said, "Would
you like the baked salmon *en croute* with wild rice and dried cherry pilaf?
Or maybe the rosemary roasted chicken with *harryco vairs* and braised
whatever it is?"

"On-*deev,*" his daughter said.

"Oh, is that French, too?"

"I don't know what it is," Abby said. "Maybe it's *en*-dive."

No one was sure what *en croute* meant either but they settled on the salmon for Helen. A woman wielding silver tongs served them two rolls apiece, each topped with a worm of caramelized onion; the butter came in spheres stacked in a triangle, like little cannonballs.

Elliott did all the ordering. The waiter kept his hands crossed in front of his black cummerbund and wrote nothing down. He was tall and thin, and he hadn't grown into the nose that protruded aggressively from his narrow face. His hair was the color that mothers used to call dishwater blond. "Very good, sir," he murmured after each item. "Very good."

He wasn't handsome, but he was young and self-possessed. *I was like that once,* Elliott thought, *but better-looking.* "I don't suppose you'd tell me if it wasn't very good," he said.

"Dad," Abby hissed.

"I'm just teasing him, Abby. He can take it." Elliott looked to the waiter to confirm this.

"It's all good, sir."

Abby coolly detached herself from their interaction—Elliott could tell she was trying to be dignified, to let the help stay help—and he was unable to stop himself from goading her. "My daughter," he said to the young man, "she's easily embarrassed."

In the light slanting through the window, her eyes were a startling pale shade of blue. The waiter grinned. *Too pretty for you, kid,* Elliott thought. When he was that age, he'd been a hot ticket; he'd had two girl-friends at once, both cheerleaders. Linda and Bobbi had powdered cheeks and soft, eager lips, and it was for their sake that he finally told his mother he'd rather cut off his legs at the knee than become the priest she was hoping for.

"*Please,*" his daughter said, when the waiter had gone. "Just please."

When Abby came home after her first semester of college, her voice at the dinner table was loud and bright and she would not touch the chicken; Elliott thought she sounded hysterical. She called her new friends—coddled eighteen-year-olds, all of them—"women," which he considered an abrupt, undeserved promotion into experience and adult-hood. Abby's legs were unshaven and she wore a style of batik skirt he re-membered from the seventies, and if it had been ugly then, it was even uglier twenty years later. He hated to imagine where she'd gotten it—a dirty salvage store or some community swap meet.

Her arms and shoulders had seemed rounder, and her womanly bottom had shocked him: the ten pounds he knew she'd gain had gone straight to it. She was hypersensitive, ready to pounce on anything he said. She appeared to think she had to defend women and minorities against him. Him! A private-school headmaster who'd spent the last ten years of his life trying to get female and black students to attend his little academy. Helen was incapable of being annoyed by Abby and her strident, vaguely articulated new beliefs. At each meal she cooked twice as many vegetables and piled her daughter's plate high with them.

Now Abby was thin again and unfamiliar to him in a new way: burnished, intermittently scornful, with larger breasts. He thought perhaps she was even taller.

"Please what?" he said, but it was the Tanqueray talking.

She turned away from him and took a sip of her water. He wondered, without wanting to, how many boys at her fine liberal arts college had appreciated her blossoming.

The food, when it came, was embellished with sauces and creams, and something frothy and green lay puddled alongside Elliott's potatoes. He asked the waiter what it was.

"Parsley foam, sir," the boy said, gliding away. "It's a new twist on the garnish."

"Well, it's certainly interesting," Elliott said. "It looks like soap scum. Parsley foam. I thought maybe they had a dishwashing problem." He scraped his steak free of its accoutrements; the herbs, the innovative garnish, and the tiny rings of fried shallots lay in a small mound in the corner of his plate. "It's not Pizza Villa, is it?"

Abby held up a piece of string that had come tied around what looked like a miniature purse made out of cabbage. "My food's wrapped up—like a present."

"It looks like something only a rabbit would love," he said.

"At least nothing died to make it."

"That cabbage isn't alive," he said. "Or those tomatoes. If that's what those are."

"*Dad,* of course they're tomatoes. What else would they be?"

"I don't know, something really French," he said.

His wife ate slowly. The pink fish, stripped of its pastry crust—so that was what *en croute* meant—looked naked and fleshy, and the dried cherries were the deep blackish red of blood clots.

But, he had to admit, everything was delicious. He felt the softening bloom of the alcohol, the gin's slight heat in his throat, and it slowed his blood and calmed him. He ordered another as the waiter slid by. Two was the limit, but he would truly enjoy them both.

"Did you know the dining room is round so that no one would ever feel banished to a corner?" he asked Abby.

"You're making that up."

"I'm not." He had once convinced her that the trees grew straighter in New Hampshire than they did in Ohio; it had something to do with latitude, with weather patterns. Elliott had a reputation for small-scale trickeries, but he fancied they were funny, whereas there was nothing amusing about this pretentious pink room. The woman at the front desk had told him about the shape. "I guess it's not really your crowd here, is it?"

Abby sliced into her cabbage; she was not very graceful with her knife. "I brought a book," she said.

"There are trail rides," he offered. "There's a cog railway you can take to the top of Mount Washington. You'll be able to find things to do."

"I know," she said, but she kept her voice distant, noncommittal. "Maybe I'll take a tango lesson."

"When everyone gets here, it'll be more fun."

"For *you,*" she said.

He ignored that because, ungenerous though it was, she had a point. His friends would all say how much she'd grown up, and she would be pleased and embarrassed by their fleeting attention, and then she'd be left alone, a spectator to their nostalgia.

"Eva said we could have a—you know," Helen said.

"A what?"

Her eyes searched his face, as if she were reading something there. "A picnic," she said finally.

"That's a good idea," he said. "Who doesn't like a picnic?"

Actually, he didn't, but it was typical of Eva Schmidt to plan something like that; she liked to make things special. She'd been Helen's best friend in New Hampshire, and she'd sent Helen bright, newsy letters once a week ever since that first seizure. She'd also put her lawyer husband, Henry, up to calling Elliott now and then to check in. They were good people—less entertaining but more reliable than their neighbors, Ruth and Dom Callahan, who were also dear friends but had never quite abandoned the self-indulgence of their youth.

The waiter who had delivered their food had been replaced by another tall kid with dark hair and a clever, insinuating sort of grace; he was exceptionally attentive to them. When Abby returned to the table after redoing her hair in the bathroom (she'd had it up, but now it fell around her shoulders in brown waves), he sprinted over to pull out her chair. Elliott saw their eyes meet and a smile crack open the boy's face like an egg. Abby ducked her head and blushed, and then the waiter looked up at Elliott, his dignified but obsequious expression already back in place. *Maybe not too pretty for you,* Elliott thought, *but don't get any ideas.*

Their dinners were cleared and their desserts brought out. They could mark the time by the coming and going of strangers, by the business of consumption and digestion. The band had moved from Bach to Sinatra to Berlin, and now they were embarking on "The Blue Danube." Out the window the clouds had broken and then reassembled themselves into thick masses, and the setting sun made a gilded ridge along the spine of the mountains.

Elliott watched a couple walk hand in hand to the dance floor and join the others already there, turning in desultory circles. Abby eyed the dancers as well, and he wondered if she wished she were waltzing with her boyfriend. Not that kids knew how to waltz these days. His students kicked and flailed their arms at each other as if dance were a form of combat. His daughter tucked her hands under her chin, looking wistful. Who was she missing? The boyfriend? Some lacrosse-playing Choate graduate in Connecticut?

The waiter slid by again, close behind Abby's chair, and something white fell from his right hand. He stooped to pick it up—it was a napkin. His shoulder, as he rose, caught a piece of Abby's hair, and for a moment, that one soft curl lifted, too. Then it slipped back down his jacket, clinging to it, tender as a caress.

Elliott felt his breath inexplicably catch in his throat. Outside in the gathering dusk, a tree shivered and trembled with birds.

It's bedtime, and there are only two pills to take, one a cellulose capsule full of gray powder and the other a white thing that looks like aspirin but has an odor that is chemical and bitter. It lies in the warm cup of Helen's palm like a lost button.

What a luxury it had been to put only food in the body—what ease, all those years she never even took vitamins. No Advil or Tylenol, either, not until the headaches, pinwheels of pain that whirled behind her left ear, then rose to her forehead before descending to the base of her skull. They've gotten better, but still Elliott rubs her back when they're bad. He pushes his thumbs deep into her muscles, and sometimes it's too much to take in at once, the pain in her head and the delicious hard sweetness of his hands.

"What do you think?" he says. His long body is on the bed, rigid and heavy, like a felled tree. "About this place?"

"I think it's fantastic."

Everywhere she looks, someone's bowing at her or tipping his hat.

There are silk walls in the lobby powder rooms, there are silver candle-sticks on the mantels, there are bowls of roses everywhere. An air of po-litesse hanging over the place like a mist.

In her bathroom the soaps are wrapped in powder-blue paper, and there are pretty cobalt bottles of cleansers and unguents. There are silver towel racks and a deep sink with two taps, one for hot water and one for cold. Above the sink, the mirror in its heavy silver frame greets Helen with her own face, gently distorted in the rippled old glass, as if she has come to visit some other version of herself.

She imagines that this self is new and improved, no longer something that has to be driven to sterile offices with taupe-colored walls and walked down long, overlit hospital corridors to be examined by affectless, competent strangers. Her body was once sealed and private, but now every week there is a new person touching it, sticking a needle in it, pho-tographing it with a special camera. There are medicines she's told to swallow and lotions she's supposed to use.

She goes to a support group for cancer patients now and then, and one day someone in a waiting room gave her a copper bracelet and prom-ised it would balance all her electromagnetic energies. This someone was bald like Helen, with a swollen, moon-shaped face and wide, frightened eyes—this someone, huddled inside her faded cardigan, looked *done for.* Helen took the bracelet, but she kept it sealed in a plastic bag, as if it were contaminated.

Nothing in the public property that is her body works the way it used to. She's like the old dishwasher in the kitchen: the lights go on, the water runs, and it tries—oh, it tries—to wash the forks the way it once did. But still they come out dull and sticky, with bits of food wedged in their tines.

She swallows her pills, both at the same time: she's a pro. She can do four at once if she feels like it. Next she squirts toothpaste on her tooth-brush, brushes her teeth, and rinses her mouth with Scope. Sometimes she can't believe she keeps doing these things. Sometimes she thinks, *Fuck the teeth, I have cancer.*

But she always puts the toothpaste on her brush anyway. What is she but a gathering of affections, a collection of habits? What, after all, is anyone?

In the emergency room waiting area, Elliott had sat on a hard plastic chair beneath the television, so that all the people in the room were turned toward him, their faces tipped up, inexpressive and contained. Cool bluish light shifted and flickered across their foreheads. He could hear gunfire and shouts: above him the cops were chasing the bad guys. A little boy climbed up on a neighboring chair and sat companionably beside him for a few minutes before wandering back to his mother. Elliott looked in everyone's eyes and tried to imagine who in the room had it worse, and as the hours went by and he was not allowed to see Helen, he began to suspect that it was he and his wife.

Later, he and the admitting physician rode silently in an elevator to the ICU. On the second floor, the metal doors opened and a nurse pushed an entire bed in between the two of them. There was an old man on the bed, pressed between tight sheets so that only his head and neck were visible. Elliott stood over him as he lay senseless, his mouth open, his skin shadowless in the institutional light.

The nurse was chewing gum, and the cloying strawberry smell of it filled the car. Her hair was slicked back into a ponytail except for a high puff of bangs in front, stiff and round and yellow as a dahlia; her eyes were lined with black and her lips were thin. She looked like one of Helen's girls from court, he thought—the skinny ones who hung out in the Kroger parking lot, drinking rum in Slurpee cups while their boyfriends chewed Skoal and compared the engines of their Pontiacs.

"When seizures happen in a series like this, it's called *status epilepticus*," the doctor said, leading Elliott down a hall. He had fleshy cheeks and eyebrows like gray slashes of fur above his eyes. "It is often fatal. But in your wife's case, it was not."

In a small white room, Helen lay sleeping, a tube thicker than a garden hose curving down her throat and an IV dripping something into the back of her hand. Her dark hair spilled over the pillow. He sank into a chair and watched her until she woke and reached out for him.

"She can't talk," a fat nurse said. "Because of the tube." She was frighteningly matter-of-fact, the way she switched one bag with another, changing whatever it was they were pumping into his wife. "Sometimes they try but it's best not to encourage them."

That was before anyone knew what was wrong. Head injury, epilepsy, meningitis, encephalitis, tetanus, heatstroke, tapeworms, carbon monoxide poisoning, malaria, rabies, African sleeping sickness, shellfish poisoning, electrocution, lupus, Rocky Mountain spotted fever, syphilis, whooping cough: all could cause seizures.

Three weeks later, after the biopsy, Dr. Buxbaum told him it was a malignant tumor. Elliott heard the news alone, in the doctor's book-lined office at the university hospital. Through the window he saw a patch of white Ohio sky, a pigeon in a bare tree.

Dr. Buxbaum had a wide, full mouth and sympathetic eyes; she was short and delicate and beautiful. The first time they met, Elliott had felt—to his discredit, he knew—a faint but undeniable welling of doubt in her abilities. How could this small, lovely woman be the hospital's best oncologist? But she had reassured him with the frankness of her manner and the Yale diplomas on her walls.

There were things they could do, Dr. Buxbaum told him, and they would certainly do them: radiation, chemotherapy, steroids, anticonvulsants. She folded her hands together and tucked them under her chin. "In cases like these, a cure should not be considered the only successful outcome of treatment," she said. Her voice was low and compassionate—the kind of tone one never wanted to hear from a doctor.

Outside, the pigeon fluffed his feathers and hunkered down. His branch trembled in a gust of wind.

"A happy death," Elliott heard himself say.

"Pardon?"

"It's what we said in Catholic school when we didn't like one of the fathers. 'Let us pray for his happy death.'"

She knitted her brows.

"It was a joke," he said. "We meant it as a joke."

He put his hands on the edge of the desk, appealing to this woman as if it were possible for her to make anything different. He had a vision of his wife, waiting down the hall in a polka-dotted hospital gown tied with thin strips of cotton, a shaved patch on the side of her skull and staples holding the skin together in a red welt, and then he imagined his daughter, studying in a library in Connecticut. *What am I going to tell them?* he asked himself. *What am I going to say?* Helen had had some *headaches.*

Dr. Buxbaum handed him a box of tissues. "Considering the size of the tumor, she is in remarkable shape. A positive outlook is beneficial, and it may be in her best interest to keep such an outlook as long as possible."

What he understood her to mean was: *Don't tell her she's doomed.* And yes, he believed she was right.

Elliott had bought a pack of Merits on the way home, and without ceremony or regret he lit his first cigarette in six years. The inhale made him gag, but in a satisfying way. *Oh Helen.* When he'd found her, he'd thought she was taking a nap on the floor—she could be odd like that— and then he had thought she'd slipped and hit her head. He'd taken her to the hospital across the creek, and they in turn had sent her to the one in Columbus, and here it was, three weeks later, and she had an inoperable anaplastic astrocytoma.

That night, instead of going to bed, he drove to the school where he had been headmaster for ten years. The campus looked like a tiny frontier town, its buildings darkly outlined against a dark sky. To stand in the center of the quad was to feel himself in the middle of a tranquil composition: here were the trees, here was the main office, there was the science building. Everything was in its proper place. The ground was frosty, and he stamped his feet to hear the crackle of the frozen grass. The fluorescent bulb over the entrance to the gym gave off a high, persistent whine.

Night had always been his time for optimism. For planning. When everyone else was asleep, an order seemed to settle over the world. His mind awoke and his thoughts ran quick and smooth. He had made his best plans after midnight: how to take the Carlisle School coed, how to start a successful capital campaign, how to recruit young, ambitious teachers from the best colleges to work for room, board, and a salary too low to be called modest.

As he stood in the center of an enterprise that he had brought up from the brink of failure, Elliott felt as if he had never seen it before. He knew that a different life was coming to him. He saw it like a wave on the horizon, advancing mutely, inexorably. It would wash over the farms and the soybean fields, and it would cover this campus and flow east into town and into his neighborhood, where it would heave up his front steps and enter his house, and it would sweep away everything he knew and leave something else, something ravaged and desolate, in its place.

As he smoked, he inventoried his character, the way a person checks and rechecks his luggage in the final hours before a long trip. This was preparation—this helped stave off shock. He reassured himself about his strength, his deep sense of responsibility. He was not forgetful or superstitious or self-absorbed, and he excelled at the bureaucracy and paperwork of living: bank statements, bills, schedules, lists. He did not relish leisure, and he saw duty not as a burden but as an opportunity. In short, by nature and habit, he was as well equipped to face disaster as anyone he knew.

After a few more minutes, Elliott decided it was time to go back to his house. He walked through the sparkling grass to his car.

There were always miracles to hope for. Even Dr. Buxbaum had said she'd seen her share of them.

Now, beside him, Helen slept soundly. In this unfamiliar bed with its fading flowered quilt, he sat up straight as if listening to a lecture. Tonight, grief had his full attention.

A faint breeze set the black leaves of the trees to whispering as Abby picked her way through the gardens behind the hotel. It was still new to her to be out so late without permission, and she could feel faint ripples of the thrill she'd had those first curfewless weeks of college, walking down the lamplit paths, hearing music and voices from open dorm windows rolling out over the lawns. At the edge of campus, she'd listened to the cars along the road into town, the hiss of their passing punctuated by bass from the bands at the student pub. She'd loved the exquisite loneliness of those walks, which seemed to her like part of the solitary reckoning one should feel when embarking on a new life. The faces of the people she met on the path were gray and indistinguishable, but she felt like she was glowing in her borrowed clothes, radiating the promise of her future.

But in the blossomy frivolousness of spring, when her mother was being dosed with X rays and poisoned with chemotherapy, Abby had wandered down paths beneath lighted windows in the lilac-scented air and understood that the whole world had shifted and that no one in Connecticut noticed it but her. Her new friends were good to her, but they couldn't help it that they were still happy, and that they lived in a world that suddenly she did not.

She opened the pool gate. The bright umbrellas had been folded for the night, and empty chaise longues reclined in evenly spaced rows. A filter in the corner of the pool made a low gurgling sound that mimicked water lapping at the shore of a lake. Abby sat down at the edge and put her feet in.

The hotel, illuminated by spotlights, seemed to float above its lawn. There were people on the porch, and the sound of their laughter came in pulses. She had stolen one of her father's cigarettes but had not taken any matches, and anyway, she didn't want to smoke it. She wanted to sit there until someone interesting discovered her.

Back in Ohio, Kevin would be home from his summer job as a dishwasher at the Branding Iron, and he would be sitting down to write her a letter. He'd promised to, anyway, though she had protested—she would be gone only a week.

They'd started going out their senior year in high school, during homecoming, when the hallways were strung with orange and black crepe paper. The whole student body had crammed into the gym bleachers for a pep rally, and the marching band and baton corps, roundly ridiculed at all other times, sparked in their fellow students an almost patriotic fervor. Abby and Kevin had bonded in their scorn for it, and in their hatred of calculus. She had never had a boyfriend before, and at the time she loved him, or thought she did, and every new feeling, each new conversation, was met with a kind of gleeful, giddy surprise.

Kevin wanted to stay faithful when they went to college, and Abby had agreed because it seemed easier that way. She'd thought he would end up kissing someone on his dorm hall, as she had, and then start secretly dating, as she had not. She had hoped, honestly, to lose him to a Notre Dame blonde. There was a boy she'd liked in Connecticut, a sophomore from New York City. He was charming and vaguely deceitful, with dark hair and a handsome, sullen face; he was Italian. He had kissed her on the path near the amphitheater and told her she should wear tighter jeans.

She would not go back to his room with him, and not long after that night he'd started dating someone else. But Kevin had remained loyal—even more so after the news about her mother. He'd written and called and offered to visit, and she let him think that her failure to respond was all due to her concern for her mother.

The day after she got home from college, Kevin had driven over in his dad's Cutlass with a bouquet of Queen Anne's lace from the meadow by the railroad tracks. He had a fine-boned face and a flush of freckles on his cheeks. They sat on the front porch and he couldn't stop touching her.

Abby, who was by then a new person, read his attentions as sexual desperation. She observed him with detached curiosity, as if he were the boyfriend of an old good friend of hers. Kevin hadn't been able to persuade her to have sex with him before they left for school, and she supposed he was determined to now. He always wanted to watch movies in his basement, with its long pullout couch and lockable door, so that two minutes after the opening credit sequence ended, he could be lying next to her, his hand on her waistband and his breath on her neck. Feeling like he was kissing her to death, Abby would say something about her mother and begin to look sad, and then poor Kevin would stop and put his arms around her, tenderness welling up in him as reliably as his preceding desire.

She didn't assume that he was still a virgin, nor did she think herself such a prize—but Kevin, as kind as he was, was no doubt anxious to get what he believed had been promised him. He'd kissed her first nearly two years earlier, and by now, she imagined, he must see sex with her as a moral right.

She heard the scrape of metal on concrete and lifted her head. There was the backlit figure of a man at the gate, his face invisible but his hair illuminated in a fringe of bright gold. She sat up straighter, eager for—for what?

"Excuse me," he called. "The pool is closed for the evening. You'll have to come out."

Abby felt her cheeks flush—at her dumb hopefulness, at being caught. Did she think he had come to rescue her somehow? She rose, slipping on her sandals, and walked through the gate that he held open for her without meeting his eyes.

"Have a pleasant night," he said.

Back in her room, she flung her purse to the floor and flopped down on her twin-size bed, scattering the decorative pillows. There was a vase of dried strawflowers on the bedside table, and, on the turned-down sheet, one lonely chocolate in gold foil. On the little writing desk was the stack of quarters her father had pressed into her hand after dinner. "For what?" she'd asked. "For video games," he'd said. "There's a whole room of them in the basement." She hated video games and would have thought he'd know this, but she had taken his quarters anyway.

She knocked them off the table in one bored sweep of her hand, and as she bent down to retrieve them, she noticed a piece of paper on the carpet near the door. It was a receipt from a drugstore, but it wasn't hers. She picked it up. On one side it marked the purchase of Ivory soap, a notebook, and Wise potato chips. On the other was handwriting in a neat blue cursive. *Hello, pretty. Meet me for a drink? Hancock's in the basement, 11 P.M.*

Abby held the receipt lightly between her fingers and turned it front to back, rereading both sides. She tried to parse the list of items purchased into some kind of additional message. The person had spent three dollars and eighty-nine cents. There was a fifty-cent charge for Misc. What sort of notebook had he bought—college-ruled? Blank? What was Misc.? There was a red smudge in the corner, and this also seemed mysterious.

Her mother had once sent Abby secret-admirer notes in the mail (*I think you are the nicest girl in the world!*), somehow not foreseeing the devastating disappointment that knowledge of the notes' source would one day bring. But this note, with its neat handwriting and correct spelling, was not from her mother.

It was almost midnight—too late to go to Hancock's and see who had written her. Abby wondered if she ought to find it creepy. But the soap reassured her; it was such a simple, familiar need. Then, too, the writer had called her pretty. She read the note a dozen more times and then folded it up and tucked it amid the neat little balls of her socks, aware of a kind of uneasy hope. She hadn't seen any guests her age, but obviously there was at least one hidden among the elderly with their novels and the middle-aged with their golf clubs. Now, she thought, there might be something to look forward to.

The old hotel creaked and groaned, settling in to itself. The window was a porthole looking out over the dark sea of the lawn. Later, when she was in bed, the rain finally came, and the trees surrounding the hotel were full of its noise.

TUESDAY

Awakened from his fitful doze by a high, eerie tendril of sound, Elliott lay in his hotel room, reluctantly but undeniably alert. A note rose and faded and rose again with forlorn insistence, two distinct syllables, like a woman calling out in a language he couldn't understand: *Nee-ah! Nee-ah!* Faint as it was, it echoed inside his head, and in the early unnatural hours of the morning he heard it as a kind of warning.

He focused all his attention on that shrill cry, as if he could interpret what terrible secret it sought to tell him. *Nee-ah!* it said again. *Nee-ah!* Elliott blinked, waking further, and then it came to him: it was the peacock, pacing in the gardens below the window. *Fucking bird,* he thought, and sighed. He lay very still, willing sleep to return, but he felt the thoughts of the day already assembling themselves, impatient, needy, bleak.

Beside him there was Helen in her deep, animal slumber. Her right arm lay across his chest, her palm open on the pocket of his pajamas.

Some mornings he used to wake to find her smiling, pressing against him, pulling him up from the deep caverns of sleep with a cunningly placed hand. He would resist—unconsciousness was so sublime—but she would ease a leg over his. And then, slow, stupid, he would open his eyes, his heartbeat already surging.

He'd be lying to himself if he didn't admit a certain dull thrum of resentment: he didn't know why she couldn't prefer doing it *before* they went to sleep, like regular people. But in the darkness, with the long warmth of Helen beneath him and the fuzz of dreams between them, he woke to his body and found in it wells of pleasure that surprised him, that rippled through him and through Helen and out into the room, as if their soft urgent motions brought energy into the dawn.

At breakfast on those mornings, she was grinning and girlish, pleased with herself. She flirted with him over her cereal and giggled when he tapped her gently on her round bottom.

Slowly the curtains brightened and the room's black thinned to a cool gray. Shadowy forms resolved themselves into dresser, armoire, television, chair. He put his hand on Helen's warm shoulder and felt the cycle of breath—the slow rise and the measured release. In the dim room, her hairless head looked as if it were carved from marble.

He rose and dressed without turning on the light. Shutting the door softly behind him, he went downstairs, through the lobby, and out to the back veranda. The sky was orange shot through with pink, and in the gardens a thin mist coiled around the granite boulders and drifted past clusters of lilies. Birds dodged in and out of the pillars, twittering and diving. The maple trees sighed in the breeze as the sky grew pinker, and then a golden yellow came up and dissolved into a pale blue, the color of a ribbon on an Easter dress.

The Duke lurched along beneath the wrought-iron café tables, pecking between the flagstones. A squirrel appeared on the porch and worked its way in fits and starts toward Elliott, looking wary but hopeful. He put his hand in his pocket, and the squirrel, thinking he was reaching for food, moved closer, its eyes bright and beseeching.

Though he'd only been trying to tease his daughter when he told her the trees grew straighter in New Hampshire, Elliott really did think they looked different here—leafier and cleaner, more properly treelike, and far superior to the unlovely buckeye and sweet gum of Ohio, both of which had leaves that hardly turned color in the fall but merely bleached themselves a wan yellow and then dropped. Here, in a couple of months, the woods would be on fire with red and orange and the roads would be clogged by the leaf-peepers he had, as a younger man, decried—and yet imagined that he and Helen might someday become.

The first time Elliott saw Helen they were juniors in college and she was wearing a skirt that was shorter than regulation, and even from far away he could tell she was nervous about it, though her strong legs and large steps would have told a less perceptive man otherwise. It was one of those October days when the slanted sunlight shone clean and brilliant on the campus and the air was crisp, even though it was still warm—it felt like spring, but more golden and poignant.

Helen was walking with Laurie Morelli, who popped her gum in psychology class and crossed her slim, pretty ankles in the aisle where the boys couldn't help but admire them. Laurie had borrowed a pen from Elliott once, and now he found himself on his feet, waving at them. "Hey Morelli," he called. "You owe me a pen."

Laurie and her friend stopped in the middle of the sidewalk. The maple above them dappled their faces and their smooth bare arms. He approached them quickly, his pulse as hard as if he had just finished a sprint, his spirit already soaring.

Laurie bent her dark head and fished around in her purse until she pulled out a pencil. "This is all I have."

"That's no pen," he said. "It's not even sharp." Even as he said the words, though, he regretted his ploy. He didn't want to seem like someone to whom a pen would matter so much. "I mean . . ." he said, and then trailed off.

The green-eyed girl in the short skirt watched him with a bit of a smile on her lips. She wore a white blouse with a Peter Pan collar and that plaid skirt over white tights. Her face was round, open, and friendly, her brows perfect arches. She had high cheekbones and a long slender nose with a bit of extra flesh on its tip, like a flourish. Her heavy, wavy brown hair was swept back in a headband, and she had on lip gloss, just the faintest touch. "I have a pen," she said.

"I can't take yours," he said. "You don't owe me one."

"Here." She gave it to Laurie. "It's hers now."

Laurie accepted the pen but looked confused.

"Now give it to him," directed the lovely person.

Laurie held the pen out to Elliott. It was a blue ballpoint that said MCDERMOTT PHARMACY on the side, and it was warm from being in the girl's hand.

"There—so now we're even," Laurie said.

"But we're not, really." He turned to Laurie's friend. "I don't know your name," he said.

"Helen," she answered. Her full smile came out—deep dimples, teeth slightly, appealingly crooked—and it was not too much to say that he was dazzled by it.

"Helen's out a pen," he said to Laurie, who all of a sudden seemed unconscionably dull and inane.

"I have hundreds of them," Helen said. "Boxes upon boxes."

"She's not lying—she really does," Laurie said. "They're from her stepdad's pharmacy, and she gets them for free. We're late."

"Where are you going?"

"Swim class," Helen said. She gave her shining hair a casual but deliberate toss, which he read as a signal to him. Elliott thought of those strong legs coming out of a bathing suit, drops of water beading on the shins, the naked feet, the shadow of muscle down her thigh, the neat round calf he could cup in his palm. He watched the girls hurry down the path. He felt elated.

The next time he saw Helen he asked her out on a date. She had another boy's ring, but she agreed to go to dinner with Elliott anyway—a dinner he paid for with money meant for the next semester's books. She wore a different, longer skirt, and she brought him a dozen more pens. She sang along to Petula Clark on the jukebox and told him that the pharmacy belonged to the people she'd gone to live with after her parents died. The McDermotts had been her parents' best friends. *An orphan!* Elliott thought, reaching across the table for her hand. She seemed even more beautiful then. As he watched her sip her cherry Coke, served by a girl in lederhosen in the silly old German restaurant he'd brought her to, he realized that Helen reminded him faintly of his prettiest sister, and this made her seem even more intimately his, not in an incestuous way but in a way that spoke of familiarity and comfort.

Elliott and Helen, HelenandElliott, college sweethearts. Laurie Morelli called them Ellen and Helliott and took credit for their happiness. They looked good together—everyone said so. They had dark hair, light eyes, and good midwestern faces. The top of her head came to just under his shoulder. She made him feel gigantic, protective, lucky.

They'd been married on a day like this one, bright blue and green, in the chapel on that very campus, a year after they graduated. The day after the ceremony, they'd driven west to go camping—another first for them both—and he had cooked them breakfast every morning on their new Coleman stove. Eggs and bacon were his specialty, and the only things he knew how to make. He was enthralled with everything on that trip: the musty, delicious smell of the borrowed tent, the thrill of zipping their two sleeping bags together, the chilly damp mornings raucous with birds. That was twenty years ago, and it felt like that—more, even.

A couple wearing matching polo shirts strolled through the garden beneath him, and another early riser peeked into the empty dining room, and soon enough the smell of waffles and coffee beckoned to Elliott. He stood on his bad knees and reentered the hotel. The building seemed to yawn and stretch, and water rushed through the pipes like something alive.

He passed his fellow guests in the halls without acknowledgment. Along the wall by the phone bank, a man squatted, the receiver held tight against his cheek. "What did the fish say when he ran into the wall? No no no! Jesus, Kate, wait till it's over, it's a three-second joke! The fish! The fish, when he ran into the wall, he said, 'Dam!'"

Upstairs in the warm room, Elliott lifted the shade and his wife turned sleepily onto her side. He sat down with the *Eagle,* dispensing with it in moments, and turned to the front section of *The Wall Street Journal,* which he had taken from the lobby. It had a coffee stain in one corner. He scanned the headlines only; he did not like a used paper.

Helen sat up slowly and swung her legs over the edge of the bed. In two decades—before all this—he'd never gotten up before she did. She looked down at her feet and then up at the brightness streaming in through the window and squinted.

"I suppose you want me to get you those pills you like," Elliott said. He folded the paper and set it carefully on the side table. From the bathroom he retrieved the pills from the compartment that said TUESDAY A.M. and brought them to her with a glass of tepid water. He tipped them into her hand, and one by one she took them.

"Clothes, too," he said, taking away her glass. "Let's see what looks good for today."

"I can find my own clothes, Elliott," she said.

He went through the drawers anyway, pulling out underwear, a blue-and-white-striped shirt, a pair of soft blue pants. These were gifts from his three sisters, who had visited in the spring and bought Helen shirts without buttons and pants without zippers, everything in happy primary colors so she could mix and match.

He had protested when his sisters came home from the mall. "But these are so ugly!" he'd said, loath to hurt their feelings but unable to contain himself. They were the sort of clothes a mother might buy for a child eager to dress herself. Theresa, who was the eldest, sat him down. She said, "Listen, maybe they're not her style exactly, but they're cheerful. And this is not a very happy thing to say, but there may come a time when your wife won't be able to figure out a zipper."

He thought of that red plaid skirt she'd worn the first day he saw her—its shortness, its sharp pleats, its bewitching girlishness. *Your wife won't be able to figure out a zipper.* That was the sort of sentence that woke him in the middle of the night, if he'd gotten to sleep in the first place.

"Where did I put your socks?" Elliott said. "I didn't forget your socks, did I? That would be really stupid."

A few moments later he found them in the drawer he had reserved for his underwear and shook his head at the misplacement.

"Elliott," Helen said quietly, "really."

"Oh I'm just trying to speed things along. I'm starving." But he made himself sit back down in the hard blue chair. He stared at the paper while Helen slowly dressed, brushed her teeth, and found her shoes. He waited until she was ready. "Let's go eat bacon," he said, and he held out his hand to her.

Out of the corner of her eye, Abby watched her mother navigating the buffet table, on which grapes, oranges, and strawberries lay in gleaming heaps. Steam from the chafing dishes rose in white twists above the shiny curds of scrambled eggs and strips of bacon curling in their own fat. Helen moved from the pastries and fruits at one end to the pancakes at the other, her plate clutched in her left hand and her right hovering above the bounty.

"Shouldn't you be with her?" Abby asked.

Elliott didn't look up. "She doesn't like being coddled."

Helen seemed to decide upon fruit salad and scrambled eggs, and then she shuffled back for a muffin. When she got to the end of the buffet, she turned in the light-filled room and took a few steps in the wrong direction. Men and women streamed around her as she stopped and stood, looking for her family.

"*Dad*," Abby said, and this time he got up. He walked a little ways toward Helen, waving, and then she saw him and waved back, smiling uncertainly.

Her face had grown rounder without becoming fleshier, and the outer corners of her eyes had begun to slant down beneath her thinning eyebrows. Abby didn't know when this had happened; she supposed it had been gradual, while she was away at school. Nor did she know the cause—whether it was the cancer or the drugs that were supposed to fight it that gave Helen this look of soft, blurred sadness. It had frightened Abby when she came home in the spring, though now she could almost reconcile it to what she remembered: the bright pale eyes, the laughing mouth, the quick-moving expressions.

"I like the—" Helen said, sitting down. "The . . ." She pointed. "You know."

"The buffet," Elliott said.

"Right," Helen said.

A crescendo of laughter rose from a table of middle-aged men and women. One of their number, a bearded man with binoculars slung across his chest, was flapping his arms and extending his neck absurdly. Two of them got up and passed by the Hansens' table on their way for seconds. "—strange markings for an eastern finch, and larger than I would have—" one was saying.

Helen picked up her muffin. "There's so much food," she said.

"It's the buffiest buffet I've ever seen," Elliott agreed.

A waiter appeared with a silver pitcher. "Would you care for some juice?" His voice broke as he asked.

"Yes, please," her mother said, and smiled sweetly at him. "It's good for me."

"Can't you see yourself coming here one day to write?" Abby's father asked her. "Marguerite at the front desk said that a lot of authors come here for the peace and quiet."

Abby swirled a spoon in her yogurt. Marguerite! Whoever she was, Abby did not believe her, and anyway, she didn't want to write. She had made up the idea about writing to get her father off her back when she dropped biology. And she knew her father's true motive in asking the question, which was to suggest that this place had a culture besides tennis and golf. As if she cared: she'd never had melons and kiwis and scones laid out like this for breakfast, never had a man hovering at her elbow, asking if he could make her waffles—Belgian, multigrain, blueberry, any kind she wanted.

"I don't know, maybe," she said. "I like the breakfast."

A few feet away, the bird-watchers saw everything with their sharp old eyes, and Abby could imagine them taking notes. *The older female moves uncertainly. She has a peculiar headcovering different from other members of her species. Her family group—especially the male—is attentive to her.*

"So what's on tap for today?" her father asked.

Abby broke off a piece of a croissant and dipped it into her coffee. "I don't know," she said. "I'm going to take a walk, I guess."

"You know, I was outside earlier," Elliott said. "It was like a symphony of birds."

God, she thought, he was *trying* again. She never should have said that thing about the writing. "Sounds nice," she said.

He passed Helen the butter. "Here, honey—here. Use my knife, that other one is too small."

Helen looked up at Abby. "Isn't he thoughtful?" she asked.

Once her mother had been the kind of person who would drink her coffee, eat her breakfast, and put on her makeup at the same time, all while driving a stick shift in traffic to work. Abby had also seen her read a magazine behind the wheel, though only on highways. It was unheard of to find her needing help like this. *What's happened to you?* she wanted to ask. Though she couldn't ask, because she knew.

It wasn't her mother's fault. And still Abby resented her, her sudden meekness and gratitude, even more than her father's new, unwearying solicitousness. It upset the long-established family order, which had placed Abby and Helen on one side and Elliott on the other. Of course they all loved each other, but their love had not precluded alliances. Abby wanted back the mother she was used to. She wanted her back and on her side.

"Here, Helen," her father said, "don't you want some cream?"

The parents of the adolescent, having established that it has been offered sufficient nourishment, turn to their own feeding needs. They engage in an elaborate dance of sharing and reciprocity: "Try this," the male seems to say; "Thank you, please try this," one imagines the female responding.

Abby pushed back her chair. "Maybe I'll just go now. I'm not that hungry."

Her mother looked up from her breakfast, a grape skewered on a fork halfway to her mouth. "Will you come back soon?" she asked.

"I'll find you later."

Abby thought her father might stop her, but he only looked at her with displeasure. She made herself as tall and thin and light as possible—*the adolescent, testing her independence, leaves the security of the nest*—and she drew a line to the door, and on that line she stepped one foot in front of the other, and in this way carried herself outside.

Past the tennis courts at the bottom of the hill, Abby crossed a small swift creek on a covered footbridge. On the other side the path divided, to the right hugging the perimeter of the golf course and to the left following the creek into the woods. A golf cart went buzzing by a few yards away, and then another chased it. Boys in yellow shirts drove them one-handed, their right arm flung casually along the back of the passenger seat and their eyes invisible behind sunglasses.

Abby's stomach ached a little, and whether this was from hunger or guilt she wasn't sure. Though she was ashamed of her behavior, she could not entirely blame herself—or rather, she blamed and excused herself in the same breath.

She took the path that led into the trees, wishing she'd found her admirer at breakfast, because by now she was tired of solitary walks in well-tended woods. On her college campus, it had seemed like every cluster of elms shaded people wearing rag wool socks and carrying well-thumbed copies of books by Adorno or Lacan—people who liked college and believed in it. Their thoughts and interests had become incomprehensible to Abby; nothing in a book meant anything. *If society . . . is really one of rackets, then its most faithful model is the precise opposite of the collective, namely the individual as monad. . . . The thematics of this science is henceforth suspended, in effect, at the primordial position of the signifier and the signified as being distinct orders separated initially by a barrier resisting signification*. . . . She viewed such sentences—if she bothered to read them at all—as lines from a remote, irrelevant language. She was exempt from comprehension, attention, effort. Nothing typed, nothing xeroxed, nothing written on a chalkboard mattered. There was only one question that did, and only one answer that was acceptable: *Will my mother be okay? Yes.*

To ensure such an answer, it was important to keep to particular sources of information; there were rules as to how and when such a query should be posed. For example, it was never asked of a person—her father, say, or a doctor. It was a question for the world to answer.

She had established the habit one morning on her way to biology, as she walked along a path lined with magnolias. *If I can hit the trunk of the nearest tree with a rock,* she said to herself, *my mother will be okay.* The trunk was spindly, and her aim wasn't something to bet on. But she bent down and picked up a piece of gravel from the path and sent it spinning through the air, arcing high and then falling down, descending way too fast—and just when it seemed ready to hit the ground, the rock collided with the tree trunk with a satisfying crack. There was a tiny chip in the bark six inches above the grass. Proof. Proof! Abby felt exhilaration and relief. There it was, the answer. She didn't bother going to biology after that.

Will my mother be okay? It was a question she kept asking, and she found ways to keep being reassured. If she could close her eyes and run through a field for ten seconds without opening them, her mother would get better. If she could find three yellow flowers next to one another, if she watched the clock until it hit 3:33, if a squirrel flicked its tail, if a blue car drove by on the road, her mother would be fine. There were innumerable tests, and Abby was sure to choose those that gave her the answer she sought. (Never again, after that first toss, did she risk the wrong answer on a test she might fail.)

She passed a stand of birches, their ghostly white bark peeling in thin coils, and an old padlocked tennis court beneath their shade—abandoned, it seemed, in favor of the newer courts closer to the hotel. As the path carved further into the woods, the ground changed from pebbles to loam, and the rustling leaves said, *Hush, hush*. When she came to another trail that split off into deeper woods, she took it, and watched the trees slowly change from deciduous to evergreen.

Because she didn't know these woods, she was afraid to bet on them. She just walked in the aqueous light, her footsteps on the carpet of pine needles as faint and regular as a heartbeat. She imagined that her admirer, whoever he was, had seen her enter the forest, and even now he was watching her through the trees, steadily gaining on her. She saw him in rumpled navy pants and an unironed oxford; she gave him light brown hair bleached gold at its tips, as if he spent long afternoons on sailboats. She'd seen his type in Connecticut, though they didn't go to her school; they passed along the highway in old Saab convertibles, their fine narrow noses pointing them onward. Had Abby paused to look more closely at her imagined admirer, she might have recognized him, with shame, as someone from a Ralph Lauren ad—but she did not look closely. He was a faint bright hope coming after her. He would find her on the path, tears sparkling in her eyes—*What is wrong, my beauty?* he would ask. And she would say, *My mother is sick and I am alone.* He would wrap his arms around her and promise to take care of her; he would bring her to his family home on Nantucket.

She tried to walk gracefully, in an attitude that was anticipatory and reverent. She pinched her cheeks to bring up their color. Her fingernails were dirty, and she hoped he wouldn't notice.

She stopped for a moment, listening for him, though there was nothing but a faint, ceaseless whisper of air. A low stone wall, crumbling and useless, separated trees from more trees, and the rocks that marked the path glowed green with moss. The farther into the distance she looked, the dimmer it was—it was like looking ahead in time, into night—and there was a sense of aliveness everywhere.

Suddenly she was frightened. What if she'd taken a turn she didn't remember? And who knew how many paths the hotel kept and how long it would take for anyone to find her? She turned and began jogging back the way she'd come, trying to keep her breathing steady. The woods kept their stillness, their august obliviousness. She stumbled and cursed and kept going, not slowing down until she came to the wide main path. Two people shot by her on mountain bikes. "Watch where you're going!" she cried, though they'd hardly been within a yard of her.

As she neared the dilapidated tennis court, she was surprised to find it occupied. Two girls, one with red hair and one with a long yellow ponytail, stood in the stippled shadows, and on the other side of the net were two dark-haired boys. They lobbed a ball back and forth across the cracked asphalt. "Not so hard," one of the girls called plaintively. "I don't want to sweat."

The girls wore denim skirts and flip-flops, and they moved with graceful languor. Abby thought that one of the boys was her waiter, the one who had told them about the parsley foam. Who were the others? Behind the rusting fence they wandered here and there, swinging their racquets, engaged in a conversation she couldn't hear. Invisible, Abby passed by them, envying their camaraderie.

"Hey wait!" a girl's voice cried then, and Abby turned, thinking she had been summoned. But the girl was bending over, looking for something.

One of the boys hopped the net, and together they squatted down, scanning the surface of the court for whatever had been lost. The tennis ball rolled away into a corner.

Abby felt her solitude acutely. It had been that way since March. And she'd walked in enough woods feeling inexpressibly sad, longing for some sort of comfort, to know that comfort never came. No one ever looked up from his book, no one ever followed her or called her name. And yet she kept on wearing pretty clothes to walk beneath the trees, crying for her mother, counting birds and stones that would prophesy her recovery. And waiting to be rescued—knowing, without wanting to, that what drove her to pace the hard-packed dirt paths was grief but what kept her on them was desire.

Above her, the dark silhouette of a bird sliced across the sky, and the red roof of the hotel seemed to burn over the trees.

"Mr. Hansen, sir, you have a message," Marguerite called, waving at him from behind the hulking lobby desk.

Elliott had just coaxed Helen into bed for her midmorning rest, though she had refused to get under the covers or take off her shoes. After a moment of protest, she'd let him drape a blanket over her legs and bring her another pillow. "You stay out of trouble," he'd said, kissing her, and she'd stuck out her tongue at him.

Marguerite handed him a piece of paper. "A Mrs. Ford for you," she said, and Elliott noticed how large and white her teeth were.

"My secretary," he explained. "No one respects a vacation anymore, do they?"

Marguerite threw up her hands. "Don't call back!" she cried. "Ignorance is bliss."

He winked at her and then walked to the phone bank around the corner from the dining room. In under a month, the Carlisle School would be back in session. Though he'd expected to take comfort in the requirements of leadership and the familiarity of routine, for the first time in the decade of his directorship, he dreaded the start of the school year. His office, with its white cinder-block walls and folding tables stacked with neat piles of paper, had begun to feel like a cell in the county jail.

He planned to lean as much as possible on Susan Ford, who wore pressed wool suits from Sears and called him Principal Hansen when students were present and Mr. Hansen when they were not. While he was here at the Presidential, she was watering his office plants and pinging her hard heels down the long silent hallways, addressing the summer duties he used to handle—scheduling building maintenance, tracking late applicants, phoning parents—with efficiency and a grim pride. She took his dictation in her old-fashioned shorthand and kept his pencils sharp as pins. As far as he knew, she had never forgotten an appointment, never lost a note or message, never let him dangle a single modifier. With her assistance—she was less a secretary than an assistant principal when it came down to it—he had brought the Carlisle School up from a third-rate boys' academy to a promising coed college prep that shepherded its students through four years of progressive education before shipping them off to Earlham and Denison and other fine midwestern colleges, and occasionally even an Ivy or two.

He called her collect, and she answered on the first ring. "Thank you," she said. "You know I wouldn't normally bother you."

On the wall beside the phone someone had written *I ♡ Jamie* in a round adolescent hand. "What's shaking?" he asked.

He heard her take a sip of something and then cough delicately. "I spoke to the headmaster at Chase Academy this morning," she said.

Elliott's interest was piqued. Chase was barely a step down from Exeter; it was in a whole other league of private school.

"He asked me to have you call him as soon as possible. I told him that you were on vacation, but that didn't dissuade him. 'It is a matter of supreme importance,' he said."

"Really," Elliott said. "*Supreme* importance?"

"Well, he is a pompous old windbag. But he did sound serious."

He rubbed his eyes and blinked at *I ♡ Jamie.* "Interesting."

"It is," Mrs. Ford agreed. "Would you like his number?"

He wrote it on the wall beneath Jamie's name and then wondered what in the world had possessed him to do that. He tried to wipe the numbers away, but they only smeared into one another.

"That's all," Mrs. Ford said. "I'll let you get back to your vacation. Give Helen and Abby my best." She hung up before he could say goodbye.

Elliott waited a minute or two before dialing the number. The secretary put him on hold, and then Barney Russell's asthmatic voice came wheezing into his ear. They'd met each other half a dozen times at educational conferences and seminars, and last year Barney had requested a copy of a paper Elliott had given on motivating underachievers—not that Barney'd encountered many of those at Chase.

"Elliott," Barney gasped. "You're just the man I want to talk to. Listen, I've got a meeting in thirty seconds, so let me just run with this, all right? I will be retiring at the end of this fall term—it's a bit sudden, but it's necessary—and I am specifically requesting that you throw your hat into the ring for my chair. We'll conduct a national search because the board requires it, but I couldn't be more confident that you are the man for the job. You just send along your CV and one of those letters, and we'll schedule a campus visit as soon as the school year starts. Then we'll go from there."

Taken aback, Elliott fumbled for an appropriate response. "That is quite a surprise. But is everything all right, Barney? You're just retiring?"

"Thank you for your concern. It's a bit of a health thing—nothing life-threatening. But between that and my, shall we say, advancing age, it seemed like it was time to step away from the lectern, so to speak. We need a younger man—a leader, someone with drive. I know this is all very abrupt, and for that I apologize, but I've got three math teachers in the hallway I've been putting off for months, and I'm certain they're going to come after me with protractors. Finish out your vacation, Elliott, and call me when you get back. We have much to discuss."

Out on the front porch, Elliott lit his first cigarette of the day. He took such pleasure in it: the dry hot air, the crackling of the diminutive fire, the smoke spiraling up like incense. After a few puffs came the light-headedness, then the swell of nausea. The morning cigarette didn't mess around; it scraped down his throat and reached into his guts and wrung them out like an old towel. It was his favorite.

He lingered in the shade, watching the activity beneath the porte cochere: the opening and shutting of car doors, the loading and unloading of suitcases, the efficient exchange of keys, greetings, tips. All the women were blond and the men wore pastel shirts, and the valets and bellhops bustled around in their smart uniforms. Elliott wondered what brought these Yankees to a place like this, and what pleasures they expected—surely there were golf and spas in their hometowns. People had too much money, he thought, and they spent it in so many stupid ways. They ought to find a cause, a philanthropic enterprise.

So Barney Russell, Chase headmaster, thought Elliott Hansen should replace him. The idea seemed simultaneously perfect and preposterous. Chase had everything: endowment, infrastructure, legacy, academics. Its student body was ethnically and economically diverse and most of its faculty had Ph.D.s; its politics were liberal and its alumni repeatedly cited their four years there as some of the most enriching of their lives. There was an organic *farm* attached, for God's sake, and students ate what they learned how to grow on the ivy-covered campus in picturesque town-square-and-white-steepled-church Vermont.

In Elliott's first year at Carlisle, twenty kids had set fire to their shoes in the center of the quad in response to a change in the lights-out policy. In his second year, someone chalked "motherfucker" on all the buildings. In his third, he busted two boys for growing pot in their closet. (He couldn't help being a trifle impressed—they'd had grow lamps, a ventilation system, everything.) But what problems had he had since? Some smoking, a bit of drugs, but really, *nothing*. It wasn't bragging to say that he'd turned the place around.

A few yards away, a kid was sweeping the wide gray floorboards, and Elliott watched the broom arc from side to side as he finished his cigarette and dropped it into his cold coffee. He decided to walk the circuit of the veranda, and he lit another cigarette.

Over the past ten years, Elliott had shaped Carlisle into his school, bent not to his whims but to his carefully held belief in hard work, personal accountability, and community consciousness. He'd chosen Carlisle over a continued university career because he felt that college students were past molding, and that if one wanted to build future good citizens, it was better to start such work closer to puberty. He gave all his energy to his academy, and in turn his students loved their school with a loyalty they later proved through well-attended class reunions and modest but consistent financial gifts. There was an honor code, an emphasis on creativity over test scores, a scholarship fund he worked tirelessly to build. Carlisle was Elliott.

But it was also a self of which he had begun to grow tired. It never stopped striving, and nothing was ever easy. Despite all of Elliott's efforts, Carlisle was still underfunded and underrecognized. It was a school with patches on its jeans, whereas Chase was an academy in wing tips and a bespoke English suit. Chase's coffers were full, its architecture was important, and its grounds were marked by sturdy maples nearly as old as the republic. *Otium sine litteris mors est et hominis vivi sepultura* was etched into marble in the high arch above the library: *Leisure without study is death; it is as a tomb for the living man.* Elliott longed for that order, that rigor, cloaked as it would be in Chase's material comforts and the stately, reassuring whisper of tradition.

He thought about telling Helen his news. She'd always maintained that he wasn't sufficiently recognized for his efforts. At Chase there would be a house for them to move into, a brick Georgian with leaded windows and oak staircases, right across the street from the library. He'd have two vice principals, one for academics, the other for community life. The school grounds were an arboretum, and every single goddamn plant had a sign on it, so the kids were always learning. The New England aster: *Aster novae-angliae.* Sugar maple: *Acer saccharum.* It was as if Chase students never had to wonder about anything.

He walked by where he'd sat earlier that morning, above the landscaped patios, the eruptions of flowers amid the deep shades of green. A woman in a straw hat was taking pictures of the peacock, though he dragged his train behind him like a bundle of sticks. "Come on, pretty-pretty," Elliott heard her say. "Show us your shiny tail."

"His name's the Duke," Elliott called, and she turned, squinting up to the sky, as if the voice had been God's.

Though back in Ohio, the heat shimmered up from the pavement in visible waves and the petunias in the downtown flower boxes wilted by eleven, here a clean cool breeze shivered through dignified evergreens, shifting the cast of their long blue shadows and making a rustling sound like tissue paper being crumpled in a fist.

Elliott and Helen had moved to New Hampshire right after their honeymoon. With its regal colonials and small photogenic towns, its blue-skied winters and its famous falls, New England made him feel as if he'd moved into a postcard or a bank calendar. The flintiness of the air, the pillowy shapes of the clouds, and the heavy green dragonflies all seemed so acutely familiar and beloved.

He'd been young here, and he allowed himself to imagine for a moment that he could come back.

He wouldn't tell Helen about Chase, he decided. It was easier not to. And it would hardly be the biggest secret he was keeping from her, would it?

Elliott finished his cigarette as he rounded the corner to arrive at the entrance to the hotel. A large man in lavender pants heaved himself out of the way as the sweeping employee advanced, pushing a handful of leaves and a few crumpled paper napkins in front of his broom.

"I hope you don't have to sweep the whole way around," Elliott said as the boy came alongside him.

The kid looked up at him with a disingenuous smile—the kind of friendliness bought by a meager hourly wage—and then stepped back. Elliott, too, felt himself start. The kid's smile, which had faded, quickly returned, wider, and Elliott saw in those blue darting eyes a flicker of an old challenge. He *knew* this kid. *Helen* knew this kid.

"Vic Libby," Elliott said.

"Yes, sir, I'm him." The boy had dark, almost black hair, a suntanned face, and a slouching, insouciant posture. He wore his pants low on his hips, so the cuffs dragged along the floor.

"I'm *he*," Elliott said without thinking. "What an incredible surprise—what a small world. What are you doing here? How are you?"

Five years ago Vic had been a junior at Carlisle, admitted in the second semester because Helen had begged Elliott to accept him. Vic wasn't finding the right influences at the public high school, she said. He'd been arrested twice—a curfew violation, perhaps, or marijuana possession—but Elliott couldn't remember the particulars. "I don't want to keep seeing him in juvenile court," Helen had said. He'd be eighteen soon enough, was Elliott's way of thinking. His wife had persisted, though, and Elliott, who respected her dedication to the kid and to her delinquents in general, had given in.

"I'm gainfully employed," Vic said, passing the broom handle from palm to palm. "So I guess I'm doing all right."

"That's great, just great." Elliott was having trouble understanding why, nine hundred miles from where he had last seen Vic Libby, he had come upon him sweeping a porch. "Did your parents move to New Hampshire?"

"You mean my uncle? No, he's still in town, but my grandpa lives over in Conway. I'm staying with him for the summer."

"Well that's just great," Elliott said. "Just great." He'd forgotten the kid's parents were AWOL.

"I guess." Vic was still smiling.

Helen had claimed that Vic was extremely intelligent, but he'd never distinguished himself at Carlisle. He'd made friends easily enough, even though he never seemed particularly interested in them. He had been quiet, a little sly, and ultimately, a forgettable person, contrary to Helen's expectations.

"So you're working at the Presidential," Elliott said.

"Yes, sir. It's my third summer."

"Best hotel in New Hampshire."

The cigarette butt that Elliott had crushed out lay on the porch between them. Of course he had busted Vic for smoking—that much Elliott remembered clearly. He'd gone back to work late one night and spotted Vic squatting by the gym doors, exhaling a sizable puff of smoke. Other kids tried to hide or even make a dash for it, and the runners learned how fast Elliott was—he'd been a sprinter in college. Vic had merely stood up and waited, calmly finishing his cigarette as Elliott approached. Elliott had admired Vic's ready acceptance of culpability, and as they walked back to the boys' dorm without speaking Elliott felt almost a sense of camaraderie. He'd loved his late-night cigarettes, too, almost as much as his morning ones. He hadn't kicked Vic out then, though he could have. He'd given the boy another chance.

Now they both looked at the butt on the floorboards, and Elliott saw the wheels in Vic's mind beginning to turn, processing this piddling hypocrisy. He was tempted to make a joke or to explain—*extenuating circumstances, I only just started again*—but instead he kept his mouth shut.

Vic nudged his broom toward it. "I should get that," he said.

Elliott stepped back. "Certainly," he said.

"How's Mrs. Hansen?"

Elliott gazed out over the hotel lawn and did not feel awkward about smoking anymore. "She's been very sick."

"What's wrong?" Vic's voice had lost all its irony. "What's the matter?"

His obvious concern took Elliott by surprise. He'd always assumed that the affection between Vic and Helen ran primarily in one direction. "She has cancer."

Vic set the broom against the side of the hotel, where it leaned for a moment before clattering to the floor. "You're kidding," he said. "I'm sorry . . . Is she . . . I hope she's okay."

"As do we all."

They stood in silence for a while, not looking at each other. Elliott considered asking Vic if he wanted to see her, but then he decided against it.

"Well," Vic said, "I should finish up. Tell her I said hello."

"You bet," Elliott said.

Vic picked up the broom and began to sweep himself away, but then he turned and called over his shoulder. "What about Pig? How's Pig?"

He was so openly looking for good news. Pig! Elliott had forgotten she'd come from Vic.

"Pig's doing just fine," Elliott said, as if he had any idea.

Abby sat between her parents on a padded silk bench in the corner of the ballroom and tried not to fidget too much. They had eaten lunch on the patio, then browsed through the gift shop, and now they were watching strangers navigate the box step.

The dance instructor had waves of iron-gray hair that never moved, not even when he stood in front of the fan that kept the long sheer curtains swaying. In his gray pleated slacks and gray short-sleeved shirt, he was a study in slender monochrome. "She goes back, see, and he goes forward, see, at the same time, and then they both step out to the side, and then for the man, left foot closes to right foot, yes, like that . . . Wait, no, the other foot, my dear, the other one . . ." His slippers whispered along the floor.

This was her father's idea of a good activity: stimulation without any actual effort. Abby had suggested a trail ride, and he had shaken his head at her, disappointed at her thoughtlessness. "Your mother has to save up her energy for tomorrow," he'd said, "for when the Schmidts and the Callahans get here."

Now he was saying, for what seemed like the millionth time, "Vic Libby. Imagine the chances."

Helen had expressed her desire to see Vic, and Abby had pretended not to remember who he was, though she could picture him clearly: the skinny body and slightly stooped shoulders, the face with its amused reserve, the long nose and thick-lashed blue eyes under close dark brows. Vic should have been handsome, but somehow the whole was less than the sum of its parts, and his looks—striking, she might say, or at least interesting—were part of his inscrutability. He had been an aloof, broody senior when she was a freshman, and she had been afraid of him in the way she had been afraid of everyone sixteen and older.

They had no classes together, and though they ate lunch during the same period, Vic spent his break on the concrete patio known as the Senior Courtyard, outside the cafeteria. In the warm weather, the twelfth-graders sprawled along old carved-up wooden benches, and in the cold, they huddled in their coats, the smoke from their cigarettes almost indistinguishable from the steam of their breath. She supposed herself invisible to all of them, and to Vic especially—for being younger, for having such do-gooders for parents. But sometimes when she passed him in the hallway his posture betrayed an awareness of her, and as she began to watch him more closely, it seemed possible that his aloofness was designed to hide a certain curiosity about who she was. After a while she even began to think he might like her a little. And then that spring he had come up to her in a roomful of people and kissed her.

"I spoke to Eva earlier," her father said. "She's making lobster rolls for the picnic tomorrow."

"Fancy," her mother said.

Closest to them, a practiced elderly couple stepped lightly and with confidence in a tight circle. To their right, two blond women who had been alternating parts began to argue about whose turn it was to lead.

"Why don't you dance?" Helen asked Abby, swaying to the music.

"By myself?"

"He would dance with you," she said, nodding toward the instructor, assuming, as all mothers did, that special attention would be paid to her child.

"I think he looks busy," Abby said. "Anyway, I like sitting here. With you," she added.

The party where Vic had kissed her was at Calvin Miller's because his parents were away and they didn't care what trouble he got into as long as the house was clean when they got home. Abby had lied and told her mother she was going to Frances's house, and by eleven o'clock she was wobbling in her heels, slightly tipsy and needing a bathroom. She had seen Vic on the front porch with a group of people she didn't know, and she thought he might have waved in her direction.

There were beer cans on every available surface, and she couldn't find Frances or any of the friends she had come with. Calvin's big white dog trotted by, brushing against her leg and leaving a dusting of fur on her jeans. She was trying to clean them off when Vic came up behind her and spun her around, and before she could say a word the kiss had happened. His lips were cool at first but they warmed against hers, sweet and insistent, and in those few seconds she felt swelling inside her an unfamiliar and thrilling recklessness. He put his hands on her cheeks, and her own hands, possessed of a new, private volition, reached for the place where his untucked shirt had shifted to the side to expose smooth bare skin.

Someone passed through the hallway carrying a TV set. "Hey, Vic, get a room," he said.

With Vic's mouth on hers, Abby became someone else. She eradicated her parents—the mother who'd come to school to give an antidrug presentation, the father who'd set her curfew an hour and a half earlier than anyone else's. With her arms around Vic, she shook off her reputation for shyness, even prudery, in one brilliant public display. She felt his warm skin under her palms, the edge of his jeans against her pinky. She wanted to fall into his chest, to bury her face in his flannel shirt. She suddenly understood what parties were for.

When he pulled away, she had a hard time catching her breath, and she looked up at him with surprise on her face. He looked back with the same expression.

"Oh, shit, I thought you were Mandy," Vic said. He put his hand to his temple. She saw that he was very drunk. "Sorry," he said. "Sorry. Amy?" he asked, but he was already backing away from her.

When she found the bathroom, she locked the door and stared at herself in the mirror, and the face that looked back was blurry and ashamed. How stupid she was! She washed her hands, pinched her cheeks, and put on some of Calvin's mother's lipstick. She was not uglier than Mandy, but it didn't matter—she had so quickly given herself to a person who meant to kiss someone else.

"This is pretty cool, isn't it?" her father said now. "This guy's a real professional. But what else would you expect from the best hotel in New Hampshire?"

"Oh stop," Abby said.

The instructor never stayed still but flitted and slid from one couple to the next, touching their shoulders, encouraging them. "*One* two three, *one* two three," he said, his arms counting this out. "The body is in four-four time—that is its natural pulse. The heart goes one-two-three-four, one-two-three-four. It is crucial, okay? But it's boring! The waltz, in 3/4 time—that, my friends, that is the pulse of joy."

"What did he say?" her mother asked.

"He said that waltzing makes you happy," said her father.

"See? That's why I think Abby should waltz."

Abby tugged at a loose thread on the bench, and a tiny corner of the fabric began to unravel. "I'm perfectly happy," she said.

"You've got to feel the way your feet make contact with the wood," the instructor called. The sheers at the window behind him billowed and collapsed over and over again, like giant lungs. "Let it be soft and light as a kiss . . ."

For the rest of the school year, Abby never once met Vic's eyes. But she watched for him, and she always knew where he was, and when the bell rang after last period and he got into his car, it was like saying goodbye to a special part of herself. He had been her first French kiss.

She supposed that Vic had gone off to college—if he had gotten in—to make out with new strangers at bigger, better parties. By her sophomore year she had almost forgotten him, and it was hard to understand how he had once seemed so important to her, so grown-up and intimidating. She supposed it was a sign of how dumb she had been. What had he ever done but confuse her with someone else and bring her mother a cat? Here he was, working in a hotel for the third summer in a row, and he was still sweeping up porches. She felt almost sorry for him, and she decided that if they ran into each other, she would be cool but friendly. She would mention college in Connecticut and her trip to New York City, and he would realize that she was not the silly girl she had been four years ago in high school. She imagined coming upon him in the midst of some janitorial duty while she walked hand in hand with her secret admirer. That—*that*—would show him.

Then the unpleasant truth of the matter struck her, and when it did so, she wondered how she could have failed to figure it out before. Vic had written the note—of course he had. Here they were in the middle of nowhere New Hampshire, and he had found a familiar face—a vaguely familiar face, anyway—and was trying to hit on it. Vic Libby! She'd waltzed into this fancy hotel with a piece of her midwestern past clinging to her like toilet paper on the heel of a shoe.

Oh, how much she had wanted her admirer to be someone exciting: some tanned, windblown boy with a rope bracelet on his brown wrist, some beautiful Yankee who wore a canvas belt with pictures of sailboats on it. Or someone from Manhattan or even Brooklyn, someone who skied or traveled or played the guitar. Someone who had been to Paris, someone who read books, someone who went to Amherst.

But no, it was Vic who admired her, and he hadn't called her "pretty" because she *was* pretty, he had called her that because he never could quite remember her name.

Pig had been a present from Vic, an unexpected and impossible to return present. Neither Elliott nor Helen had seen the kid in over a year, but there he was, under their porch awning, taller and broader and nineteen years old. He'd cut his hair, and he was carrying a cardboard box with a pink ribbon drawn on it in Magic Marker. Inside the box, atop a faded hand towel, was a tiny, mewing kitten, its eyes still cloudy blue and its fur so long and fine that each little hair seemed tipped with light.

"Her name's Pig," Vic said, holding out the box.

They had buried Licorice two years before and they were catless. Abby and Helen insisted they keep the kitten, though Abby wanted to rename her—Trixie or Pixie or Moxie or something. Elliott, in protest, suggested Dog. But Helen thought Pig was funny, and since Vic had intended the kitten for her, the name stuck.

Elliott did not particularly like cats, but Pig, who grew plump and affectionate, worked her way into his heart. Late at night when everyone else was asleep, Pig and Elliott sat together in the kitchen, he sipping a gin to relax, she crouched attentively at his feet, eyes half open and tail flicking back and forth across the linoleum. She liked to be close to him, but she never presumed to climb onto his lap, and he liked such perceptive deference. Sometimes when he was feeling womanish he would lift her high in the air with one hand, so that her legs dangled helplessly down while her quick heart fluttered against his palm. He'd knuckle her head and say, "You fat cat, you dumb furball," in tones that were soft and full of tenderness. When she purred her whole body trembled.

After a year of silent nocturnal companionship, he loved her better than Helen or Abby did and had taught her how to stand on her hind legs. "Pig, up!" he would say. "Pig, up!" And after pausing—she always made it seem like she was debating whether to obey—she'd lift her front paws and half stand, half squat on her haunches like some fat, green-eyed meerkat. This was a big hit: everyone loved it that Elliott, with his professed dislike for anything that didn't shit in a toilet, had trained a cat. It was a great party trick.

But when Helen fell ill, Pig became a different animal. She began crying all the time, and pacing the halls, and staring, frightened and baleful, from beneath the furniture. She wouldn't stay in the kitchen with him, though Elliott still sat there every night, working through a liter of Tanqueray and feeling fear like he had never felt before.

Pig hissed at the women Elliott invited to keep Helen company that spring: Kathleen Mackey, who came to bake quickbreads; Carole Weiss, who drove Helen to the park where they watched kids feed the ducks; Lauren Carpenter, who brought dollar annuals and clay planters to encourage Helen to work with her hands. These women tried to pet Pig and she ran from them. Then, at night, she started throwing up.

Elliott tried new food, less food, hairball remedy—everything—but it didn't matter. Pig left hairballs on the carpet in the living room, in the corners of the hall, on counters she'd never even tried to get onto before. Elliott put mousetraps on the dining room table, covered carefully with pieces of newspaper, in the hopes that she would set them off and be frightened from the table before she had the chance to vomit on it. But Pig, oh Pig, she barfed right on top of the business section.

He almost could have admired her—there was the purity of her confusion and her suffering, the terrible, precise way in which she acted out what he himself could not. But instead, overwhelmed by all that he had to care for, he decided to give Pig away.

Mrs. Ford found someone who agreed to take her, and the woman drove over one afternoon in an old wood-paneled station wagon. She had five cats already but she couldn't resist a story like Pig's, like Helen's. Abby was just home from college, and she was with him there on the driveway, sobbing, having exhausted all pleas for clemency. Elliott told himself he wasn't sorry; he knew what his priorities were. But he felt a sharp ache in his throat when he saw the way Pig scrambled out of her new owner's arms and leaped over the seats into the back of her car. He could see the tip of her tail twitching in the corner of the window. She began to cry, and her howls came at him high and confused.

She had six toes on her front paws and a white-tipped tail, like that of a fox. She used to sit outside the bathroom door when he took his morning shower, and when he walked to the kitchen to refill his coffee, she followed close at his heels. She spent her days stretched out along the ledge of the picture window, her fur warm and almost golden in the sun.

Across the creek, the hospital generator kicked on, and then Elliott couldn't hear her cries anymore. It was over, he told himself. He would miss her, he really would, but he had cleaned up his last hairball, brushed the last cat hair from the sofa. He would sit in the kitchen by himself at night.

Then through the dirty back window, he saw Pig stand up on her hind legs, the way he had taught her. It had taken weeks. He'd cut a block of cheese into cubes and put them in a Ziploc bag, and these were what he used to reward her. She was a willing student, and in himself he found a new and surprising patience. Sometimes he'd thought about teaching her other things, like how to roll over, fetch, or speak, but he'd never gotten around to it.

In the rear of the station wagon, Pig's ears were pitched forward, and he saw her eyes as wide and green as leaves. *See what I can do!* she seemed to say to him. *Look at how I stand!*

"Oh, Pig!" Abby said. His daughter clenched her hands at her stomach as if she were going to be sick.

The hospital generators shut off again, and before the woman started her car to take Pig away, he heard the cat howl again. She was still balanced on her hind legs, looking out the window, and her urgent, confused keening seemed to cohere into language. *Where,* she cried, *are you sending me, your good kitty, your furball, your own little night friend?*

He held his breath as they pulled away, as Pig lost her balance and fell out of sight. He wasn't—he couldn't be—sorry.

After dinner, Abby watched a documentary about the Peruvian rain forest in her parents' room while her mother got ready for bed and her father made notes in his planner, and then she wandered into her own prim little room, feeling like the embodiment of boredom.

She chipped a flake of white paint from the windowsill and then another. Next she stared for a long time at the cover of *The Mill on the Floss*. She had missed the afternoon trail ride, as well as the lecture on the hotel's stonemasonry. She had seen no admirer—no Vic—and her waiter at dinner had been at least forty, with the same wet, protruding lips as her physics teacher.

She contemplated going for another nighttime walk, but instead she stood in front of the bathroom mirror, inspecting her teeth and wishing for the one hundredth time that she had been better about wearing her retainer. She braided and unbraided her hair, then clipped her toenails, then filled the long white tub with water and half a bottle of bubble bath.

This was something to do, she thought as she sank into the heat.

Her toes popped up at the far end of the tub like tiny pink faces, and she watched them curl and flex as if they belonged to someone else. Lately she'd had a similar feeling when she caught an unexpected sight of herself in a window or a hallway mirror; she looked different from the way she was used to looking, and when she wasn't prepared, her image came as a surprise. The only thing she had done on purpose was pluck her eyebrows (Lizzie had taught her how). But the overall effect was somehow significant: it was as if she had always been slightly blurry, and now she had come sharply into focus. She'd lost her first-semester-of-college fat—"You're not fat, sweetie," her mother had said, "you're just a tiny bit *softer*"—but the breasts that had swelled with her weight hadn't shrunk down with the rest of her, and now, floating there beneath the lavender-scented bubbles, they seemed as if they would be hers forever, these fleshy, plump strangers.

Kevin had been glad to meet them, and he made their acquaintance as often as she would let him, cupping them and kissing them with a reverence she found embarrassing. She waited to feel something during these amatory sessions—she had *before;* she wasn't frigid—but it seemed to her that with the new body had come a strange disassociation from it, as if it refused to function properly until she was more familiar with its layout and dimensions. Poor Kevin. She kissed him back primarily to be polite.

After a few more minutes of listening to the bubbles hiss as they shrank and died, she was hot and bored again. She'd forgotten how little she enjoyed baths.

She wondered if she should have been so quick to dismiss Vic as a companion. At least he was a person to talk to, someone to play pinball with or something. He could entertain her by trying to guess her name. *Annie?* he would say. *Katie? Becky?*

She climbed out of the bath, wrapped herself in a white hotel robe, and wandered into her bedroom. And there it was on the floor, another folded piece of paper, this one ripped from a spiral-bound notebook (thin-ruled, her favorite). She tiptoed toward it and picked it up. *How about tonight? Same time, same place—Hancock's, 11.*

She wondered if Vic looked different, if he had grown a beard or shaved his head or built up muscles. Everyone at the hotel was so well kept, and she hoped that this had rubbed off on him; in high school he'd dressed in pilled flannel button-downs over old T-shirts.

How about tonight? Well, how about it? It was that or go to bed, twitching with loneliness and ennui. She stirred her finger in the bowl of dusty potpourri on her nightstand, sending up the smell of old dead roses. She pretended that she didn't know which she would choose, even as she reached for her lilac blouse instead of her nightgown and felt beneath the bed for her good sandals.

Abby made her way along the dim halls of the hotel's lowest story, past the locked gift shop and a room emitting the soft, erratic blips of arcade games. The walls were lined with black-and-white photographs of the men who'd built the hotel, and they gazed out at Abby with grave, antique faces.

She paused at Hancock's threshold. Behind a large wooden bar, a man leaned against the cash register with his eyes closed. To Abby's left, a white-haired couple sat without speaking, directing all their attention to their drinks. There was a table of men in golf shirts, a loner in a suit, and a trio of women in the corner. She saw no face she knew, so she stood self-consciously in her nice blouse. The bartender opened his eyes and, noting that she was not yet in need of his services, closed them again.

Then a hand waved from a corner, and a person Abby only vaguely recognized got up as she approached. He was tall, with dark hair and deep-set eyes of an indiscernible color. The arms of the sweater he had tossed over his shoulders seemed to embrace him lightly around the neck.

"You came," he said in a voice that held a trace of an English accent. He extended his hand, and when she automatically gave him hers, he brought it to his lips and kissed it. "But you look stunned that you did." He had a slender face, a broad nose, and an amused, almost feminine mouth.

"It's just—I thought you were going to be a different person," she said. She tried to make her confusion less obvious; she'd been so convinced that Vic was the author of the notes.

"You have another man writing to you?" He smiled.

"There's someone I know working here," she said. "I just assumed . . ." She held her purse tightly in front of her as if to shield herself. She didn't know who this person was, and she wondered if it was a bad idea to be here—if she ought to turn around, go back to her room, and finally start reading *The Mill on the Floss*.

"What's his name?"

"It doesn't really matter," she said, taking a small step backward. "I don't know him that well."

"I'm sorry if I startled you," he said, seeming genuinely chagrined. "I wouldn't normally write a note like that—I know it's a little creepy. But I saw you in the dining room, and you were so pretty in your white dress. If we'd been at a party I'd have come up to you and introduced myself, but I couldn't see how that was going to work while I was refilling your water glass."

He told her his name was Alex and that he had waited on her in the latter half of dinner the night before. Because he was looking at her intently and she didn't know what to say yet, she offered up what she had promised herself she wouldn't admit. "I'm not twenty-one," she said.

"I didn't think so," he said. "I'm barely myself. Anyway, Owen doesn't mind. He's pretty much napping back there."

Alex indicated that she should sit. His fingers were long and pale, with fine black hairs settled between the knuckles and white half-moons on his nails. He had piano player's hands, she thought, though there was something delicately simian about them.

He smiled at her, his whole face welcoming. "Please," he said.

She hesitated, and inside that pause she told herself that this was an experience and she ought to try to have it—she shouldn't be a chicken. Also, there was nothing else she felt like doing; her room didn't even have a television.

So she sat down. There was a bowl of olives and a bottle of wine and two glasses on the table.

"It's a Sancerre," Alex said, turning the bottle around so she could read the label. "It has good acidity and crispness, but it's what you might call a nervous wine. That's what I'd tell you if you were thinking about ordering it." He poured a glass for her and topped his off. "Sancerres are out of favor at the moment. They're from the Loire Valley, which is south and east of Paris . . . Paris, France."

"Oh, right," Abby said, still feeling somewhat anxious. "*That* Paris."

He laughed. "You're charming. Where did you come from?"

She was emboldened by even the slightest hint of success, and she thought his accent was nice. "Room 403," she said. "As you know."

"Funny," he said. "But really."

In college she had experimented with "My parents live in Ohio," as if she could no longer be associated with it. But here it seemed pointless to dissemble, so she told him the truth. "Go Buckeyes," she said.

"I've never known what a buckeye was."

"It's our state tree," she said, hearing, as she did, the old A-student earnestness sneak into her voice. "It has a little nut thing that's shiny and brown, which is supposed to look like the eye of a buck."

She grasped her glass by its neck, unsure what to say next. But Alex, it seemed, was willing to take up the slack. He was also an only child, the son of two retired lawyers. His parents were older—his mother was in her sixties, and his father was almost eighty—and they lived in Washington, D.C., where he had gone to an all-boys' school with the children of senators, though he'd attended fourth and fifth grade in the English town where his father had grown up. He'd been a high school long jumper and had played cello for five years. He was going to be a senior at Colby, and he was studying creative writing. He acknowledged that his college wasn't as good as hers, but he had read *Moby-Dick* and *Swann's Way* and could ski.

"I'm reading DeLillo right now," he said. "*Libra.* Not his best."

Abby, still accustomed to the shufflers and mumblers of high school, was surprised by his easy monologue. She liked that he thought he had so much to offer a conversation. And he kept complimenting her, which made it hard to remain uncharmed; in the light of his admiration, she felt herself becoming more winning.

"You're lucky to work in a place like this," she said, glancing around appreciatively at the fireplace, at the polished stone walls, at the fine dark portraits of stern-looking New Englanders.

"You might think it's nice now, but it's nothing like it was. Back when they opened the hotel, even the *maids* had maids, and all the chefs were from Paris."

"Which Paris would that be again?"

Alex laughed and plucked an olive from the bowl. In the background, Billy Joel opined about Catholic girls and the bartender turned the television to a soccer match.

"The one in France," Alex said. "The Presidential's degraded now, but a certain je ne sais quoi remains. I take notes. I'm thinking of a play. A sort of *Upstairs, Downstairs* thing."

"Is it a comedy?"

"So far," he said.

Since Abby could not bring herself to even *read* a book—how long had she been carting *The Mill on the Floss* around?—she felt that his voluntary labor spoke well of his ambitions and said so. He told her his real project was a novel that he'd been working on forever, and the play was just a distraction. Something light and easy.

"Going to a movie is easy," Abby said. "Or taking a walk."

The affable expression he'd been wearing disappeared, and Alex looked at her as if he were about to tell her an important secret. "It's easy because it's terrible," he said. "The book is a whole other thing." He tapped his finger on the table for emphasis. "I've been working on it for four years."

Abby had assumed him a dilettante—it was the accent, the affected flourishes to his speech. "What's it about?"

"I can't talk about it," he said. "I sound like a complete jackass. Let's talk about you instead. You are interesting, and I am interested."

"I'm not interesting," she said. She thought of Lizzie's easy way with a conversation, which was aided by her lack of fidelity to the truth of any particular event. "My friends are interesting. It's too bad they aren't here for you to talk to." She supposed she was fishing for another compliment, but this time he failed to offer one.

"Funny, I've got friends here, but they're not that interesting. Actually that's not true. They're interesting enough. But I've been living with them for three months now, and we've talked about everything there is to talk about twice."

He refilled her glass, and as the wine settled in Abby's stomach she relaxed farther into the booth. Alex wasn't the admirer she'd imagined for herself, but she liked him. She was intrigued by his confidence and his pomposity, and he did seem to want to please her. She told him a funny story about Lizzie falling asleep in philosophy class, and she made sure to mention her trip to New York and the art she'd seen at the Met; she supposed she wanted to impress him, too.

"You look like the kind of girl who likes poets," he said.

"I like poetry," she said. "My opinion of poets varies." She didn't know why she'd said that—she'd never met a poet, had she?

He took a pen from his pocket and a cocktail napkin from the table. He bent his head in concentration and after a few moments he pushed the napkin to her. In the cramped, neat hand she now recognized, he had written:

> *This night is like perfume,*
> *And you are a rose in the darkness.*
> *Autumn is coming.*
> *Beauty is a moral hidden in your tales. Your eyes*
> *Are like pools, like jewels,*
> *Like flowers on a flowering branch.*
> *In this night we shall go out*
> *Beneath the trembling firmament,*
> *Singing songs to call down the stars.*

When she had finished reading, she looked up at him. She didn't know if it was something he'd made up or memorized, or if it was supposed to be about her, or what she ought to say. Also she wasn't entirely sure of her taste, but she thought it might be a very bad poem. This must have shown on her face, because he began to laugh.

"And *that*," he said, "is a horrible Neruda knockoff."

"Oh," she said, feeling both relieved and deflated.

"'Darting sapphire night-bird, from you I learn the feathery shape of hope.' I think I'm good, don't you? You just need certain words—such as 'night,' 'beauty,' and the name of a flower or a stone. There should be an animal and a body part and the moon or a star. Then you address the poem to a 'you' and aim for a kind of earthy transcendence." He drained the last of the bottle into their glasses. "Actually that's a ridiculous thing to say. Neruda did much more than the odes. You could hold his communism against him, but other than that . . ."

"I haven't really read him much," Abby said. She hadn't read him at all.

"Did you see that?" Alex exclaimed. On TV, men from countries she'd never been to ran up and down a wide green field. "Eight was completely offsides."

She asked him if he was a soccer fan. Then: "Sorry, I mean *football,*" she said in a bad British accent.

"You've got a mean streak," he said. He reached out with one finger and began to trace it along her arm. He didn't look at her but kept his eyes on the game. His touch was gentle, and it sent tingling waves along her skin, in places he touched and in places he didn't. In mild disbelief, she followed the trail of his hand. She studied his profile, the epicene elegance of it. He was a pretty boy, and she liked pretty boys.

"Do you play tennis?" he asked.

"No, I don't. I mean, I've done it before, just never very well."

"But maybe you'd like to play it with me."

He leaned closer, and she saw that his eyes had a ring of brown that surrounded a ring of green, and then the black pupil like a bull's-eye. He had lovely lashes, dark and thick and heavy, and there were two small moles on his cheek, one above the other, like a colon.

"I don't think I can," Abby said.

Alex slipped his cool hand around her wrist. "It's so easy," he said. "Here, stand up." When she obeyed him, he came around to stand behind her, his chest pressing against her back and his arm close along hers. With the hand that circled her wrist, he mimed a swing. She felt the swooping rush, slowed down and sensual. Three times their arms sent an invisible ball across an invisible net. His breath flurried past her ear.

"See?" he said. "I used to teach it when I was in high school."

There was a kind of vibration in her insides, a thrumming that was gentle but insistent. His body against hers was warm and suggestive, and the unfamiliarity of it, the emphatic solidity of it, was like speech beneath speech—a language new to her but not so hard to interpret. She turned to face him. He held lightly to her wrist.

He was waiting for her to answer, and she found it hard to look at him, so she stared at his shoulder in its pressed white shirt and the arm of the blue sweater that draped over it. "I can't," she said. She couldn't play tennis with him—she had to be with her mother. Also she was terrible at it and would be humiliated.

"Tennis," he said again.

She wondered if it was something other than tennis he was asking about, if he had a subtler but more significant question to which she was still saying no.

"What are you going to do all day? Lie around by the pool looking gorgeous? You could be getting exercise on the tennis court. Everyone needs exercise, Abby."

"Laps," she said. She noticed how his shirt moved when he spoke, how its shadows shifted slightly and the white became pearly gray in the creases. "I can do laps."

"That pool is an obstacle course of wizened old women. You don't belong with them, love. You're too fresh."

"Goal!" the bartender cried.

Alex glanced toward the TV. He let go of her wrist. "Twenty bucks! Never bet against the Brazilians."

"Did you lose?"

"I don't know—did I?" he asked.

The old couple Abby had seen when she first walked in had ordered a carafe of punch, and a group of festively dressed men and women had gathered around the bar. But she was standing up, and it was late, and it seemed that she ought to go. What if her father opened the door to her room, thinking it was the bathroom, and saw that she was gone?

On TV, it was yellow shirts against blue, little figures dodging, feinting, sending the ball plumb down the field or high into wild flight. She used to play soccer. Her favorite position was the bench.

Helen dreams she meets her parents, rosy-cheeked and dressed for Mass, in the lobby of a vast apartment building. She is amazed: they aren't dead at all, and they were never even sick—they've just moved to another city, to this impressive art deco high-rise. How stupid she has been, not knowing all these years! Her mother's hair is dark and shiny, and her father looks like he's been golfing every afternoon. Helen takes their hands, almost weeping with happiness, and she thinks, *Why didn't you call? Why didn't you write?*

She wakes slowly and with the profoundest regret. Beside her, Elliott lies still, but she knows he isn't sleeping; he rouses her with the taut silence of his body. She can feel his worry, and she knows that she can't help him because she is the cause of it.

She breathes deeply, closes her eyes, and tries to conjure her parents again, but instead she sees Vic Libby, the first time he came into her office at the juvenile court on judge's orders, looking like her father did when he was young. They both had that Irish wrong-side-of-the-tracks pugnacity, that intelligence, that wariness. It was what had endeared Vic to her in the beginning. And what was so strange about that? It was a face she'd missed for thirty years.

In their initial meeting, Vic had admired the pillows on her plastic institutional couch. She'd appliquéd them herself, and he was the only person to have guessed that. She supposed this predisposed her to like him, too—not because he'd complimented her but because, unlike most of the kids she counseled, Vic was capable of noticing things that mattered to other people.

Then he'd made fun of her inspirational posters and the sign on her door that asked WHY BE NORMAL?

"People have certain expectations about the accoutrements of counseling," she told him. "Like the way dentists have to put up posters about your teeth, and gym teachers are required to have a plaque that says IT's NOT WHETHER YOU WIN OR LOSE, IT'S HOW YOU PLAY THE GAME." She glanced at her walls. "SMILE! IT'S CONTAGIOUS!"

And he *had* smiled. In fact he'd laughed. "That is so fucking stupid," he said, and though she didn't say so, she thought he was right.

The people at the court were into early intervention that year, and they saw Vic as a kid who wasn't too deep into trouble but was probably headed there. They decided not to wait until he became an arsonist, so they sent him to Helen. He was a sophomore then, lean and canny. The notes from his intake interview said that his mother was in California, that his father had no known current address, and that Vic was being raised by his maternal uncle on the east side of town. Beneath the heading "Traits," Helen's colleague had written "defiant, antisocial, remorseless." In truth Vic was none of those things—or at least no more so than most teenagers. Nor did he lie, a tendency so frustratingly exhibited by the majority of Helen's juvenile offenders.

Most of her kids were devious, some were belligerent, and others were so sweet it was impossible to believe they'd done what their files said they had. And she'd loved all of them, or almost all of them. Usually, they were in trouble for their poor choices in group activities: they'd been busted for partying, fighting, or racing down the wide, temptingly straight lanes of Winter Street. Helen knew that had she herself ever truly misbehaved, she would have required the encouragement and example of bolder, more reckless people. But Vic's crimes—curfew violations, criminal trespassing—were all solitary. Helen found a certain perversity in that. And maybe there was even something a tiny bit admirable about a person self-assured enough to make his bad decisions independently.

Then there was his sense of humor. He'd smashed the plaster busts of the U.S. presidents that lined the high school's main hallway—but only the Republicans, beginning with Taft. Twice he'd risen before dawn to chain the school doors shut.

For his community service, Helen had signed Vic up to plant trees in one of the municipal parks, and one day on a run she'd passed him shoveling mulch around a new sapling. He'd called out to her.

"Flowering dogwood," he said, gesturing to the tree. "The twelfth one I've planted."

"It'll be gorgeous next spring," Helen said. She was sweaty and breathing hard.

"How far do you go?" he asked.

"On my run? About five, six miles on the weekends. Less during the week."

"That's a lot," he said.

"You're getting sunburned," she told him.

"I'm done for the day. This was my last one. I'd do more, but they're out of trees."

"Well, you can come over to my house, then," Helen said. "I've got plenty of yard work."

She'd been teasing, but he'd actually done it: she was watering the roses when he pulled up in his uncle's car. Her first instinct was to send him home again—it really wasn't proper, and how did he know her address, anyway?—but she didn't want to hurt his feelings. He was still just a boy, a sixteen-year-old boy. And she could use the help; Elliott was at Carlisle, and Abby, who wouldn't have been that useful, was at a rehearsal for the seventh-grade play. Vic kicked his toes in the bark mulch while Helen thought about it, and after what was a fairly casual internal debate, she motioned him into the garage, where she gave him a bottle of sunscreen and a pair of hedge clippers.

Vic's parents had been a couple of teenagers who'd pawned him off on his grandparents, and when his grandparents got tired of running around after him, they sent him to raise himself at his uncle Mike's house. That was how Vic told it, anyway. His story wasn't the worst Helen had heard, not by a long shot, but it touched her, and she wondered if it was because she heard in it a faint echo of her own long-ago abandonment. His parents had decamped, hers had died; they were both, in a way, orphans.

There was a part of her that wanted to show him a picture of her father when he was still so handsome. Sean Murphy, black Irish, foreman at the barge company. Helen had adored him. Each night after dinner he'd put Helen on one knee and Susan on the other, and Mary Pat would bring him a drink, and as the night wore on he'd grow more charming and sentimental. He sang "Hang down your head, Tom Dooley / Hang down your head and cry . . ."

He had a fatal heart attack at forty-five, when Helen was ten. At the wake on the *River Queen,* big men from the barges and skinny men from the business office ate heat-lamped chicken and sang his praises, and to Helen they had all seemed like monsters, like loud, red-faced giants.

Three years later, Mary Pat died of cancer, and Helen and Susan were alone until the McDermotts took them in. The story got into the newspaper, and for a while they were a little bit famous, the poor Murphy girls.

Vic had clipped the arbor vitae into fine, straight columnar forms and then helped her weed the flowerbeds. Mostly they worked in comfortable silence. And when she sent him home, she did so with a check for twenty dollars and an admonition to spend it on some kind of activity that wouldn't get him into more trouble.

For so many of her kids, she just did what she could, understanding that whether or not they'd straighten themselves out was unknowable and beyond her control. But that day she realized Vic would make it, and that, too, made him dear to her. Yes, she'd loved all her kids, but there were some she loved more.

Still feigning sleep, Helen rolls onto her side and puts her hand over her husband's heart.

WEDNESDAY

Elliott felt fatigue in the marrow of his bones—a dull, insistent sensation that was not pain but pain's close relative, working to reacquaint him with the architecture of his body, its joints and struts and trusses. He held an empty ceramic mug tightly in both hands, as if, by pressure and concentration, he could squeeze more coffee out of it. The dining room seemed too far away, so he sat by the lobby fireplace with its red roses—fake, he noted—and hoped that some waiter, some valet, some Good Samaritan would come by with a gallon of coffee and a big bowl of sugar, because the Schmidts and the Callahans would be arriving in the afternoon and he needed to feel alive enough to receive them.

Sheila, the Presidential's special events manager, sat on the couch across from him with a clipboard balanced on her knee, ready to help him pick the menu for the party on Friday.

"This is just a treat for me," she told him. She was a carefully powdered and painted fiftysomething in a crisply ironed blouse and a silk jacket with narrow shoulders. "We do dozens of weddings every summer, and I love them, but they can be so stressful. I think it's wonderful that you're celebrating an anniversary like this. Twelve is the ideal number of people, too—it's just enough to make it feel like a real party."

"Would you like to come and give the speech?" Elliott asked.

She laughed a gay butterfly laugh. Of course she could never do such a thing, but she did hope to help him plan the perfect event. She had reserved the Gold Room, where an important treaty had been signed on the very same table at which the Hansen party would be eating; Sheila couldn't remember the details of the settlement itself, but there was a plaque describing it on the wall. If Elliott would like live music, her daughter played in a string quartet procurable for a very reasonable rate. Sheila was sure everyone would like the filet mignon, which was one of the hotel's specialties, though she could also recommend the roast chicken.

She handed him a list of menu possibilities, and Elliott wondered if it would be inappropriate to ask her to get him coffee while he read the list through. He'd never really planned a party. A wedding anniversary: how did it go? He tried to remember how his own wedding had been managed. Helen must have planned everything, since he certainly hadn't. His sole preparatory act had been to buy a fine new charcoal-gray suit. He was finishing his master's thesis, and then defending it, and even marrying Helen on that halcyon August day—standing before the priest alongside a woman he loved like no other—had felt like another kind of graduation ceremony.

"I love the salmon as well, but some people don't like fish," Sheila said. Her hair was held back on one side by a tortoiseshell clip, and when she moved, the air she displaced smelled dry and floral, like a sachet kept in an empty drawer. "I don't know why it is, but men never want to order the fish. Women will pick it, though—they like that or the chicken."

"Men prefer larger animals," Elliott said. "It's an ego thing."

Sheila laughed. "It's all about the conquest, isn't it?" she said, leaning forward, smiling, the color rising in her cheeks, and Elliott swore—though he must be mistaken—that she was attempting to flirt with him. Involuntarily he shrank back, and immediately Sheila's coyness vanished;

brisk professionalism settled over her face like a veil. "The salmon is an excellent dish," she said.

He raised his coffee cup and shook it. "Is there waiter service out here?"

"When the lobby bar opens, there's table service. Do you need coffee?"

"Badly."

"I'll get you some."

"I wouldn't ask—" he began.

"Sit tight, I'll be right back," she said, already striding purposefully on her way, and as he watched her cross the room in her old-fashioned spectator shoes, it occurred to him that it had been months since someone had done him a favor not motivated at least in some part by pity. He felt a warm, if fleeting, affection for her.

The menu Sheila had given him was numbing in its breadth. He was reminded of his trips to the grocery store after Helen came home from the hospital, already impaired, already having relinquished all domestic responsibilities to him. How he stood gripping the greasy plastic handle of an empty shopping cart, stumped by the produce section, all of his intelligence and resourcefulness nullified. What was he supposed to do with all those misted, glistening leaves and fruits? There were carrots in mesh bags, carrots gathered into bunches with their frilly green tops still attached, and carrots in plastic tubs, cut into matchsticks, their flesh already dry and pale. There were five different . . . breeds? species? . . . of apple. Was it peaches Helen didn't like, or nectarines? Elliott forgot his own tastes as well, and bought radishes in a neat red bundle. He hated radishes. It took weeks to learn his way around the aisles, to parse the system of classification that kept Windex on one side of a store and paper towels on the other when their relationship to each other seemed so fundamentally clear. Once, instead of buying a head of iceberg lettuce, he had brought home a green cabbage.

The women at the checkout counters took a special interest in him, at first for his helplessness and later for his competence. They learned his name from his checks and called him by it; he had once caught one of them putting on lipstick before he got to her in line. Elliott hadn't worn a wedding ring in sixteen years, not since Abby had sent his and Helen's swirling down the toilet bowl during her flushing phase, and he understood that this contributed to his warm reception.

Sheila came back with two mugs of coffee and a Danish on a china plate. "They're getting ready to close up, but I swiped a pastry." She sat down across from him again. "Any thoughts?"

He thought that he had gotten himself in over his head—all these people coming and him having to host them. He thought that if Helen were well, he would have had only to take her out to a nice dinner in Columbus. He looked into Sheila's soft brown eyes. "I'm having a tough time deciding," he said. He was still in that supermarket aisle, bewildered. *Does my daughter like spinach? Does a red onion taste different from a white? What's the difference, really, between penne and rigatoni?*

"You can think about it for a while if you like," she said.

"If we met tomorrow or the next day, I could bring Eva along."

"Eva is your wife?"

"No, just someone with good taste."

"I'm sure you have excellent taste, Mr. Hansen," Sheila said. "Don't sell yourself short."

"This has never really been my realm of expertise."

"You're the yard-work type," she said. "And the type to pick out wines. By 'type' I mean simply 'male.' My husband could hardly tell salmon from catfish, but he could tell a Château de Fieuzal from a Château la Louvière with a single sniff." She folded one of the sample menus into small squares. "And he kept an exquisite lawn."

Hearing her use of the past tense, Elliott shifted habitually, easily, into counseling mode and fixed Sheila with a sympathetic eye. "Did he—"

"He's passed," Sheila said. "A spontaneous splenic rupture. One day he didn't feel well after dinner, and the next thing you knew, he was gone."

"I'm so sorry to hear that." He put his hand on the table between them, as if, were he closer, he would have placed it comfortingly on her shoulder.

She gazed into her coffee mug. "He was a remarkable person. He could remember anything anyone ever said to him, any movie he'd ever seen or book he ever read. It was like living with an encyclopedia. You could ask him anything. What did Margaret Thatcher study in school? What did Pauline—our daughter—wear to her junior prom? He'd say 'Chemistry, and a one-shouldered floor-length white dress with a blue satin sash.'" Sheila's voice had taken on a hint of remonstrance, as if Elliott had been unwilling to appreciate her husband as much as the man deserved. "He taught himself to play the piano at forty. He wasn't brilliant, but he was quite good, and for our own twentieth wedding anniversary, he composed a minuet for me. He and Paula performed it—a duet."

"He does sound like a remarkable man," Elliott said. "A man of many talents."

"Yes," Sheila said. "That's exactly what he was." She fiddled with the clasp on her bracelet. "But I don't know why I've told you this. You just want to know if you should have salmon or steak."

"You shouldn't apologize."

"You have a kind face—that's what it is. It must be."

Elliott could have mentioned Helen, which would have eased Sheila's embarrassment and forged a kind of tentative connection between them. It was good to have something in common with a stranger, good to not be alone in distress. But he merely smiled at her as kindly as he could.

"Anyway," she said, "I'll leave you for now. Let's talk tomorrow or the day after. You're not a large party, so we don't need a lot of warning. And if you do get the quartet, make sure you say hi to Pauline. She's the one with the short dark hair. She just cut it all off last week." Sheila reached across the table to shake Elliott's hand, and though his was sticky from the bit of Danish he had just broken off, he placed it firmly around hers. She blinked at him, and it seemed like they were comrades.

"Have a wonderful day," he said. "You're doing a great job."

After she left him, he lingered over his coffee. He was due to meet Abby and Helen at the pool, but he liked his seat in the lobby and the public invisibility it afforded, there amid the maids and the entering and departing guests. He leaned back, just for a moment, and closed his eyes.

In the hot glare of the sun, the cells of Abby's skin felt as if they were constricting, desiccating, becoming bright and hard as grains of sand. She had rolled up her shorts and pushed the sleeves of her shirt over her shoulders, and every once in a while she dipped her fingers into a glass of water and flicked cool droplets on her face and arms. She was thinking about Alex, who had kissed her once on each cheek before sending her off to bed with a promise that he would find something besides tennis to entertain her.

He did not quite benefit from scrutiny in the bright, sober light of day, when Abby recognized her slight distaste for the pretensions—the flattery, the unwarranted English accent—that had so easily won her over the night before. But she was unfamiliar with love that didn't involve at least a grain of contempt: for years she'd been listening to her classmates badmouth their boyfriends, and she had always been a trifle skeptical of Kevin. She'd thought herself better than Vic, too, even when she was half in love with him. So the trace of scorn she acknowledged did not necessarily lessen Alex's appeal as a companion.

She wondered how much of his attention was due to her charms and how much to his boredom. When she considered herself through Alex's eyes, her faults seemed clear: shyness, a certain confusion as to the proper steps in the dance of flirtation, her being there with her parents. She wanted him to think her sophisticated and experienced when, more likely, he would see her as young, innocent, provincial. This was another thing to ponder as she tried to defend herself against the mixed opinions she had attributed to him.

"Stop it," cried a high, plaintive voice, and Abby opened her eyes to see the boys who reminded her of Tracey's horrible children spitting water at each other in the shallow end. By the pool bar, a little cedar-shake hut, a woman in a fluttering caftan reclined on a lounger. She slid a page of a magazine along her wrist and then sniffed at it absently.

Helen napped in the shade a few feet away, unintentionally patriotic in a red bandanna, a blue shirt, and white shorts. She had her earphones on, and beside her on the grass she'd set up a still life of sustenance: banana, water, croissant, Ensure. Her hands lay folded on her chest, and her rib cage gently rose and fell. Above her the leaves of a birch tree trembled, and the dappled light shifted over her body. It was one of those times when Abby looked at her and had to remind herself: *That person is my mother.*

When they first moved to Ohio, Abby had had a babysitter named Bertie. Bertie drove an old Dodge Dart and wore sweaters fuzzed with the hair of her cat. Slow, dim, and joyless, she was the precise opposite of Abby's mother, who said they must be patient with Bertie because she'd had a stroke when she was twenty-eight. It just happened one morning, Helen said, when Bertie was putting on a pair of panty hose.

Bertie, with her short black hair and round white face, had been a bank teller downtown. When she could not remember the word she wanted—the thing that Abby was supposed to use in the backyard (a rake), or the thing that was blocking the steps to the garage (Abby's pogo stick)—her pale soft hands would move in a circle, paddling the air, as if language floated invisibly around her and she could somehow stir it up into her mouth.

Abby was nine years old. Adult incompetence embarrassed and infuriated her. She almost always knew what Bertie was trying to say, and she almost always let her struggle anyway. "The what?" Abby would cry. "The *what?*"

Beside her, Helen sat up and took off her headphones. "I think I fell asleep," she said. "It's nice, isn't it?"

The drink hut's window slid open, and Abby could see the flash of someone's shirt inside. From the ballroom, the faint notes of a piano concerto came floating toward them. It *was* nice: the hedges were trimmed so neatly; climbing roses clung to the fence that enclosed the pool; on either side of the gate, tiny purple flowers spilled down the sides of stone planters. "It's very pretty," Abby said.

"I think so, too." Helen twisted her watch around on her wrist, exposing a band of paler skin. "Can you see what time it is?"

Abby leaned over to look. "Almost noon."

Helen smiled at that. "Good. Our friends should be here soon."

Abby would be glad when they arrived, too, because they would keep her parents occupied, thereby directing their attention, such as it was, away from her. As the lone adolescent, she would be left out, and that would be just fine.

"Are you going to swim?" her mother asked.

"I don't have my suit on."

"I do," Helen said. "Under these things."

"Those are shorts."

"I know."

The boys clambered out of the water and circled the deck, leaving a trail of small footprints that evaporated one by one. Their mother held out towels, and they collapsed into them, spent and sleepy.

"Are you hungry? Do you want a sandwich? Something to drink?" Abby asked.

"I'm fine." Helen began to untie her tennis shoes. "Twenty years . . ."

"Your china anniversary," Abby said, watching as her mother removed her shoes and then her socks. "You're supposed to get a tea set or something. It's Tracey's anniversary, too. You know, the lady—the *woman*, I mean—whose kids I'm watching. For her it's ten years. We looked up all the presents you're supposed to get. Ten is the tin anniversary, but Tracey said it's diamonds."

"I hope she gets some," Helen said.

"She probably will."

Helen pulled her chair closer to Abby's. "I want to be in the sun," she said. Her nose was pink from the day before, and there was a slight flush to her cheeks.

"I don't think you're supposed to be," Abby said. "You could get burned." When her mother didn't answer, she added, "Because of the chemo?"

"I'm not doing that right now."

"But still. There's, like, a sensitivity or something."

Her mother stepped carefully out of her shorts and shirt and then tossed a plastic bottle of sunscreen at Abby. "That's what this is for."

Though Abby's aunts had bought Helen a new wardrobe of summer knits, no one had thought to get her a new bathing suit. The elastic had lost its stretch and she had gotten so thin that the Lycra hung loosely on her, like an ugly flowered blouse.

"Ready," Helen said, and pointed to her back.

Abby knelt on the rough concrete behind her mother. The tail flap of Helen's bandanna had come loose from its knot, and it fluttered lightly in the wind that rippled the glassy deep end of the pool and set the bright pansies to bobbing. One strap of her mother's bathing suit slid down her shoulder, and Abby caught a glimpse of white, diminished breast.

"I looked for Vic this morning," her mother said. "I thought he'd be on the porch."

"Maybe he was mucking out the stables." It gave Abby some satisfaction to imagine him knee-deep in horse manure.

"He's afraid of them. Horses."

"How do you know?"

"He told me."

"Why?"

"I don't remember." Her mother leaned forward and clasped her knees, baring her long narrow back. "Are you going to put it on?"

Abby squeezed the bottle with both hands and squirted a dribble of sunscreen down her mother's spine. Helen flinched and immediately Abby was sorry—she knew she was supposed to rub it between her palms first to warm it up. Helen had always done that for her.

Abby watched the white glops sliding down her mother's back. Helen waited. Then, hesitantly, reluctantly, Abby began to rub the lotion in, feeling the triangular planes of her mother's shoulder blades and the peaked, countable knobs of her spine. Beneath Abby's palms, Helen's skin seemed thin and slack, as if it didn't fit her right either.

"That's really nice," her mother said.

The pure, shy pleasure in her voice dug a pit of guilt in Abby's stomach. How hard was it to give her this? She summoned all the tenderness she had and sent it into her hands. She smoothed the sunscreen into her mother's bony shoulders, her lower back, slipping her fingers under the loose straps of the bathing suit. As the lotion was absorbed, Abby's hands met the warm skin, and the sensation was one of almost unbearable intimacy. She could feel her mother needing this, and her desire and fragility were strange and frightening. Abby drew her index finger lightly up her mother's spine, all the way to her neck, until the bandanna brushed against her wrist. "All set," she said softly.

Helen sighed. "You're so good at that. Can you do it some more?"

"I got it everywhere."

"I think you missed some spots."

"Very funny." Abby laid her cheek on top of her mother's head. The bandanna was warm from the sun and it smelled like fabric softener. She felt a surge of love so strong and painful that her breath caught in her throat.

"Oh, honey," her mother said.

Abby sat back in her chair and wiped her eyes and handed her mother the bottle. "Can you do the rest yourself?"

"I think I want to go in the water."

"But you just got all that stuff on."

"I can put it on again."

You mean I *can,* Abby thought. "Why don't you wait for Dad?"

But Helen was already walking toward the pool. At the shallow end, she took a step down, holding on to the railing, and the water lapped at her ankles.

"Why don't you stay there?" Abby called. "You can sit, you know—you can sit and put your feet in."

Abby was sure her mother heard her but pretended not to. Still grasping the railing, Helen walked down the tiled stairs until she was up to her waist. She kept her arms extended, her hands hovering above the rippling water as if she were afraid to get them wet. Abby remembered those hands cupped under her legs and shoulders as she tried to learn how to float. She was five or six then, in the Callahans' pool, with the sun glinting on the water and Ruth Callahan on the deck, saying, "My girls could float when they were four!" Abby recalled acutely the reassuring gentleness of those hands, and her panicked thrill when they were pulled away.

Helen knelt down, sinking into the water so that only her head was above it, and Abby sat up straighter in her chair. She said to herself, *If I can hold my breath for a minute, she won't try to swim.* She reached for her mother's watch, already counting one thousand one, one thousand two . . .

Abby was only up to twenty, not even feeling it—she thought she could hold her breath for an hour, if that was what it took—when her mother stuck out her arms and pushed forward with her legs and began swimming.

Helen had had an effortless crawl; when the Hansens went to the beach for vacation, she took twice-daily swims out past the waves, parallel to the shore, her arms windmilling up and her legs scissoring straight and sure for what seemed like miles. Abby used to follow her along the sand, pretending to gather shells but actually waiting and worrying, never comforted until Helen had returned to shore, giddy and breathless.

Now Helen held her head high and tense, kicking up water droplets that rose spangling in the sun. She moved forward, slowly and resolutely, to where the pool floor cut away sharply and the water became a deeper blue. Her scooped hands pedaled under the surface: she was dog-paddling.

The Presidential Hotel employed masseuses, maids, busboys, bell-hops, bartenders, caddies, waiters, valets, chefs, dance teachers, and groundskeepers, but not one lifeguard. To reassure Abby about the safety of her mother in that sliding, treacherous water, there was one lone Sty-rofoam ring, striped maroon and white, and a long metal pole with a hook on the end. Abby scrambled out of her chair to stand at the edge of the pool, her body poised for rescue.

Helen's brow was tight with determination as she moved forward by agonizing, splashing inches. It seemed that at any moment something could go wrong: she might breathe in water or grow tired; she might begin to sink down under the surface.

"Oh please," Abby whispered. "Oh please."

Stubbornly her mother went on, and Abby walked along the edge above her. Helen passed the six-foot marker, the seven, the eight. At nine she stopped and rested, treading water.

"Are you okay?" Abby said, but her mother didn't answer.

One of the little boys was bouncing lightly on the end of the board, waiting for Helen to move out of the way. The other walked in circles in the shade, humming to himself, wearing his towel like a cape.

"Why don't you swim to the side?" Abby said.

Still her mother didn't answer, but began her torturous dog paddle again. Abby shut her eyes and thought, *Oh God, don't drown, don't drown,* and by the time she opened them, Helen had reached the deep end of the pool. Abby experienced a surge of relief that was followed just as quickly by something that felt almost like fury: her mother never should have frightened her like that. Helen gripped the tiled edge, shaded by the div-ing board, panting a little. The boy took a running leap from the end of the board and landed right where she had been.

Abby pointed to the ladder. "Look," she said. "You can climb out here. You must be cold. I'll bring you a towel."

"I'm going back," her mother said.

"No, you're not."

Her mother turned away, and Abby wondered if she was going to have to jump in the water in her clothes. But instead of swimming again, Helen edged along the wall, pulling herself hand over hand, down the length of the pool until her feet could safely touch bottom.

"*Please* come get into your towel," Abby said.

But her mother opened her mouth in a great wide O, sucked in her breath, and dove underwater. Beneath the surface, her body was distorted, wavering, inching forward. Her bandanna remained floating, a bright jellyfish. A few feet away from the wall, Helen rose up, smiling and gasping, her bald head shining.

"Oh," she cried. The water beaded on her skin and slid down in rivulets. Her ears stuck out on either side of her skull, lonely and absurd, and the scar from the biopsy was a vivid pink line. Helen put her hands over the sides of her head, as if this would cover it.

It seemed to Abby that every petal on the rosebushes and every leaf on the suspended geraniums had turned to watch. She could feel the people on the porch leaning over to look. There was a blue jay in the tree, and his call was sharp and derisive. The windows of the hotel were a hundred dark eyes.

Helen reached for the bandanna and tried to slip it back on, but it was still knotted, and it sat as uselessly as a crumpled napkin on top of her head.

Abby cried out, "No, that's not it!"

"Oh, honey," Abby's father said, walking through the gate. "Let me help you with that. Hand it to me."

Even into the afternoon, the long halls of the hotel kept the cool stillness of the morning. From the ballroom came the faint notes of some Spanish-sounding number and the occasional encouraging bark of a dance instructor: "Hips, people! Stay loose!"

Elliott and Helen had taken a turn around the veranda, and now they sat in the airy conservatory, Elliott paging through the newspaper even though it was past two and the news already seemed to belong to the day before. He read without comprehension an editorial about NASA and a recipe for Moroccan lamb. His wife had finished writing the postcards they'd picked out from the gift shop (*We are haveing a great time in the sun and swiming in the bool*), and now she sat looking out the window. She was disappointed not to have run into Vic yet, but she was having one of her better days; the swim had done her good.

Abby appeared in the doorway in a tank top and a skirt that ended six inches above her knees. "There you are," she said. "I saw a Volvo with a KEATS license plate drive up. Is that them?"

Elliott resisted the urge to comment on her clothes and turned his mind toward his friends. It was beginning, it was all starting now. He held out his hand to his smiling wife, and together they walked out to the front porch, with Abby trailing behind.

Climbing out of the Volvo's backseat, Eva Schmidt saw them and, with no small effort, composed her face, smoothing away her obvious surprise at finding Helen so transformed. She came up the steps with her arms outstretched, and Helen walked right into them. They held each other for a long time.

"It's so good to see you," Eva said, stepping back. She wore her hair cut short and pearls in her ears, and she looked just as she had when Elliott saw her two years ago—petite and efficient and maternal. "I'm so glad we're here. I've been thinking about you every single day. You know we wanted to come visit you earlier, but Elliott made us wait. Oh, my dear Helen, you're so tiny. We've got to get you fattened up."

"Skinny is the thing I have going for me," Helen said.

Eva laughed. "Nonsense," she said, and cupped Helen's cheeks.

Ruth Callahan approached in a cloud of linen—flowing pants that rippled about her legs and a blouse with long, flapping sleeves. Her dark hair was swept back in a headband. Elliott had never thought her particularly alluring, but she had memorable features: a wide, ironic mouth, an aggressive nose, large eyes under a broad forehead. "It's been too long, too long—do you hear me?" she said. She, too, looked rattled by the sight of Helen.

"Don't cry, Helen," Eva said. "There's nothing to cry about! We're here! We're here! We're going to have a picnic."

Helen wiped her eyes. "I'm sorry," she said. "I'm happy."

"We know, sweetie," Eva said. "We're happy, too."

Tan, angular Ruth came over to Elliott and put her arms around his waist.

"You look wonderful," he told her.

"I am merely well moisturized," she said, and her hands swept up to touch her face and then descended again. When she leaned in to kiss him, he smelled the same perfume she had always worn, something deep and sweet and earthy.

"And Eva," he said, "you look lovely, too."

She pinched his arm affectionately. "You don't need to flatter *me*. Go say hi to the boys."

Down by the car, the husbands came over to greet him. "Hansen," Eva's husband said, taking his hand. "It's good to see you again." Henry was short and broad-shouldered, an ex–rugby player. Though middle age had thickened him around the middle and given him a ruddy, jowly look, it actually suited him; it had softened the blunt planes of his face and mellowed his general demeanor.

"Well met, friend," said Ruth's husband. Dom had been a prep school tennis player three decades ago, and he wore his hair in that privileged, rakish fashion still, with long bangs in front that he kept swept off to the side. Now he was an assistant professor of English, specializing in Romantic poetry; his financial comfort he owed to an enterprising earlier generation of bankers and inventors. The Volvo was his, though Elliott assumed the vanity plates had been Ruth's idea.

Helen and Abby came down the stairs to meet them. Everyone agreed that Abby had grown, and Eva said she was gorgeous, but Ruth demurred, saying she didn't want Abby to get a big head.

The suitcases were stacked on the porch and the bellhops were waiting in their maroon suits, but still everyone lingered under the porte cochere. A swallow whose nest sat cupped in the ironwork of the light fixture flew in and out between the pillars, and the peacock trundled over to eye them.

"Is he friendly?" Ruth wondered. She took a few steps toward him, clicking her tongue, and he let her get quite close before shying away to observe things from an unassailable distance.

"In my experience, he's more inclined to be friendly if you have food," Elliott said. "They call him the Duke."

"As in John Wayne?" Henry asked, and Elliott shrugged.

"Well, I'll just have to get some food, then," Ruth said. "I love peacocks; I think they're so beautiful."

"Everyone thinks peacocks are beautiful," said her husband, which made Ruth roll her eyes.

"Are you hungry?" Eva asked Helen. She pointed to a large wicker basket, out of which poked Tupperware containers and the slender green necks of wine bottles. "It's late for lunch, but I've brought about a hundred pounds of food."

"Do you want to go up to your rooms first?" Elliott asked.

"Nah, we'll have our bags sent up," Henry said. "Let's take a look around and then eat."

Dom said he would check them in, and the rest of them walked out to the back veranda so Elliott could show them the view. The porch was mostly empty, and Elliott wondered, not for the first time, where everyone was. All in all, he'd seen more staff than guests, and while there'd been the occasional middle-aged face to provide a necessary gravitas, in general they had been attended to by well-scrubbed, deferential adolescents.

Ruth fell onto a wicker love seat and patted the cushion beside her. "Come here and sit by me, Elliott. You got sun and it makes you look rugged and handsome."

She was trading flattery for flattery, he thought; he'd seen himself in the mirror and he knew he looked like hell. He also knew the sharp eye with which old friends examined each other. There was the mapping of new wrinkles, the quick appraisal of other novelties: a heavy new watch (an inheritance?), a mole that hadn't been there before (something one ought to get looked at?). How did a person measure up? If the years were kind to a friend, might they be kind to one's own beloved, declining self?

"This view is incredible," Eva said. She bent far over the railing. "And there's a little café thing down there. Right underneath us."

"He keeps saying it's the best hotel in New Hampshire," Abby said.

"What about that Foxmoor by the Sea or whatever it's called?" Ruth asked. "I used to hear wonderful things about it."

"Shuttered," Dom said, striding over to Henry to hand him his room keys, "and it was floridly ornate. French Regency by way of the county fair fun house. I went to a Coleridge conference there once." He pulled out a pair of pocket binoculars and trained them on the mountains, on the evergreens, on a woman sunbathing by the pool. "My paper was on

Coleridge and the picturesque. Or something like that. Coleridge and dreams? It was only a couple years ago, and already I can't remember it." He rubbed his mustache thoughtfully.

"It must have been incredibly fascinating," Ruth said, mugging for Helen's benefit.

They seemed self-conscious, performing a familiar marital dance without much enthusiasm. But Helen was amused, and Elliott allowed himself a brief moment of self-congratulation: this was just what she needed.

Abby, who said she had seen a good place for the picnic, led them down to the hotel's lower story, past the patio, and along a sloping path over the creek and into the woods. Elliott walked with Helen's hand in his, and he could feel her excitement. "Careful of the branches there," he said, and she elbowed him lightly in the ribs.

The path brought them to a place where a bend in the stream made a small, rocky beach and a cluster of boulders sheltered a shallow pool. The water was pale green and little fish darted about in it, thin and silvery as knives.

"'Brook! whose society the Poet seeks, / Intent his wasted spirits to renew,'" Dom said happily.

Eva and Ruth spread out layers of blankets for Helen to sit on, and when they worried that it wasn't enough—she was so thin—Eva sent Henry back to the hotel for a pillow. "He likes to be useful," she assured Helen. Henry waved, acquiescing like a good sport, already jogging away.

"No sense in serving off the ground like a bunch of animals," Dom said, unfolding a small table. "I've told you about Armond's, haven't I, Elliott? How they do milk-fed suckling pigs?"

"Yes, you've mentioned it," Elliott said.

Ruth, helping Eva unload the basket, said, "They look like toddlers. It's just terrible."

"You name your size, they slaughter it, and then they deliver it to you on ice."

"See what I mean?" Ruth said. "Terrible."

"Ruth eats the suckling pig if you slice it up for her, " Dom said. "So it's not a moral argument she's making, but an aesthetic one, which takes the heat out of her objection."

Sunlight filtered through tiny apertures between the maple leaves. Abby had climbed to the top of one of the boulders and was gazing picturesquely downstream. If anyone were a bit closer to her, Elliott thought, they'd be able to see up that skirt of hers.

Ruth held up a lighter for the cigarette Elliott had unconsciously taken out of its pack. He'd meant to hide his vice from them, but he found he could relinquish such a secret without regret.

"You know Dom's aunt had a stroke last year," Ruth said.

"I'm sorry to hear that."

Her eyes were large and brown and rimmed with kohl, and her wooden bracelets clacked down her wrists as she lit herself one of her Mores. She had a few good years left, he thought. A few more years before the silks and the wild prints, the flowing scarves, began to look ridiculous, before she became a scarecrow draped in bright cloth.

"No, no, don't worry—she's fine. It was the weirdest thing. She was in the stroke ward, and you know what that's like. Everyone is drooling in their wheelchairs and pissing into tubes, and she seemed completely all right—she'd even managed to put lipstick on—but all she could talk about was deep knee bends." Ruth inhaled, and as she pulled the cigarette away from her lips Elliott heard a slight popping noise. "Literally, that was it. She started doing them in her hospital room. Then she went home, where Dom's uncle, who is a saint, took care of her, and she kept doing them. She worked very hard on her technique. And so nine months went by while she did the knee bends, and then all of a sudden it was like a light turned on in her mind. At breakfast she asked her husband if he had cleaned out the gutters, and by dinnertime she could talk about everything she used to talk about. She was just like her old self! Except that she had the legs of a woman half her age."

Elliott smiled. "That's a funny story."

"Oh, it's all right." Ruth knocked her hard hip against his. She said, "You're going to die for this picnic. For the lobster rolls? Eva even made the *buns.*"

"Come and get it," Eva called to them, holding out plates, and Dom moved over on the blanket so Abby could sit next to him.

" 'I put my faith in knee bends,' she says," Ruth said, poking him. "Get it? Knee bends instead of Jesus?"

"Ha," Elliott said. He was reminded of how frank and godless she was—they all were—how unconcerned with questions of the eternal. He'd been that way, too, of course, ever since, at twenty-two, he was finally done with Catholic school.

Henry returned with the pillow for Helen, and they all settled in and began to eat. There was a sweetness to this, Elliott thought, to the simple act of feeding oneself in the company of friends. He felt a sensual pleasure in the weather, and in the wine's benevolent influence. Shadows shifted over his friends' faces, and behind them the water rushed ceaselessly over the rocks, whispering and splashing. Little cotton-puff clouds slid by overhead one by one, and to Elliott, watching them disappear behind the high bank of trees on the other side of the stream, it seemed as if he could see time passing in their wake.

"'I heard a thousand blended notes, / While in a grove I sate reclined, / In that sweet mood when pleasant thoughts / Bring sad thoughts to the mind. . . . ' That's Wordsworth," Dom says, settling in beside Helen.

The others are cleaning up the picnic behind them; Helen can hear the rustle of garbage bags, the shaking of blankets, the brushing off of pants. It feels selfish to sit here by the water, but she's doing it because Eva told her to. Eva said she wasn't to lift a finger for anything.

Dom hands her a pinecone. "Here," he says, "throw it in and make a wish."

"That's not how it goes," she says.

"What, you want a penny? A quarter? You might brain the fish."

Still he holds out the pinecone, so she takes it from his palm. It's light, the size and shape of an egg, and its spines are sticky with sap. Helen passes it from hand to hand as if she needs time to think of a wish. She doesn't, of course—there's only one wish, and it doesn't even need language, it is in every cell of her body. It's hammered out in her pulse, it swells in each dilation of her lungs, and it rushes along in her veins like blood. *Make it go away.* She lets the wish rise up with all its deep, somatic power, and then she flings the pinecone, which lands in the center of the pool and floats.

"Now that's a good sign," Dom says.

As if he has any idea, Helen thinks, eyeing him. He used to have a beard, and now that he has shaved it off, his chin seems small and vulnerable.

Water skimmers gather in a still pocket in the shade, their minuscule legs outstretched. Where their feet touch, they make a dimple in the water.

Dom pushes up his sleeves. The dark hairs on his forearm lie in one direction, like river grass bent in a current. He reaches down and scoops up a handful of pinecones and holds them out to her. "Do you need more wishes? How many wishes do you want? We've got these to start with."

Fifteen years ago, seventeen maybe, something like that, Dom used to love her, and the memory of this fills her with regret. But regret for what, she wonders, or for whom? Does she wish things had been different, and if so, how? She isn't sure. She knows only that now it seems like anything at all could have happened then, and they would still be here by this green, rushing creek. She could have loved him back or told his wife; she could have stayed in New Hampshire or moved to Alaska; she could have become a lawyer or joined the circus. It wouldn't have mattered what she did, because nothing could change what life had in store for her.

Still, she thinks, *maybe if I am really good, then everything bad will go away.*

She picks another pinecone from his palm and flings it into the water—with the same wish sent from heart, from fingertip, from gut—where the water skimmers are, scattering them, and then Dom throws one, too, and together they watch the ripples they make swell and touch and roll into each other.

"Hey," said a voice. "I know you."

Abby, half dozing in the hot tub in the shade of a blue spruce, sat up with a start, and there he was, Vic Libby, the kisser of wrong girls, sitting not two feet away from her. She'd almost forgotten about him; it was as if Alex, who'd left another note while she was on the picnic (*I came to entertain you but you were gone! Where are you, pretty Abby?*) had somehow canceled him out.

Vic wore a white uniform, and he looked taller and more substantial than she remembered him, though he sat slouched down on a deck chair. His blue eyes were a little hooded in his narrow, almost handsome face, and the arms he crossed over his chest were brown and smooth and dry. He seemed vaguely amused.

"You're the Hansen girl." He gazed up at the sky as if her name would be written there. And maybe it was. "Abby," he said. "Abby Hansen. What's with the fruit?"

The lemon wedges she'd taken from the picnic basket sat beside her on a paper plate. "I put it on my hair," she said, sinking lower into the tub. She was hot all of a sudden, not from the water but from the humiliation he reminded her of.

"What for?"

She couldn't believe he was here and that he was asking her about hair care. Her freshman year, she'd memorized his license plate and could recognize his car simply by the low, rattling sound its engine made, and she wished she could go back in time to tell her younger self not to be so incomparably stupid. "It's supposed to make highlights," she said.

"Do you want to be a blonde or something?"

"No." She touched a stiff, lemony curl.

"You do look different."

"It hasn't worked yet."

He held a branch of the blue spruce in his hand, and one by one he picked off its needles and put them in a pile on his knee. "I guess it's been a while."

"It has," Abby said.

They were alone in a copse of trees. Behind Vic, the big shiny leaves of a rhododendron glinted as if they were made out of plastic.

"I wondered when I'd see you. I ran into your dad yesterday."

She nodded, making circles in the water with her feet. "He told me. He kept saying, 'Small world, small world.'"

Vic laughed. "Diplomatic like always. I don't think he liked me much."

"He kicked you out of Carlisle, didn't he?"

"I like to think of it as more of a mutual thing." Vic scraped the pine needles into a smaller, neater pile and then brushed them off in one quick swipe.

"What'd you do?"

"Acid," he said. "On a field trip to the Columbus art museum."

Because of her mother's work at the court, Abby had always thought that drugs were bad, but she knew that part of being less of a baby was revising that opinion. "Sounds like a fun time," she said.

"I've had funner," he said.

"So what are you doing here?"

He gestured to the uniform. "Working."

"I know that, but why here?"

"My grandpa lives a few minutes away, and I'm helping him build a boat."

"A sailboat?"

"More of a fishing boat."

"I hate fishing," Abby said.

The jets in the hot tub shut off, and the water hissed and then stilled. Abby became conscious of herself in her bathing suit, her bare legs and her new strange breasts now visible. She stirred the water with her arms.

Vic walked over to the control knob and the water bubbled up again. "He's a pretentious bastard, isn't he?"

"Who?"

"That waiter of yours."

She gave him a sharp look. "Were you spying?"

"I guess he's read a lot of books or something," Vic said. "That impresses you. Reading. It's not that hard, you know. 'Elderly persons and infants, persons with medical problems such as heart conditions, low or high blood pressure, pregnancy, obesity, circulatory system problems, diabetes, and other health conditions requiring medical care, and persons using medication should consult a physician before using the hot tub.' See?"

"That's not the same thing at all," she said. "Alex chooses to read, and you choose to fish."

"I don't fish. I'm just building a boat. It's a favor," he said. "And I *do* read."

"Signs," she said.

Vic smiled, looking at her carefully with those heavy-lidded eyes, as if remembering when she was fourteen, flat-chested and timid in tapered jeans and that frosted pink lipstick she'd worn because she didn't know any better. He seemed comfortable, though, and interested in talking to her, as if he was sure they'd once been friends. She stared at his feet; they'd never said ten words to each other.

"It's actually a canoe," he said.

"What?"

"The boat I'm building." He leaned forward, reaching out toward her, and she drew back; she thought he was going to touch her shoulder or her hair. But his hand dipped down to scoop up some of the pine needles from the swirling water. He flicked them into the grass.

"Oh," she said, and then was at a loss.

"When am I going to run into your mom?" he asked. "*She'll* be happy to see me—she loved me."

Abby wondered how true that really was, but she supposed it was rude to say so. It was strange to think of Vic talking to her mother every week, strange to imagine him on Helen's office couch, playing with the Silly Putty or the marbles or the mini-puzzles she kept on the coffee table. What had they talked about? What had he thought of her poor earnest mother? Had he been kind to her?

"As my dad probably told you, she's sick," Abby said. "She has can-cer." When Vic didn't say anything, she said, "Brain cancer." In a dark, barely acknowledged part of her, she felt a kind of terrible elation: it was electrifying to be the bearer of such awful news.

Vic looked away. "Jesus Christ," he said to the trees. "Fuck." Then he got down off the chair and sat next to her plate of lemons on the deck.

"You could say that," she said.

"Is she okay?"

"I don't know," Abby said. There was a burning behind her eyes, and she blinked rapidly to stop it. "I mean, she's really sick. But she's going to get better." She stopped, uncertain. On whose authority did she say this—the squirrel she'd bet on? Yet telling Vic made it seem more true.

Vic patted his chest, a gesture she recognized from her father: he was looking for a pack of cigarettes.

"I've got a Merit in my purse," she offered, thinking of the one she had taken from her father's pack. "It's probably a little bent."

He shook his head. "I quit," he said. "I just forgot for a second." He ran his hands through his hair, and when he stopped, it stuck out from his head in new directions. "I want to see her."

"We've got a lot of people here. She gets tired. Overwhelmed." Abby wasn't sure whom she wanted to protect—her mother, Vic, or herself.

"Come on," he said, the impatience clear in his voice.

"Well it's not like I can make an appointment for you. But we sit on the porch a lot. Sort of outside the conservatory. Will you get me a towel?" She pointed to the stack of them all the way down by the pool.

He nodded, and she watched the bright white of his uniform against the green grass and the orange daylilies, and then she closed her eyes until she heard his footsteps on the stairs.

"Here you go," he said.

She climbed out of the water, careful to show herself as little as possible because her old bathing suit, a modest one-piece, didn't look so modest on her anymore. Vic, gazing away into the trees, didn't turn toward her until she was wrapped up.

"I guess I'll see you around," he said. "I'm on in five."

"What's the white for?"

"Kitchen prep."

"Do you ever wait tables?"

He shook his head. "They save that for the charmers. And by 'charmers,' I mean ass-kissers and lapdogs. Like your Alex." He laughed.

When he had gone, she followed in his footsteps back to the hotel, conscious of her bare legs and the way the lemon juice had made her hair sticky and stiff as straw. *She loved me,* Vic had said. *Sure,* Abby might have replied, *she loved all the delinquents.* Or: *I used to love you, too, back when I was dumb*—because something in her wanted to hurt his feelings. But maybe it mattered that Vic knew her mother when she was still herself, the Helen Hansen who would run five miles, read the paper front to back, and fix Abby's school lunch all before seven A.M., the Helen Hansen who could fill the home-team bleachers with lawbreaking juveniles indebted to her for her aid and advocacy. This could not be said of anyone Abby had met at college, and suddenly Vic seemed dear to her again, and she was sorry she hadn't been nicer.

"Here we go, 437," Eva said.

She slid a key into the lock, and Elliott followed her inside and set what was left of their picnic on the bed. The Schmidts' room was smaller than his and Helen's, with gray walls, a white dresser, and a deep armchair beneath the window. Eva opened the wicker basket and began taking out the Tupperware and the wineglasses—Dom had also insisted on stemware—to wash in the bathroom.

"Not bad," Elliott said, flipping the TV on and then off again.

"It's wonderful. Of course, I'd sleep on a cot in the kitchen."

The water splashed in the sink, and Eva pushed up her sleeves and began to scrub things with the speed born of habit, laying them aside on a folded bath towel to dry. He watched her reflection in the mirror—the soft set of her mouth, the quick, efficient movements of her arms. Even her body seemed designed with graceful economy; there were no unnecessary flourishes, no immodest lines, no features that didn't match the others.

Her house, an airy old colonial on the green crest of Putney Hill, complemented her person. The flagstone kitchen was lined with neat shelves of home-canned vegetables and summer preserves. Hand-hooked rugs were placed in front of comfortable love seats. In the bathroom hung thick cotton towels in cranberry, navy, and white, colors that Elliott thought of as particularly New England, and the soap was shaped like shells or little pieces of fruit. Though Elliott usually met such über-domesticity with suspicion—it seemed selfish to him, even small-minded—in Eva's case, he had always relished it. Her kindness to herself made her kinder to others. And beneath the housewifely flourishes lay congenital Yankee austerity: rooms were uncluttered and beds were high and hard. There was none of the midwestern fondness for calico and gingham; Eva had no quilted tea cozies, macramé owls, or carved wooden geese in aprons and hats. When the Hansens went to New Hampshire for a visit, her home's graciousness relaxed him like a soft hand on his brow.

She held a wineglass up to the light, turning it this way and that. "Does this look clean to you?"

He shrugged, and she dunked it in the sink.

"It was such a pretty drive up," she said. "I can't believe we've never been here before. We were going to come one year—Henry had planned a skiing trip—but that was the winter Rachel broke her arm, and it was also around the time when Henry's mother died, so we didn't make it." She held out another glass to him. "What about this one?"

He knew she wasn't really asking his opinion but merely trying to include him. "Looks clean," he said. "No harm in giving it a rinse, though."

He went to the window and looked down over the pool. There were a couple of kids in the shallow end and a boy in red swimming trunks climbing onto the diving board. He was going to tell Eva about Helen in a minute, and maybe afterward everything would be different.

The boy in the red trunks was tentative at first, but he began to bounce higher, and soon the board was bending deeply toward the water and flinging him up, over and over. The other kids in the pool stopped to watch him. Elliott counted ten, eleven, twelve, then nineteen, twenty, and still the boy bounced, higher and higher as if that were all he ever planned to do. "Twenty-five," Elliott whispered, "twenty-six," and then finally, after one last tremendous leap, the boy launched himself into a high pike dive. He seemed to hang in the air for a moment, touching his toes, still in the dry, familiar world, his shadow a blur on the water.

That boy was Eva, Elliott thought, Eva right now. And in a way, she, too, must know what was coming next, the way the boy knew as he plunged down into the water with hardly a splash.

Steam billowed up from the faucet, fogging the bathroom mirror, obscuring Eva's reflection. "How's business?" he asked, to delay a bit longer. She had a store full of lovely, unnecessary things: soaps wrapped in flowered paper, lace-edged nightgowns, scented candles, crystal boxes of potpourri.

"It's going along. We got a nice write-up in the *Monitor.* They took an awful picture of me, otherwise I might have sent it to you."

"Send it anyway," he said. "Helen would love to see it."

"She seems in good spirits. I guess I wasn't sure what she would be like—I don't know if it's better or worse than what I expected."

He sat down on the arm of a chair, and it tipped under his weight. He adjusted himself but did not sit all the way down. There was a doily peeking out between his legs, and another on the chair's right arm, draped like a tiny lace veil. He plucked them off and folded them and placed them on top of the television.

Eva stood before him. The front of her shirt was splashed with water, and she was patting at it with a towel. "I'm afraid," she said.

Sunlight through the window lit up a wave in her hair and made her ear glow pink. He thought about telling her to sit down, but that seemed theatrical. He said, "It doesn't look good."

Eva blinked and waited for him to continue.

"It's the tumor's shape," he said. "It can't be surgically removed. So they give you the other options: radiation, which destroys healthy tissue along with the cancer, and chemotherapy, which is poison. You sign up for that, as bad as it sounds, and then you realize that the tumor is too spread out to target with radiation and that chemotherapy drugs are only minimally successful at crossing the blood-brain barrier."

Eva sank down onto the bed. "What does that mean?"

"They said she would live about nine months."

"From now?" she whispered.

"From then," he said.

"But that was March! Oh God—I knew it was bad," she said. "But I thought . . . I don't know—I thought . . . Couldn't they have said *years*? Couldn't they give her that?"

Elliott shook his head. There had been hope for a while, and that was what he'd held on to. When Helen had begun treatment, the tumor had shrunk measurably at first. That was the kind of news he'd told people readily. He'd said things like *You know Helen—she's a fighter.*

Eva put her hands over her face and was quiet for a long time. He had a desire to take her into his arms. Or—no—to be taken in hers. He wanted to lie down on her bed. He wanted, suddenly, to sleep.

He leaned back in the chair and looked at the ceiling. There was a water spot in the corner shaped like a half-peeled banana and a crack in the plaster running jagged down the wall. He thought there would be a sense of relief now that the facts were shared, but somehow it only emphasized his solitude.

After a few minutes he went and sat down on the bed next to her. He put his arm across her shoulders, and she pressed in to him, and he could smell the flowery shampoo she used. There was just a bit more to tell. So he held Eva close and explained that, in the opinions of both himself and Helen's doctors, Helen was doing as well as she was solely because she was willful and capable of hope. If that hope were taken away, he said, she would collapse, and the end would come that much faster.

He felt Eva shivering against him, a warm wetness blooming on his shirt. "She doesn't know?"

"No," he said. "And Abby doesn't, either. The time line, I mean. Just you."

"Oh God," she said. "I don't think you're wrong. Believe me, I can understand anything. I just . . . I just don't understand why it had to happen to her."

"I ask myself the same question."

Eva wiped her face and then got up. She began straightening the pillows on the bed, and when she was done with that, she opened the curtains wider. She ran the towel along the windowsill, and they watched the dust rise in swirling puffs.

"There are maids for that," he said. "Though obviously they don't do that good of a job."

"Cleaning is what I do," she answered.

"Me too," he said. "Now."

She folded the towel and set it on top of the dresser. "I want to help. Please tell me if there's anything I can do. Isn't there something I can do?"

"You can pray for the miraculous." And in a way, he did mean that. Because maybe it was their best hope. And even if it wasn't, what was the harm?

"Oh, Elliott."

"You can tell Henry for me. Ruth and Dom, too."

"Really?"

"Please."

"Why Helen?" Eva cried. "It should have been Ruth." Then she picked up the towel and flung it to the floor. "Oh God," she said. "That's not what I meant—"

"I know," Elliott said.

She sank down beside him again, and they sat quietly. In the hallway, the maids pushed their carts from room to room, calling out to one another, laughing, complaining, alive.

As the sun set on the other side of the hotel, a violet dusk spread over the trees, darkening the flamingo-pink clouds above the blunt ridge of the mountains. A few yards away, a German family took pictures of themselves, the flashes sparking on their spectacles, the children draping themselves along the porch railings. Elliott lit a cigarette and flicked the match over the edge; it landed near the peacock, who was scratching idly in the dirt with one dry, gnarled claw.

"We could play cribbage," Ruth said. "Anyone for cribbage?"

"Helen was a killer at cribbage," Dom said. "She beat me so badly the last time we played, I swore I'd never play her again."

Helen smiled, pleased to be reminded of her success, and Elliott recalled summer weekends spent at the Callahan family lake house, when they'd played games each night as if they were children: cribbage, euchre, Pictionary, and once, on a long night, I Never. The lake house was a large and rambling white cottage with long hallways, staircases leading to various stories and half-stories, a massive stone fireplace, and an air of sanctioned, genteel deterioration. Family photographs going back nearly a century leaned against the books on built-in walnut shelves. In Dom's generation, there was a passel of siblings, of cousins, who taught at minor universities up and down the East Coast, all of them epicurean, well read, and lazy; the tall, dark-haired Callahans had certain innate and inescapable traits, like a breed of fine hounds.

Elliott remembered how they used to eat lunch down on the sun-bleached dock, how the girls pestered him to take them out in the rowboat, all of them at once, Abby and Katie and Maeve and Eliza and Rachel, shoved in a tight tangle of limbs and musty orange life preservers. When Maeve Callahan, the oldest, turned thirteen, they were allowed to paddle out by themselves to the edge of the cove, where the lake became dark blue and the white sailboats sliced back and forth, inscribing circles on the water. Helen would watch them with binoculars, pretending not to be nervous.

The lake house was Helen's favorite place. She and Elliott always took the same room under the eaves, where they slept between sheets ironed and pulled tight by the housekeeper, and each night the friends circled up on the dock in the fading light and drank and talked and played their games. Amid all the pleasure, Elliott sometimes felt a rare swelling of jealousy; he wished the lake house were his to give to Helen.

"So how is Abby these days?" Dom asked. "And where'd she run off to?"

Elliott didn't know where his daughter was, but with her out of earshot, he could mention her accomplishments without her sighing and rolling her eyes at him. He told them she'd joined a singing group and was active with the campus environmentalists. "She says there's not a single cute boy at school," he said. "Isn't that funny?"

"That's what she'd like you to think," Ruth said. "I've never heard of a campus that didn't have cute boys. I've been to her school more than once, and let me tell you, there are plenty of them."

Elliott supposed she knew what she was talking about—Ruth had certainly been to more undergraduate pubs than he had. She'd begun singing and playing her guitar in coffee shops in her early thirties, when Maeve and Katie were in elementary school. Against the odds, she'd released a couple of profitable albums on small labels under her maiden name, Ruth Peel, and these days she enjoyed a modicum of fame on the campuses of liberal arts colleges. She sang about empowerment and community and the strength of women, subjects irresistible to the earnest, well-meaning minders of college entertainment budgets. Her songs were rhyming and sometimes maudlin, but she had a rich, assured voice and hundreds of fans age eighteen to twenty-two. Elliott would have brought her to Carlisle if he'd had the money.

"You could be right, Ruth," Henry said. "On the other hand, you get to be a certain age and then you can't tell who's good-looking and who's just young."

"I can tell," Dom said. Then he began to tell a story about hiring the father of one of his students to remodel a Callahan bathroom, while Ruth flicked her eyes between her husband and Helen and Eva, who were whispering to each other. The contractor was also apparently a dealer of marijuana and a committed user of his own product, Dom said. When he reached the part about the injudicious use of a sledgehammer, Helen giggled—a high, girlish laugh that rippled through the air like tiny bells. It belonged to another decade entirely, another season, some long-ago bright morning full of promise.

Everyone turned to Helen, and she looked back at them, startled. In the half-light the lines on her face were deeper and her eyes seemed sunken. "Eva told me a joke," she explained.

"What is it?" Ruth asked. "Tell us."

Elliott could see Helen growing embarrassed. "It's not a . . . punch line," she said. "It's a story."

"Sorry, it's for Helen's ears only," Eva said.

———

Elliott could see Ruth appraising her friend. She crossed her arms. "It's good that you're so funny, Evie," she said. "Since you know what they say, laughter makes the best medicine."

And there it was, poked into the conversation on the knife tip of platitude—the first public acknowledgment, slight as it was, of Helen's sickness. And it had been done in a flare-up of petulance: Ruth had felt left out. *She doesn't know,* Elliott thought, *she doesn't know yet what a horrible thing that is to say.*

"Laughter and a hell of a lot of pills," Helen said, and at that everyone roared, no one louder than Elliott, who was relieved that the tension had dissipated and was thrilled to see, for one fine moment, the return of his wife's wits. He reached out and squeezed the thin thigh above her hard knee, and she smiled at him, pleased with herself.

"You don't have a spare one of those lying around, do you?" Henry said, gesturing to Elliott's cigarette.

"Henry," Eva admonished him. "You don't smoke."

Elliott tossed the pack at him, and Henry put a cigarette in his mouth and let it hang there, unlit. "I'm just thinking about it," he said. "It suits Elliott so well." He reached for the lighter.

Eva put her hand on it. "Please," she said. "Behave."

In the old days he would have lit it just to tease her, but mellower now, he sighed and handed the cigarette back to Elliott.

Eva slid a sweater over her head; the temperature was dropping. "I could stay here for a month," she said breezily. "Was this where they filmed *The Shining*? Some big hotel in the mountains?"

"No," said Ruth, who loved Jack Nicholson, "that was in Washington."

"D.C.?"

"No, no, Evie, the *state*. The state of Washington."

"I never saw the movie," Eva said.

"Washington," said Dom thoughtfully. "Actually, I think it was Oregon. For the exterior, anyway."

They weren't really interested in the conversation they were having, Elliott thought, but they were polite, good-natured people to whom such palaver came easily. "Why don't you sing us a song?" he asked Ruth.

"Summer is my time off," she said. "Anyway, I don't have a guitar, because we couldn't fit it into the trunk with all the golf clubs."

"And your *suitcases*," Dom said.

"But that reminds me—we brought an extra set of clubs for you, Elliott," Henry said. "From Bob Mitchell. You remember him, don't you? He's moved to Concord." He pronounced the town *Con*-ked. "Isn't that right, Evie?"

"He's divorced now," Ruth said. "Christine took him to the cleaners."

"Well he kept his clubs," Henry said, and Eva confirmed and dismissed these facts simultaneously with a small nod.

Ruth said they ought to take the cog railway to the top of Mount Washington. "It's the worst weather in the world up there. The Indians called it 'home of the Great Spirit.' Though why He'd choose to live there is beyond me."

But only Ruth thought that sounded fun. Eva said she thought they ought to lie by the pool and eat chocolates. Elliott kept his mouth shut because he didn't care what they did. He lit another cigarette and inhaled deeply. Voices drifted toward them from the other end of the porch, and laughter traveled up from the pool below, and a whistle sounded from a doorway. *Everyone else in the world is having a good time,* he thought.

Ruth had begun telling a story about a dog Maeve had rescued and adopted. Though Ruth wore bracelets and heavy pendants, her long-fingered hands were always bare, and there was never any polish on her nails—in contrast to the rest of her elaborate costuming, they seemed raw and naked. When she spoke they swooped around her like hawks.

Elliott turned away. In the gardens below, the breeze shivered in the leaves and the lightning bugs flickered and pulsed.

Ruth's voice cut into his thoughts. "That's how the little fireflies call their mates, you know," she said, seeing where Elliott was looking. "You think it's so pretty, so *twinkly*, and it's just a bunch of bugs flashing 'Fuck me, fuck me, fuck me.'"

"Good God, Ruth," her husband said, "put a sock in it."

"I missed you today," Alex said, leaning in Abby's doorway. "I don't know why you played so hard to get."

He peered past her into her room. It was still uncharacteristically neat because she had been waiting for him, without admitting it to herself, for hours—it was almost midnight—and so she had made her bed and folded her clothes and then lined up her George Eliot and her notebook and pens carefully on the desk, as if she planned to study.

"I was here the whole time." She hadn't seen him at dinner, so she'd walked the entire hotel grounds afterward, hoping to run into him; his absence had made him desirable again. "You can't come in," she whispered.

"I wasn't planning on it." He held out a drooping, daisylike purple flower to her. "For you."

She said, "It's totally wilted."

"I know, I forgot to put it in a vase."

Instead of putting the flower in a glass of water, she placed it behind her ear.

"Very flattering," he said. "Now comes the part where I rescue you from your solitude and torpor. Put your shoes on. Bring a jacket, too. Mountain air, et cetera."

There was obviously no doubt in his mind that she would obey him, and it felt peculiar to be commanded so decisively. She was possessed of enough natural obstinacy that she almost shook her head. But she didn't want to be alone in her room, dying of boredom—she wanted to be out in the illicit dark while her parents slept. She slid on a pair of sandals and debated between two sweaters before taking the uglier, warmer one.

"Where are we going?" she asked.

"You have to meet everyone," he said, and tucked her arm into his.

Once they were outside, he steered her toward the parking lot on the north side of the hotel. At the far edge, near where the forest began, there was a low white building, unadorned and a bit shabby in the shadow of the Presidential.

"Ta-da!" said Alex. "Where the workers live. Which is off limits to hotel guests, naturally."

Inside was a long hallway that stank like beer and the lemony tang of industrial-strength cleaner—like college. The carpet was gray and dotted with stains. Alex strode ahead, pushing through another door and motioning Abby to follow.

She found herself in a bright kitchen where half a dozen people her age clustered around two wooden tables. Everyone looked up at them except a ponytailed girl who was peering into the oven.

"*Nous sommes arrives,*" Alex said.

"Just in time," said the girl by the oven. When she straightened up, Abby recognized her as the blonde she'd seen on the old tennis court. "They're almost done."

"Did you bring beer?" asked a tall, thin boy in a Feelies T-shirt.

"I brought Abby," Alex said.

Abby looked around at their tanned, handsome, expectant faces. She supposed she was not as exciting to them as beer would be, but they were exciting to her. The girls wore their hair long and straight, and the boys leaned back with a casual, loose-limbed confidence.

Alex went around the circle, pointing. "Molly, Ellis, Josh. At the smaller table you've got Paunch and Trey—we forget their real names, but Trey's a Third of something. Bea's there, she had her head in the oven. People, please allow me to introduce you to Abby. Oh, and over there's Pete—we like to keep him in the corner. Abby is from Iowa—" Alex said.

"Ohio."

"Yes, Iowa, and she is very charming. She is— What year are you?"

"A sophomore. It's *Ohio*."

"She's going to be a sophomore! She is with us for another . . ."

"Four days. Or three and a half."

"Another four days. I told her we would take very good care of her."

Abby stood smiling and self-conscious at the edge of the room, feeling that the flower in her hair somehow marked her as belonging to Alex. She repeated the names to herself: Josh was the one in the Feelies T-shirt, Ellis wore pigtails, Trey had bright red cheeks . . . They were almost alien in their easy, lounging grace, the self-assured way they filled the space around them. She felt like an eight-year-old who'd stumbled across the clubhouse of her camp counselors.

"Hi," she said. Her voice came out high and uncertain because she had been unprepared for this, and because she had just been introduced by a person who tossed off French in a put-on British accent. She lifted her hand in a little wave.

"I like your skirt," Molly said. She was wearing bright pink lipstick and a paper crown, and she reminded Abby of a girl she used to see in the college library. "Alex told me about you. We were hallmates last year, did he tell you that? It's my birthday."

"Happy birthday," Abby said.

Josh extracted two beers from the refrigerator and held one out to her and one to Alex. "Ohio," he said pensively. "I have a cousin there."

Ellis twirled a pigtail around her finger and wondered aloud if Alex had tried to impress Abby with his wine knowledge—"He's disgustingly proud of it," she said—while Trey just grinned at her.

She was being met, Abby thought, with a mild and friendly curiosity, and it seemed that their welcome had less to do with their interest in her than it did their affection for her companion. This was a relief: she had not been introduced to a group by one of its outcasts. Their regard for Alex made him still more appealing.

"Paunch?" Abby whispered to him.

"No, Ponch," Alex said. "Like Eric Estrada. He and Josh work at the golf course, Ellis is in the gift shop, and Bea's in the kitchen on desserts. Trey and Molly and I are waiters, and Pete waits tables too sometimes, but he also works the grounds because he's dirty."

Molly held out her hand and Josh passed her a beer. "I know at least as much about wine as Alex does, but I'm not so anxious to prove myself," Molly said.

"Cheers." Alex leaned back proprietarily against the counter. "Branches of Molly's family fought against each other in the Revolutionary War."

Molly faked a yawn. "Alex finds this fascinating for some reason."

"I'm putting it in my play." He turned to Abby. "Molly is the blue-blooded shrew."

"I get to be the maid," Bea said. "The maid has better lines."

Molly kicked an empty chair toward Abby, who sank into it gratefully. The checked linoleum floor was worn away in front of the counters and the doors, and in the far corner, balls of dust rolled lightly in the breeze coming through the window. There were old posters on the wall: a woodblock print of a forest, a faded photograph of the hotel, and a drawing of grasses overlaid with calligraphic characters.

Bea heaved a pan out of the oven, and it clattered on the stovetop. "Voilà," she said. "Molly, you want to help make your frosting?"

"Bea wants to be a pastry chef," Alex explained.

Molly rose and went to the counter. Pete leaned over and turned on a tape player.

"Not Dylan again," Josh said. He tossed an empty beer can into the air, caught it, and then winged it into the trash.

Alex positioned himself behind Abby and lay a long hand on her shoulder. "This is what we do every single night. You still think you'd like to work here?"

Ellis put on a pair of sunglasses that were lying on the table and said to Alex, "You're the one who never wants to go to a movie or leave the grounds."

"Untrue," Alex said. "I've also made Ellis a character in my play. A fat charwoman, jilted in love."

"You should have seen my red velvet cake tonight," Bea said, watching Molly stir the frosting. "It was the prettiest thing ever."

"I had that for dessert," Abby said, glad to have something to contribute. "It was amazing."

"Thank you," Bea said. "The rest of you cretins wouldn't be able to appreciate it."

When Bea put the brownies in neat little squares on a plate, everyone sang a cheerfully desultory "Happy Birthday" and then devoured them. Abby lingered on the periphery, letting the competing tracks of conversation float over her head. She understood that their nonchalance toward both the occasion and Bea's efforts was proof of their bond, the sturdiness of their friendship. Josh began talking in a German accent, imitating one of the guests, and Trey told a long joke about a man with no arms. Abby wondered if there was a special element of performance to their humor— if, by being a fresh audience, she made them more interesting to themselves. Molly told a much shorter joke about a man with no legs, and Abby watched an ivory moth that had landed with an audible plop on the screen.

Then Josh pushed his chair away from the table and got up. Abby thought he was too skinny but perhaps cuter than Alex. "Which of you losers wants to play tennis?" he asked.

"I'm in," said Molly.

"Me too," Bea said. "I don't care what you say, Pete, I love Dylan. 'Goin' to Acapulco . . . Goin' on the run . . .' Then I forget what comes next."

"Fat gut," said Pete.

"What?"

"The words to the song. He goes to see some dude called fat gut."

Ellis yawned and beckoned to Trey. "Let's go to bed," she said, and he got up obediently. Ellis went around the room, kissing everyone good night. When she came to Abby, she said, "What the hell," and kissed her on the cheek, too.

"Do you play tennis?" Bea asked Abby, who shook her head and wondered what it was with these people and tennis.

"For some reason she won't," Alex said.

"Never mind—you can keep score," Bea said, and put the last crumbs of brownie into her mouth.

Josh put a few extra beers in the pockets of his shorts; Molly tripped over a chair and started giggling; Ponch picked up a handful of rackets and pushed through the screen door.

Pete leaned back against the wall and said, "'Hard wind on soft wheat thinks it has conquered that which only bends, then grows.'"

"What?" Abby asked.

"It's the poster. What it means in Japanese. I saw you looking at it."

"Oh," Abby said. "Thanks."

"Later," said Pete.

Outside, the night had grown cooler, and Abby pulled her sweater around her shoulders. The girls led the way, still giggling, then Molly dropped back and fell in step beside her.

"Did Alex tell you it was his idea to come work here, and he got me into it? Then we met these guys. Bea used to have a crush on Pete but then she stopped. Trey is actually in love with Josie who is away this week but he's settling for Ellis, who is sort of a slut. Bea is my best friend and Alex is second. Josh and I kissed one night when we were drunk. We thought he was gay but then it turned out that he was just politer than the rest of us. Hannah who also isn't here this week we don't like, but we do like her boyfriend, Jose, who works on the grounds crew. He's twenty-six. We get our pot from a guy in the kitchen—his name is Mark but everyone calls him the Mayor. You're not the first guest Alex has brought us but you're the only one we might like. Don't get on Bea's team if you want to win, her backhand is horrible."

Molly's warm breath in Abby's ear was intimate and exciting. Abby felt a quick rush of affection and had the sudden surprising urge to put her arm around Molly's waist. In front of them, someone turned on a flashlight as they went into the woods, heading down to the shabby court Abby had seen her first day, lit now by a humming old lamp.

Once inside the chain-link fence, Molly and Bea and Ponch and Josh moved in and out of the light, the ball spinning across where Abby could see it and then vanishing again. She was buoyant and pleased and a little light-headed. She felt lucky to have met these people, lucky not to be alone. She took another sip of beer, though she supposed she shouldn't; it was going to her head.

On all sides the trees loomed, and the night was alive with sound: with the crickets and the breeze and the volleys and the laughter. Alex and Abby stood beside each other, silent but for their breathing, the backs of their hands almost touching. She had read somewhere that everyone's hands hung at the same distance from the ground, no matter how tall they were, and she wondered if it was true. She could feel the way the air warmed around him, and it reminded her of when he came to her doorway to urge her out, and she had felt him impatient, hot, alive.

Lizzie claimed that people had auras, and though Abby had never really believed it, maybe it wasn't crazy. Maybe Alex's aura and her aura were brushing up against each other, and their bodies were exchanging information wordlessly, below thought. Molecules from him were streaming into the night, communicating with molecules from her.

"It's only for you I'm not in there slaughtering them all," Alex said.

"You should go if you want," she said. "I can watch."

"They've got four. Anyway, I'd rather be with you, in case you can't tell. Shall we take a walk?"

He took a step backward and then turned on his heel. She watched the blue of his shirt dimming as he walked away. She thought of Kevin for one moment, not with guilt or regret but with a cool, exceedingly mild affection, and then she followed Alex into the woods.

No one noticed them leaving. Or else, Abby thought, they had expected this. She wondered how many times Alex had appeared in the kitchen with a girl from the hotel registry. She wanted to know who those girls were and how she compared to them. Had he flattered them so much? Had he kissed them all by now?

Behind them Josh called out, but not to them, and his voice was already faint, already belonging to a different place.

Alex clicked on a penlight, and Abby watched the unsteady beam and tried not to be afraid of the dark. Pine trees, their trunks sticky with pitch, seemed to lean toward her, and she felt the hard resilience of the earth with each step. Alex looked back at her every once in a while, and each time he did, she smiled at him, though she didn't think he could see her.

They emerged on the edge of the golf course, a green-black undulating wave that seemed to curve up at its edges like a huge shallow bowl.

"Back nine, eleventh hole, par five," Alex said.

"Are you a golfer, too?"

"Absolutely not."

Side by side they walked onto the fairway, their shoulders not touching, their hands not touching. The night was cool and Abby shivered, exquisitely aware of everything from ground to tree to sky. Even her body seemed to be pushing at its boundaries, as if it wanted to expand into the night. It was a strange but not unpleasant feeling—a mixture of animation and stasis, somehow, and attributable to what? Beer? Nerves? Alex?

Far away they could see the yellow windows of the hotel. In the dark sky, a few clouds still lingered, gray and thin, like torn pieces of linen.

"Do you want to sit?" Alex motioned to a golf cart parked under a willow tree.

"Did someone run out of gas?"

"Not literally. We keep it for the old men who realize halfway through their game that eighteen holes is a long way to walk in August."

He motioned for Abby to lead the way, and she pushed aside the willow fronds and climbed into the cart. The seats were smooth white leather and smelled faintly of gasoline and cologne. The fingers of the tree swayed before them, a curtain between them and the night.

Alex put his hand on the seat next to her hand. He was right there beside her, tall and solid on the padded bench. She had him all to herself, and she was acutely conscious of his body, the way his chest rose and fell beneath his shirt. The way it seemed that she could see a tiny vein ticking in his neck. The way his hair curled over his collar and his jaw made a sharp line against the leaves. He placed his little finger over hers, so their pinkies made an X.

All her attention was focused on the contact, that minute point of convergence. The willow's swishing branches traced a circle around them. To their left lay a water trap lined with golf balls—in the shallow parts, she could see them through the leaves, shining like small dim moons.

She wanted to ask Alex if she was the first girl he had brought beneath the willow tree. She wondered if he wrote those other girls poems, and if he had asked them to play tennis, and whether they had been brave enough to say yes.

She also wished they'd brought more beer with them, because her mouth felt like a deep, dry cave. She cleared her throat. "Look, see there? It's the Summer Triangle." She said this shyly—it was a kind of offering to him, as if these stars meant something special and important.

He looked up to where she pointed. "The what?"

"It's those three stars?" She extended her arm farther, and it seemed to her that it was trembling. Steady; she tried to hold it steady. "There, see?"

"I can't see it through the tree," he said. But then he leaned in very close to her, sighting along her arm where there was a break in the leaves. "Oh, that? I think I see it."

"That one on the right is called Vega. Then the one below it is Altair, and the other I can't remember."

"Aren't you smart?" he said softly.

She didn't feel smart at all—she felt fuzzy and full of wonderment. The night seemed different from any other night because she understood, finally, what it meant and how it worked. She saw that the darkness came not from the sky but out of the earth. The night crawled up from the forest floor and climbed the trunk of the trees and bled into the sky, leaving only the moon's borrowed light. The circling bats brought the night, too, ferrying darkness on their backs. The pale clouds in the black sky were the hovering remnants of daylight. Crickets marked time's passage, and she could feel the night's beating heart beneath the ground.

She was sure, in that moment, that she knew all she needed to—that there was beauty and purpose in everything, that the world was a perfect web of order and sense. She felt a reverence for the universe and for her place in it.

Alex touched her cheek lightly with his finger, and then he kissed where his finger had been. Abby's legs and arms were heavy and her head felt impossibly light. She was torn between sinking into the ground and floating away. He kissed her again, this time on her neck. His mouth lingered, and her skin seemed to flush with the warmth of it, and he was saying something she couldn't understand. He kissed along her collarbone and paused in the hollow of her clavicle.

And then he turned her toward him. She watched his shadowed face approach and his lips coming nearer until she felt them pressing against hers. They were warm and gentle, but her own mouth was suddenly nervous and hard. His hand reached for hers and squeezed it, and this friendly, reassuring gesture calmed her. She closed her eyes and let him kiss her, let her own mouth kiss him back. In her chest, a box opened and something fell out, and she was that something, and she was falling, falling, falling.

Alex pulled away and looked at her closely. He touched her eyelids, her cheeks, and her lips with his fingertips. Then he let out a wild whoop, and the next thing she knew, he had started the golf cart and they had slammed through the curtain of willow branches and they were heading out over the fairway, picking up speed, and the wind was lifting her hair and blowing it across her cheeks and the stars became lines in the sky and the trees were black blurs. They were heading for a water trap and another willow tree, but at the last minute Alex turned the cart and she went sliding into him, and she wrapped her arms around him and grabbed hold of his waist and pressed her face into his shoulder so she wouldn't cry out.

Her brain was rattling around in her skull and they were bumping over the rough and she was colliding against Alex and it seemed that she had never been this close to anyone before, this thrilled and afraid. They zigzagged across the golf course, turning onto the fairway and then spinning back out to the rough again.

"Are you feeling it yet?" Alex yelled.

She didn't answer him because she was feeling everything. Whatever he was talking about, she was feeling it, she was right there with him. He turned on the cart's headlights and she saw rabbits everywhere, dozens of long-legged rabbits streaking this way and that, darting wildly for the woods, and then he turned the lights off again and they were flying over the vast sea of the golf course and the awning of the cart was flapping crazily and Alex was laughing and she was bouncing all over and she bit her tongue and tasted blood in her mouth, bright and metallic as a penny. It was brilliant until it started to feel terribly wrong.

She clutched his arm. "Please," she said, "I think I'm sick—"

"What?" Alex yelled. He turned the cart sharply, all the way in a circle, and then turned it the other way. "Doughnuts!" he said.

"I think I'm really sick."

Alex jerked them to a stop. They were in the middle of somewhere else—the golf course, yes, but the hotel was no longer visible. There was nothing but the rolling expanse of green and their little white cart. Abby felt her pulse pounding in her ears, her throat, the backs of her eyes.

"Oh God," she said.

"Are you okay?"

"I just—" she said. "I just— I don't know. I feel funny." Nothing seemed right. Her hands tingled and her mind was full of cotton.

"You'll be fine, you're fine." He took one hand off the wheel and rubbed her neck, and she tried to think only of that. "How many brownies did you eat?"

"What?"

"How many brownies?"

"Why does that matter?"

The way he looked at her then was the way a parent might look at a pouting child, with a kind of mocking sympathy, and she began to understand what was happening. "You *have* had pot before, haven't you?" he asked.

"Yes," she said, "but it didn't feel like this. Oh my God. Oh my God, *I'm so stoned."*

"That's exactly what you should be," Alex said. He ran his fingers up and down her spine. "It's different when you eat it, you know. It takes longer, and then it builds . . ."

Certain things were clarified now, but she didn't feel any better at all. She leaned toward him and whispered, "I have to use the bathroom."

Did he recoil slightly? "Let's take this back where it's supposed to be," he said. He drove them slowly back to the willow and parked the cart where it had been. "You're sworn to secrecy, you know," he said. "I tore up some of the fairway."

"I can't believe you—you didn't tell me about the brownies." Every sentence was an effort.

"Honestly, I thought you knew. I thought Bea said something."

Abby eased herself out of the golf cart and picked her way beneath the swishing branches to the other side of the willow, steadying herself against its rough bark. This was the time when she had to reckon with herself—when she was alone, pissing, when she was at her ugliest and most common. In the dirty bathroom at a frat party, in the stalls of the dorm women's room, she would squat above the seat as the room shifted on an unfamiliar axis. She would look at her flushed face in the mirror and marvel at the stranger she saw. Who was that drunk girl?

But now there was no mirror, and she wasn't drunk. She was horribly, horribly stoned, and she felt certain she would never not be stoned, not for the rest of her whole long life.

"*Frosted* pot brownies?" she cried. "I've never heard of that!"

She lifted her skirt and lowered her underpants. She was afraid Alex would be able to hear her, so she tried to squat as close to the ground as possible. Beneath her was the great solid earth and she wanted to press her face to it. Below the grass were earthworms, millions of them, sliding through the dirt, slim and senseless tubes—nothing but mouths and anuses—eating and eliminating, living and dying in darkness . . .

When she was done, she stood, trembling. The willow tree's branches were like a woman's hair and there was a roaring in her ears. Maybe it was just the breeze kicking up, moving the branches, turning the helpless leaves . . .

Alex came around and leaned against the tree, crossing one leg over the other. "Are you all right?" he asked.

Abby turned her back to him and vomited into the grass.

THURSDAY

Elliott had needed to be prevailed upon to play golf. The night before, during the round of cocktails after dinner, the husbands had goaded him until he'd agreed to nine holes. Now he stood, grim and exhausted, in his daughter's bedroom. He'd been up since five. He had watched the ceiling brighten to gray, and then he had gone down to the porch, where he'd fed the peacock yesterday's muffin. Over the songs of the other birds—those high pips and voweless squawks—the Duke's cry had asserted itself, grand and sorrowful. *Nee-ah! Nee-ah!*

Abby, still in her nightgown, was brushing her hair, framed in the doorway of the bathroom. She had made her bed; the covers were pulled up tight and the pillows plumped. Instead of the piles of clothes he had expected, there were skirts and blouses hung in neat rows.

Elliott cleared his throat. "Your mother was up earlier, but she's gone back to bed. If you could keep an eye on her that would be helpful. Maybe hang around until she's ready to go down to breakfast."

As the brush passed through Abby's hair, single strands of it, alive with static electricity, lifted and then fell again to her shoulders. He could see her reflected greenly in the old mirror, and he was moved by her sleepy, feral loveliness. He scratched his cheek and discovered a spot he'd missed shaving.

Elliott held out a note. "This is for you." When he set it on a side table, she turned to look at it with a strained expression.

"Who's it from?"

"Your mother—who do you think? We're only playing nine holes, so I'll be back in a couple of hours. Ruth and Eva are at the patio café. You should join them when your mother gets up." He lingered, waiting for her to acquiesce.

"Is there anything else?" she asked.

His head hurt. Perhaps it was only the terrible fatigue that gave everything a fuzzy, warped aspect, the sense that the world was moving at a faster pace than he was. He felt his heart pounding, but somehow it was inside his skull. Abby had turned back to the mirror, to her own blue-eyed gaze. With her unrelenting grooming, she seemed bright and flinty and alien. He thought about asking where she'd gone after dinner, aware that his desire to know had less to do with curiosity than it did with a sense of propriety: he worried his guests would think her rude.

"Nothing else," he said.

When he shut the door, the note fluttered to the carpet. The sound of Abby's brush followed him down the hall: *swish, swish, swish.*

Henry and Dom and Elliott waited under the eaves of the clubhouse, letting the foursome ahead of them clear. Elliott wore his borrowed golf shoes uneasily; they fit well enough, but there was something distasteful about wearing another man's shoes. He had misplaced his sunglasses—he who never lost anything—and had to buy some at the pro shop. The new pair had mirrored, curved lenses and fluorescent yellow arms; he knew they looked ridiculous. "The snowboarders love that kind," Henry had said.

Elliott had never heard of snowboarders and said so. There was a swarm of insects in his head and a tingling in his right hand.

"A bunch of hotdoggers," Henry told him. "Like waterskiers on one ski. Kids in sunglasses like yours."

Elliott did not feel this had clarified things, but he let it stand.

Dom shook out his legs, warming them up. The courses were designed by someone famous and he was excited, though he would have preferred to play the eighteen-holer. "Do you have that aspirin?" he asked, and Henry handed him a travel packet.

Elliott bent over so his hands dangled inches from his feet and his sluggish blood surged to his head. His hamstrings were like steel cables, and each ball in the socket of his hipbones moved along ground glass. When he straightened up, the world faded into misty blackness and then reemerged in pixels that slowly resolved themselves into the green vista; he placed his hand on the clubhouse siding for balance.

"Head rush," he said to Henry's questioning look.

"Hair of the dog?" Dom suggested. "Something good for you, maybe, like a Bloody Mary."

"You've got to be kidding." Elliott stretched his arms out and then did a couple of squats to get things moving, and after a minute or two he could feel it working, feel his heart kicking into gear. Besides the bad knees and the exhaustion, he was in respectable shape for a man his age, and though his hair had grayed at the temples and his jawline was a bit fuller, he looked essentially as he had for two decades, especially in dim light. He appreciated this, even though his vanity had ebbed over the years, to be replaced by what were merely habits of hygiene.

Dom waved away a caddy who'd been lingering near them hopefully. He had also told the club manager that they didn't want a cart. "Waste of money," he'd said to Elliott. "We've got legs, we've got backs."

Elliott wanted a cart, purely for efficiency's sake—he didn't want to leave Helen for too long—but he allowed Dom the pleasure of denying himself something. What do you give the man who has everything? An opportunity to refuse it.

Elliott drank the last of the burned coffee he'd poured himself in the pro shop and tossed the cup into the trash can.

"Henry and I always bet," Dom said. "You want to, too?"

"Fifty, a hundred dollars," Henry said.

Elliott shrugged and agreed. It was all money he didn't have anyway. His salary at Carlisle was fifty grand and he had a daughter at a private school that cost nearly half that. Between that and the hospital bills, his debts were mounting. Which was why God made credit cards, he told himself. "Are we sure we don't want to drive?" Elliott asked one more time, looking back toward the line of neat white carts, the smart hotel insignia decorating the canopies.

"Carts are for old men," Henry said. "We are not old men."

"It's only nine holes," Dom said. "And anyway, we're up."

Elliott shouldered Bob Mitchell's Spalding clubs, each covered in a blue sock like a baby bootie, and stepped into the blinding sunlight. At the marker, they sunk their tees into the soft ground.

He felt on edge, a combination of six cups of coffee and his native competitive streak. He would hate to lose to these two, but lose he would: he hadn't played in over a year, and he'd never been very good. Helen had been a naturally gifted golfer, though she lacked the attention span for eighteen holes and had played only to humor him. She always said she thought it was more fun to take a walk somewhere. Still, she'd had that strong, graceful swing, that cool aim on the green.

After the coin toss, Dom stepped up to the tee in his madras shorts. He took a few practice swings and then sliced to the right on his shot. "This is what sharks do," he said, putting away his driver. "They start out like minnows."

Henry's first ball wobbled through the air and dropped listlessly under two hundred yards away. Elliott felt his spirits lift, and lift still higher when his swing gave him what looked like a good two-twenty down the straightaway.

"Nice," Dom said appreciatively.

"Luck," said Elliott.

The sky was cornflower blue, and fleecy clouds sat on the Presidential mountains like hats. Dom hit wide on his second try and Henry chipped up a few dozen yards. Elliott took out his four-iron for a shot that took him nearly to the green—it was an easy hole, okay, but it was not inconceivable that he'd flirt with par. He experienced the thrill of unanticipated, even inexplicable, competence.

"Lucky on that one, too—am I going to be sorry I bet you?" Henry asked.

"I hope so," Elliott said. "Though I doubt it." He fingered the monogram on his canvas bag. In a pocket he found a silver flask full of some sloshing liquid.

When he and Henry got to the green, Dom told them it was a fast one with a lot of sand behind. Elliott overshot his first putt and then played soft and light on his others; it took him three to sink it. Still, that put him a mere two over par. He began to like his hideous sunglasses, through which the world took on a dark golden sheen, as if everything were made of metal: the leaves formed of hammered copper and the grass a carpet of bronze.

He was sweating by the third tee, a gin-scented sheen on his arms. The sun caressed him, and as he walked behind his friends, he was aware of an uncharacteristic sense of lightness, even optimism. He wondered at first if he was somehow still drunk, and then it occurred to him that perhaps he was simply and unexpectedly happy.

Watching Dom and Henry consult each other over the choice of iron or wood, Elliott recalled how they used to lean over the grill at the Schmidts' Saturday barbecues, debating the doneness of the steaks. *(Give them one more minute. No way, thirty more seconds, tops.)* Those had been good nights, with the Schmidts and the Callahans and the Hansens, plus the occasional and varying fourth couple: Neil and his first wife, before they moved away and divorced, or another pair whom someone, usually Eva, had met somewhere.

The dinners always went late, and after Abby and the Schmidt and Callahan girls had fallen asleep on the TV room couches, Dom would take control of the stereo, and Helen would dance in the corner of the Schmidts' deck, her hair a corona beneath the porch light.

Elliott remembered one night when Dom would play only the Stones, and Eva came out to say there was nothing in the house but a liter of bad gin. There were no mixers, she said, there wasn't even ice. Like Helen and Ruth, she was wearing a ruffled white shirt and blue-and-white-checked bell-bottoms with a border of brilliantly red strawberries at the ankle. Helen and Eva had made them and they were ridiculous. But the wives looked girlish and playful in them, and everything had seemed especially festive.

"Ice," Helen cried when she heard the news, "who needs it?" She had one of Maeve Callahan's sparklers in her hand and she wrote *No Ice* in the air.

"Serve up a warm round," Ruth yelled. She was sitting on the edge of the hot tub with her strawberry pants rolled up to her knees and a cigarette in the mother-of-pearl holder she used only when she'd had too much to drink. Then Eva, who was always the most responsible one, fell off the deck into the bushes, nearly breaking her ankle.

Afterward Henry called Helen "No Ice." It was a good nickname to have when one was young. Oh, how they were young! He and Henry and Dom, they were young fathers with drinks in their hands, watching the wives who had brought them together dance around the yard. It was 1978 and there were females everywhere, the ones they had married and the ones they had made. There was not a single heir, not one lone little prick.

"Hansen," Henry called now. "Take a shot, why don't you? The senior citizens are catching up with us."

Dom walked over to watch Elliott line up. A band of Canada geese coasted serenely through a water guard, inclining their long black necks and making lazy circles in the water.

"Do you remember how those bastards were almost extinct?" Dom asked. "When we were kids, they rounded up what was left and sent them all over the country to make new colonies. And they just *thrived*."

"I wonder if they ever wish they hadn't," Henry said, "the way those birds shit."

"Thirty times a day, I read. I like how they do it when they're walking along. They never look back, see? To drop your turds and just keep on going—that is a life without regret."

When Elliott hit a smooth shot almost right where he wanted it, one of the geese bobbed its beak as if in approval. "Luck," he said again, crossing his fingers for more of it, and strode off to find his ball, that dimpled new friend of his.

When they met again at the green, Henry put sunscreen on his nose in a white stripe and passed it around to everyone else.

"The geese love the suburbs," Dom said. "Just like white people. They actually tamed themselves. They don't even migrate anymore."

"They just fly to Florida for vacation," Henry said.

"That's right. Condos in Orlando," said Dom. "They like to shit in the heated pools."

Elliott seemed to recall that later on the night of the strawberry bell-bottoms, they had drunk the warm gin and talked about the people they should have married. They agreed that Henry could use a woman like Ruth to keep him on his toes, and Elliott ought to be with Eva because she kept such a fastidious house. Dom and Helen, they decided, could be happy together because they would just ski and sail all the time.

There was some truth to it, Elliott allowed—Dom certainly seemed to appreciate his wife, didn't he? Elliott wasn't blind, and Dom had never been very subtle. All those poems! But Elliott hadn't minded, not even back then. Dom was too passive to cause any real trouble, and anyway, Elliott was sure that no other pairings would have lasted. However imperfect their unions, however uncomplementary their flaws, the Schmidts and the Callahans and the Hansens were married and would stay married until death did them part. He felt a certain pride in that.

He found a cap in his borrowed bag and fitted it onto his head. Of course, he thought, he would not be married much longer.

A thought to take the breath away—it did every time. And what then? What happened—*after?* There would be the shock first, inevitable despite his preparation. Then there would be the grief, and following that, the confusion and the despair and the loneliness. Months or years later, there would be a time when he would seek companionship. He thought of the women with their casseroles and the husbands for whom they cooked: Karen Morrow, who wore heavy perfume and worked at the bank right alongside her beloved Michael; Holly Huckabee, a slinky brunette married to the owner of the local movie theater. He thought of the women behind the cash registers at the grocery store, the women who drove by him in their cars, and the women who passed by his house on their evening constitutionals. *Who will I love,* he thought, *and who will love me?*

He'd read somewhere that people who lost everything in a fire or flood often felt a great and terrible relief. Waking in strange beds, in clothes they'd borrowed, they experienced a peace that was almost holy. All the physical evidence of their lives, all the years of creating and accumulating—all of that was finished, but they had themselves, inviolable. They were the few who learned that, in the end, almost nothing was worth saving.

Elliott was the person in the living room watching the floodwaters rising. Soon everything would be different forever. Like his friend Neil, he could fall in love with a woman fifteen years his junior. Like his neighbor Buck, he could work his way though a string of girlfriends, insisting each one was the next Mrs. Long. Or maybe he could get a dog and go live in the woods. He'd chop his own firewood, eat beans on toast three times a day, and piss over the railing of his front porch into a heap of pine needles.

Jesus, he said to himself, *line up your shot. Five iron, a hundred and fifty yards or so.*

By the fifth hole, Elliott's luck had started to wane, but Henry and Dom were still playing badly. Dom shanked an easy shot on six and Henry got stuck in the rough. "I'm in a tire rut," he called to them. "It looks like someone drove a Chevy through here."

Dom accused him of making excuses and then swung with way too much follow-through. The three of them watched his ball roll past the hole and down the far slope.

"You know what they say—old golfers never die, they just lose their balls." Henry grinned. "I've been waiting for a chance to say that."

Elliott realized he had expected a break in the cheerfulness, sometime when either he or one of them would reluctantly, but with a sense of duty, broach the subject of what they were doing at the hotel. But the moment never seemed right: the sun was golden, and he was one of dozens of men enjoying it, and he had never played golf so well in his whole life. Care had been lifted from his shoulders with the most exquisite and temporary release. Maybe, he thought, it was enough for now just to feel blessedly alive. He teed up for the seventh hole. He was up by at least five strokes.

Abby's mother lay on her back in the bed with a pillow over her face and her feet sticking out from beneath the sheet. Her socks had yellow pom-poms on the heels.

Abby tiptoed into the room. She had thought that the note her father held had been from Alex. He'd been so kind, walking her back to her room, a concerned, fraternal arm around her shoulder as if she were a wounded comrade. He hadn't kissed her good night, and why would he have wanted to? She had said stupid things—something about the darkness coming out of the ground, and wasn't there a bit about how plants ate the sun?—and then she had puked on her shoes. She had ruined everything, she understood that; she was a baby who couldn't be trusted with an intoxicant.

But the note had been in her mother's new, wobbly handwriting. *Abby—I work up early & went bake to sleep—hopefully till 9:30. I need to be awaken if I get "lucy" but I doute it will be a broblem.*

Abby set it down on the dresser next to her mother's wallet, still fat with things she never used anymore—her license, her credit cards, her court ID. Because Helen had had seizures, the doctors told her she couldn't drive for a year, and Abby remembered when that had seemed like the biggest problem they would face. Next to the wallet was a silk clutch that held Helen's birthstone ring, a deep blue imitation sapphire that she had been given for her sweet sixteen; a thin rope of tiny pearls; and her charm bracelet with its proud declarations: Phi Beta Kappa, Choir, Latin Club. There were a cameo pin and a ring with a piece of ebony and two chips of coral—the kind that was endangered now—and a heavy peace sign on a leather cord. "Made from policeman's bullets," Helen had said. She hardly ever wore any of these things, so they seemed to Abby like secret markers of her past.

Tangled in the chain of a silver necklace, Abby found a cloisonné brooch of a sleeping cat that Bertie had given her mother for Christmas one year. Bertie who had adored Helen. Bertie who was not so dim-witted that she didn't understand Abby's feelings for her.

One day Bertie had offered to take Abby to her house. A natural curiosity about where and how she lived almost overcame Abby's distaste of having to slow her pace to Bertie's shuffle, of having to be seen with her in public. Bertie drove them in her old Dodge to the edge of town, near the community pool and the soccer fields, across from a gas station and a Dairy Queen. The Victorian house was three stories of white slat siding with green shutters and decorative carving around the porch and eaves— it was nice. Bertie lived here? Abby thought, somewhat impressed, but then Bertie took her inside, where it was divided up into dark apartments. In the halls, the floors were wooden and slanted, and the boards were worn down to a dull patina.

Bertie had a living room and a kitchen and a little bedroom. Shy but proud, Bertie moved slowly through the apartment, directing Abby's attention to the magazines kept in neat racks, the brass clock that had been her grandfather's, the potpourri in a pink bowl. The rooms smelled like dust and old wood. There were white curtains with red flowers in the windows, and they were the only new bright thing. Bertie's calico cat crouched under a chair, squinting at them. When Bertie called, it came slinking toward them, its belly low to the ground. "Do you want to give Mittens a treat?" she asked Abby.

Abby had never seen such an ugly cat. Its eyes were close together in its fat, dumb face, and when Bertie scratched its head, it arched up to meet her hand. Bertie went into the kitchen and came back with a stiff, cold piece of cooked bacon. "Here," she said, "you can give this to her and . . . and she'll like you."

Abby didn't want Mittens to like her, but she accepted the bacon and held it in front of the cat's nose. The animal reached out and took it delicately between her teeth, then dropped it on the floor, stepped away, and watched it, her tail flicking side to side.

"She likes to pretend she's hunting," Bertie said. "Poor thing." A few seconds later, Mittens pounced.

Abby could see into Bertie's bedroom with its closet full of polyester blouses in loud, cheerful patterns. There were decorative pillows on the bed, heart-shaped crocheted things with yellowing lace, and two worn teddy bears. She was overcome by the Bertieness of everything—Bertie's curtains and her old-fashioned television set, her baby-animals calendar and her prim, flowered furniture, all the sad little flourishes: the doilies, the crocheted throw blankets, the vase full of fake carnations. She saw the smallness and the loneliness of Bertie's life, and still it did not make Abby kind to her.

She didn't know what had happened to Bertie. She just knew that the next year she'd had a babysitter named Diana, who had a quick mind and lovely long brown hair. She was a junior in high school, she wore a letterman's jacket, and there was nothing at all wrong with her.

Helen stirred beneath the covers and pulled the pillow away from her face. "I'm still tired," she said.

In the old days, Abby probably would have crawled right beside her in bed. Instead she put down the jewelry and sat on the edge of the hard damask chair. Helen turned on her side and opened her green eyes and looked at Abby.

"You don't have to get up if you don't want to," Abby said. "It's vacation."

"Did you get my note?"

"I did," Abby said. "Thanks." She dug her bare toes into the carpet. "Dad said that Ruth and Eva are downstairs, if you want to go sit with them."

"Did you eat?"

"I just woke up."

Her mother smiled. "Sleepyhead."

Abby reached out and grabbed her mother's ankle and shook it. "You're the sleepyhead."

"Lazybones," her mother said.

"Loafer," Abby said, and her mother laughed.

Helen rose carefully from the bed, already dressed in white cotton pants and a shirt with yellow dots, and went into the bathroom. Abby leaned back in the chair, hungover and sleepy. The night before felt like a half-remembered hallucination. And maybe it should, she thought, because in a way it wasn't real. *This* was what was real—her mother standing before the mirror, tightening the knot on her bandanna and looking for her shoes. *This* was where Abby's loyalties were, here in this room, with this person. It was fine if Alex and all the other people she had hoped would be her friends never talked to her again. They weren't what mattered.

"Are these what you need?" Abby asked, pointing to a pair of flat brown sandals.

"Yes, that's what I wanted," her mother said, and she slipped them on.

"All set?" Abby said brightly.

"All set."

Abby held out her chilly hand, and her mother gently took it.

Down on the patio, Ruth and Eva stood up in their big straw hats and hugged Helen and then scurried around, wanting to bring her things. Eva was smart in a lavender shirtdress, and beside her, Ruth's flowing tunic billowed out as vast and white as a sail.

"It's another stunning day," Eva said, lifting a silver pot. "Do you want tea, Helen? It's decaf."

"It's supposed to rain tomorrow," Ruth said. "Here, have a muffin or something."

Eva leaned over her teacup in its china saucer and touched Helen's arm. "I thought we could paint a little. I brought watercolors. Oh, and here." She handed Helen an extra straw hat. "To keep the sun off you. You don't need a hat, do you?" she asked Abby. "We could get you one in the gift shop."

Ruth answered for her. "Abby doesn't need a hat. Sun damage means nothing to the young."

"Right," Abby said. She was unsure whether she meant this, but she did want to be tan like Ellis and Molly and Bea.

Eva tied the ribbon of Helen's hat beneath her chin. "There you go," she said, peering into Helen's face. "That'll keep it on if there's a breeze."

Eva sat back in her chair, watching Helen as she broke open a scone. Her scrutiny irritated Abby, though it was not as bad as the way strangers looked at her mother, with curiosity and pity so plain on their faces. Yesterday a maid in the lobby had stared openly at Helen, and the elevator operator had greeted her with the patronizing cheer of an attendant in a nursing home. Here, especially, Helen stood out for her frailness; she shuffled down the hallways while bird-watchers two decades her senior went skipping off into the woods.

"So I read about this powder," Ruth was saying. "It's green and it's called something that starts with an S. It's better for you than almost anything. I was going to get some for you, Helen, but then I thought I should ask you first, to see if you were interested."

When her mother didn't answer, Abby touched her shoulder. "What do you think?" she asked.

"Okay," Helen said, smiling.

Ruth said, "The Aztecs ate it. They believed it had magic properties."

It's called spirulina, Abby thought. She knew all about it because she had it in her room upstairs, packed into a canvas bag full of potions and totems. When her mother first got sick, a coworker from the court had told them that spirulina boosted the immune system and could cure all kinds of diseases. It had sulfolipids, polysaccharides, and gamma-linolenic acid; it was the world's first superfood. Abby had bought some from an 800 number, and it came in bottles that said AS SEEN ON TV.

Someone else told Helen she must drink wheatgrass juice, and another person had said beetroot and grapes. The doctors didn't tell them these things would work, and neither did the FDA. But in those early weeks Abby found herself ready to put her faith in anything, and perhaps thereby add to the momentum of its energy, its karma, its powers of change. She was on board for crystals, hypnosis, Mass, whatever. She believed in believing. But mostly everyone thought of conventional medicine. People sent bouquets of freesia and greeting cards with warm sentiments expressed in encouraging rhymes.

Though her mother had lost interest in the spirulina, the bee pollen, the copper bracelets, and the little jade Buddha, Abby kept them with her because she did not want to be unprepared should Helen change her mind. So while her father made Helen a carefully organized pillbox with her prescription medicines arranged by the day and hour in which they must be taken, Abby kept all the totems and amulets given to her mother by women who believed in magic.

"I didn't see a health food store in town," Ruth said. "But we could ask at the front desk—maybe we should take a field trip."

"Why don't we do that later?" Eva said. "Right now I think we should paint. I think we should stay out here on the patio and paint things that are beautiful." She brought out the watercolors and passed around small rectangles of thick paper. "These are special postcards," she said to Helen. "They're very thick, see, so you can paint on them and then mail them to people."

"I've seen those before," Helen said.

"Good, then you know exactly what to do. Here are the paint sets . . . I just got this one, look how bright the colors are. Should we make flowers?" Eva asked. "Or birds, maybe?"

Helen held a brush in an unsteady hand and squinted at her postcard. "I'm going to start with that yellow," she said.

Abby drew a blue border around her card and then wondered what to do next. She ate part of a muffin, but her guts were still tender, so she tossed the rest to the Duke. Petals, loosed from some flowering bush, blew across the patio and swirled around her ankles.

"Abby's making friends with the rooster," Helen said.

"Peacock," Abby said.

"Paint an abstract," Ruth told Abby. "Everyone will have to like it because they won't be able to tell what it is or isn't supposed to be." She lit a cigarette.

Eva frowned at her, and Ruth scooted back from the table a few inches, blowing the smoke over her shoulder; when Eva still looked displeased, Ruth tossed the cigarette into the bushes. "Christ, Eva," she said, "you're like my mother. Next you're going to tell me not to put so much butter on my toast."

"Or maybe I'd just tell you to mind your manners."

Ruth sighed, and Abby watched her sharp, fierce profile. She wasn't sure how much she liked Ruth, but she appreciated her brassiness and her minor fame. At college Abby knew a girl from Austin who had a Ruth Peel poster, a silkscreened sunflower with petals shaped like thin, tall women, taped right beneath her name on the door. *I know her,* Abby had told the girl proudly. *She's one of my mom's best friends.*

"So Abby, how's that book of yours? You finish it yet?" Ruth asked.

"It's called *The Mill on the Floss.* I haven't started it."

"Maybe there's a movie version you can watch. That's what Maeve always did. Although she didn't care quite so much about perfect grades as you do. She had lots of other interests."

Abby half expected her to list them—varsity sports, glee club, whatever—but Ruth took one of the watercolor brushes and began chewing on the end of it.

Helen squinted and held up her postcard, a looping tangle of yellow lines. "I was trying to draw a flower," she said, "but I guess this is an abstract, too."

Abby said, "Or it's a buttercup in a field of other buttercups."

"It's gorgeous, I love it," Ruth said. "Send it to me."

"She could *pass* it to you, Ruth," Eva said. "Let her mail it to someone." She called a waitress over and asked for more tea. The girl bobbed her head, her cheeks plump and pink, and then smiled at Abby, who wondered if she lived in the dorm with the others, and whether she was a friend of Alex's. If so, Abby hoped he'd kept her humiliating behavior to himself.

"She's very jolly," Eva said.

"You say that because she's a little fat," said Ruth.

"I would never!"

"Fat," Ruth whispered.

"Stop it, Ruth," Eva said. "And take that brush out of your mouth. I don't want tooth marks all over it. Are you really so orally fixated?"

"That one's like a Rothko," said Abby, looking at her mother's second card, which had blocks of blue and red.

"A pardon?" Eva said.

"Rothko. He's a painter. Was a painter."

"He killed himself," Ruth said.

"Oh, Ruth," Eva said. "What is wrong with you today?"

"Well, he *did*. He sliced his wrists open."

"Are you going to paint or just sit there being obnoxious?" Eva asked.

"I'm not painting. I'm going to critique," Ruth said.

Eva flung her brush into her glass of water. "Would it kill you to be a good sport for once?"

Ruth didn't have a response for that, and Eva turned to Helen, smiling very brightly and forcedly. "Excuse me, honey," she said. "I'll be back in a minute."

"I don't know what *her* problem is," Ruth muttered, watching Eva stride away.

Their waitress came and set another pot of tea on the table. Then she reached into her pocket, extracted a folded piece of paper, and gave it to Abby.

"What's that?" Ruth demanded.

"Nothing," Abby said. "A trail ride schedule. I asked her earlier."

"Oh, please. I know you kids are sneaky!" Ruth said. "Don't think we don't know. It's just that we don't care anymore. We're done raising you. You're on your own."

"I'm only eighteen," Abby said.

"That's old enough for plenty." Ruth clapped her hands abruptly, and the sleeves of her tunic flapped together. "Spirulina," she said. "That's what it is."

In Abby's hand the note was nestled like a secret. She knew it was from Alex, and she was almost afraid to open it. She watched her mother intently place brush to paper. The lines she made were slow and unsteady—the lines of a child.

"What's that going to be?" Abby asked, unfolding the note beneath the table.

"Mountains," Helen said.

"Nice," Abby said, and her eyes flicked down to the paper.

You come to me alone, moon-bird,
hope bringing us midnight together,
our whole in one being, an eagle,
spreading black wings over the rough
terrain, hiding the moon with its coal-black
feathers, cloaking its body with the night sky.

Below it, in a different pen, Alex had written, *Note the golf imagery!* and drawn a smiley face with a puddle of barf beneath it.

"What's so funny?" her mother asked.

"Nothing," Abby said. "I just remembered something."

"*I* remember something funny," Ruth said. "Helen, how about those dresses you made for all of us that summer? The muumuus with the orange flowers?"

Her mother smiled. "They were so ugly."

Ruth rose from her chair in a surge of linen and flung her arms above her head, stretching up toward the sun. "No, they were beautiful," she said. "They were beautiful, like we were." She twirled in a circle. "But get a load of me now," she said, pointing to the draping folds of her outfit. "I was Greek when I put this on this morning, and now I look like a clothesline with a bunch of sheets on it."

Abby wished her mother would tease Ruth like she used to, but she just laughed. Then she reached out and put her hand on top of Abby's. The familiarity of this gesture, so simple and certain and old, made Abby nearly dizzy with recollected life.

"I love you," her mother whispered.

Ruth has put Helen in the middle of a flower-bed. She's sitting on a lawn chair surrounded by phlox and lilies and other flowers whose names she doesn't know. She has the pink bud of a rose tucked behind her ear, and its stem tickles where it touches her neck.

"Yes, yes, very good," Ruth is saying, "can you tilt your head a bit to the right?"

Voices lift in the air and float away. Helen catches fragments—"heard a Bicknell's thrush," someone says, "out on the toll road"—by accident, and their meaning vanishes as quickly as the sound itself. Today there are shadows climbing the columns of the hotel and nothing seems as interesting as it ought to be. She feels like her head has been wrapped in something soft and gauzy, as if she's walking around inside a ball of cotton wool. From inside the whiteness, she strains to pay attention, though everything comes to her drained of color and significance.

She wonders if this is what taking drugs is like—if the sure, sudden detachment from life bears any resemblance to being high. Did drugs make you feel more alive or less? Did the mind really expand like they said, or did it shrink down, its perceptions solipsistic but crystallized into perfect diamonds of understanding? She should have asked her kids at court. She should have laid off the "Just Say No" a little, and gotten to the bottom of the attraction. And what was so terrible about a bit of teenage rebellion? She'd been so uptight!

"Just a bit more to the right," Ruth says. She's dancing around in her extravagant clothes, her sunglasses perched on her head, searching for the right composition. Helen is used to being behind the camera, which is why it looks as if she missed every party, every holiday, for the last two decades. But not anymore. Since her eye problems, she's let Elliott take over. He's awkward at it, and he never remembers to warn anyone that he's going to press the button. But he loves to take pictures of her, in the yard, in the living room, on the porch, as if every day must be preserved. Helen tilts her head.

"Ah, there we go," Ruth says. The shutter clicks.

Oh God, Helen thinks, *I'm tired.* She's already taken one nap today and she can't just take another. But sleep—it is the sweetest thing. When she's sleeping, she's not half blind or clumsy or forgetful. She's simply herself, blissfully unconscious.

The waking is what's hard. For months she opened her eyes in the morning, that time for optimism, those hours of anything-is-possible, and believed herself to be the person she'd always been. That had been the worst part: to learn the truth each day all over again. The words that slipped away, the body that did not seem to belong to her—it took a long time for that to get any easier.

Sometimes she thinks: *What if I hadn't gone running?*

She remembers that run like it was yesterday. In the early dawn, the humming fog lights flickered and the motion-sensor porch lights snapped on as she passed by. Here and there a dog barked. She didn't meet her friend that morning, even though Rosemary, who was thin and obsessive, would jog in place in front of the bank from six to five after six every day, in case Helen wanted to join her. That morning Helen had decided to keep the run to herself, to see alone the empty streets, the frosted windows on the parked cars, and the borders of snow, the whole familiar world made strange in its dim silence.

When the Hansens first moved to Ohio, there were rumors of a flasher, an early riser who dropped his pants for lady joggers. Helen didn't know whether to believe the stories, but she figured whatever danger he might pose was only enough to make things interesting.

That last day in February the branches were black like pen scratches on an indigo sky. She wore the new high-tech water- and windproof clothes that Elliott had given her for Christmas. They made a swishing sound when she ran, so as she set out past the hospital parking lot, full even at this hour, she was accompanied by a constant, meaningless whisper. She'd run along those same streets for a decade by then. Ten years! And she'd never seen the flasher.

After a few hard, unpleasant minutes, she went into her body and the work it was doing. Her gait steadied, and her feet unerringly avoided the ice to crunch along the rime of rock salt. The warm mist of her breath met the breath of the rising world. She crossed the train tracks and passed the ghostly white barns of the fairgrounds, then turned right and went down the street where Bertie, Abby's old babysitter, lived, or used to live—she wasn't sure—and then turned right again for the last leg, the street of big old houses that led to Central Avenue and then the turnoff to her own dark house. The clouds were low and heavy, and she thought that later it would snow.

On the last day in February she had finished her run and gone into the kitchen, exhilarated and tired, to make a pot of coffee—and the next thing she knew, she was in the hospital, waking up, with Elliott's face above her looking frightened and old. There was a tube in her throat and it hurt, and iron bars gleamed on either side of her and the light was harsh and bright like sun on ice. Elliott took her hand, and she tried to say things with her eyes. She tried to think her thoughts into his head. *Please tell me what happened. What am I doing here? Tell me that everything is going to be all right.* There were instruments all around her with numbers and dials and lines and buttons. Everyone else who came into the room was very interested in the instruments, but Elliott never looked at them. He kept his eyes on her.

He still does. It's almost like they're newlyweds again. His concern for her comfort is paramount, and he acts as if she is the only thing in the world that interests him. *It's ironic, isn't it,* she thinks—*you don't have to get more attractive to catch your husband's eye; you can just get sick and ugly.*

But God she loved that old self of hers! She hadn't appreciated it enough. Why hadn't she celebrated those big strong thighs instead of trying all the time to shrink them? Why hadn't she found her feet beautiful, or her sturdy ankles? Why hadn't she loved her coarse, graying hair? Why had she not praised every perfect square inch of herself? She feels an almost unbearable ache of longing for all that doesn't belong to her anymore. She has these thin white legs, and thin white arms, and hands that seem suddenly gargantuan.

"That's enough, now, Ruth," Eva is saying. She has come out of the hotel with a hard look on her face. "You're going to get us in trouble."

She's motioning for Ruth and Helen to get out of the flower bed. In the sun her hair is like a hat of gold. Ruth, feigning deafness, keeps snapping. She takes a picture of her own feet next to a bright yellow clump of blossoms and one of Eva looking around for the groundskeeper.

"Lean over a little, will you, and sort of touch that flower with your fingertips?" Ruth says to Helen.

Helen obeys. The blossom—what kind is it? she can't remember—is bright fuchsia and its petals are silky.

"Excellent," Ruth says. "Okay, Eva, okay, nag, we're done."

Before Helen sits up, she swipes that heavy bloom right off its stem and tucks it behind her other ear. She has cancer. What, really, can anyone do to her?

Elliott kept his lucky tee in his pocket. He'd washed it in the clubhouse bathroom, and now he stroked it lightly with his thumb, a motion meant to distract him from his desire to light another cigarette—he'd been smoking too much. He cleared his throat and his daughter flicked cool blue eyes at him before opening a paper that someone had left on one of the veranda couches.

"Do you want something from the café?" he asked. "A lemonade maybe?"

Abby shook her head, but he decided that if a waiter came by he would order some anyway. He had those warm, fresh twenties in his wallet, because after the golf game was over Henry and Dom had each handed him a hundred dollars, and when he wouldn't take it they put it in his shirt pocket and told him it would be dishonorable not to accept his winnings.

"It's not so bad here, is it?" he asked. "Not too many old farts?"

Abby shook her head again, and he wanted to ask her what she was thinking. Instead he asked if she would like ice cream instead of lemon-ade.

She said, "I haven't even had lunch."

"But it's vacation. Live it up."

Helen had gone down to the pool with Eva and Ruth—they were going to do each other's toenails, Eva said—and so Elliott had asked Abby to sit with him. He thought they ought to take a little time to be together before Neil and Sylvie Wright arrived and he would have two more people to entertain and worry about.

Abby said, "I don't need any ice cream."

"This is vacation," he said again. "At the best hotel in New Hampshire. 'Need' isn't the verb we use around here. 'Want' is the ticket. 'Want.'"

He had known daughters who crawled flirtatiously into their fathers' laps, pretending to be younger and less knowledgeable about what they were doing than they were, daughters who pouted prettily and appealed for attention, practicing their feminine wiles on their poor middle-aged dads. Abby had never been like that. Between father and daughter, throughout her adolescence, there had been what felt like a mutual wariness and a deep but somehow half-thwarted admiration. Abby had loved Helen best; he could admit that. And how could he compete? Those two—they looked alike, they thought alike, of course they loved each other's company. And that was a gift, wasn't it? To find in another everything you wanted?

Elliott had turned his own stores of devotion toward his work, where it proved more useful, where it was better noticed. The only student he'd ever done poorly by was his own daughter, who had spent one miserable semester at Carlisle before he sent her to be undereducated with the rest of the town's sons and daughters at the public high school—where, it must be said, she thrived. She was conventional and ambitious, and her teachers adored her.

He was very proud of her, and that was easier than liking her sometimes. Obviously he loved her; that was a given. But liking ebbed and flowed—she could be impossible—and even his love had conditions. Helen would have thought Abby perfect no matter what she did, but Elliott felt he loved Abby more when she was achieving something. He thought this was a parent's duty. Because what else was the point of life? You were given a finite period of time on the earth, and that time should be maximized. Failure to use your gifts was a waste. Also, when Abby was achieving something, she was less of the disconcerting female that adolescence had made her—self-conscious, defensive, moody—and more something he could understand. When she performed well, she became, for a moment, sexless, victorious, triumphant. Abby in the orchestra, Abby on the soccer field—those Abbys were a delight. They made his heart swell with pride and amazement.

He'd known she would struggle in college. He'd thought, not without a twinge of sadness for her, that she would never again be the most gifted person in the room. She would have to labor; she would have to harden her intelligence. But then Helen had gotten sick, and it became ridiculous to be concerned about his daughter's intellectual life when, in an unknowable matter of months, she would be without a mother. He shouldn't worry whether or not she would find ambition—he should worry about her survival.

Oh, he loved her, loved her, and he wished she had any idea how much.

"Do you remember Bertie?" Abby asked. She was folding the newspaper into a fan.

"Sure I do," he said. "What made you think of her?"

"I don't know," Abby said. "I just did."

There was an opening there, and Elliott tested its boundaries. He could ease in, offering bits of information until they accumulated into a full picture. "Your mother has aphasia—like Bertie did," he said.

"I know." Abby closed her eyes and waved the fan in front of her face. "I never liked Bertie. She wasn't any fun."

Perhaps this wasn't the best approach. He sighed. Like all young people, Abby saw ill health as a character flaw. Elliott remembered his own impatience with his stumbling, forgetful grandfather, an embarrassment at the dinner table, spilling fruit cocktail down the front of his shirt.

"I'm sure she was fun once. But illness can change a person," he said.

"Like your mother. Things aren't easy for her anymore either." He paused, thinking about what he should say next, and that was when Helen came shuffling up the veranda. "I thought you were down at the pool," he said.

"I came up to use the bathroom," she said, sitting down next to Abby. "They should get that bird a friend."

His wife and daughter still looked like variations on a single person, one smooth and young and the other shrunken and prematurely aged. Elliott knew Abby would have bloomed like this no matter what. But there was some part of him that wondered if the two were not connected, as if his wife's vitality and loveliness were somehow seeping into his daughter, brightening her eyes, animating her movements.

"Peacocks are loners," he told his wife, though he had no idea if this was true or not.

"Yes, he's definitely happier being the only one," Abby said. She fanned her mother, who closed her eyes in pleasure.

Elliott was certain Abby didn't know what she was talking about, either, but he appreciated her support. "We should take a walk one of these days," he said to Abby. "We should spend some time."

She smiled at him, a bright and unexpected smile. "Sure. Anything you say."

"Hey," a voice called then. "Hey hey hey hey!"

And there was Neil Wright, striding onto the veranda, tan and windblown after driving from Boston in a convertible, while Sylvie, his young second wife, followed in his towering shadow, her steps graceful in sandals that matched her handbag.

It had been three years since Elliott and Neil had seen each other. "Hey hey hey hey!" Elliott called back—it was their old greeting—and Neil grabbed him in an embrace of expensive aftershave. He was almost as tall as Elliott, but he had a good thirty pounds on him, which he wore well, though he was always struggling against a tendency to grow fat.

"We took the turns at eighty-five," Neil announced. "Then we had to sit in the car for twenty minutes while Syl erased the evidence."

"It's murder on the hair," she said, tossing her head so that it swished above her shoulders. When Elliott leaned in to kiss Sylvie's cheek, somehow his lips landed on hers.

"Where's Helen?" Neil asked. "We sped all the way for her."

Neil and Sylvie had in fact been invited to arrive the previous day, but an art opening of Sylvie's had held them up. So they had not really *sped* to the hotel—a fact that would have been against Elliott's nature to mention to them.

"I'm right here," Helen said, and Elliott turned, moving aside so he wasn't in her way.

Helen sat with her legs propped up on the table. She had put on Elliott's new sunglasses, and they looked even worse on her. Elliott heard a noise behind him, a sharp intake of breath. That would be Neil, he thought, a man in full-throated denial of mortality. The British convertible, the juicy young wife: these weren't the possessions of a man who feared aging but a man who could hardly even be made to acknowledge it.

But Neil braced himself and lunged at Helen with his arms open wide. "Helen!" he cried, and she laughed from her cushioned sofa. "How is the most beautiful woman in New England?" he said. "Don't get up! You remember Sylvie, don't you? Sylvie, Helen; Helen, Sylvie . . ."

Elliott had never really shied away from expectations of death, and he'd imagined he and Helen would experience the slow, not too painful decline that they, as healthy, responsible people, should have earned. The body was a machine, and at some point parts of the machine would begin to fail, the way the Jetta had stopped going into first gear. From Elliott's new vantage point, Neil's rejection of the oblivion that awaited all of them seemed fascinating. Then again, if one wanted to talk about denial, there was Helen, whose refusal to acknowledge any of the warning signs—the headaches, the dimming vision, the time when thoughts seemed to leave her—seemed to Elliott both heroic and idiotic. Even impaired, even with only half her mind working, she was a mystery to him.

Neil and Sylvie sat down on either side of Helen, Neil's meaty tan hands enveloping Helen's completely and Sylvie smiling at them both. She had met Helen only once, on the beach three years ago. That was before the wedding, which the Hansens hadn't been able to attend.

"It's great to be here!" Neil said. "And look—here's Abby! You've grown! You're gorgeous, too. Where's everyone else?"

"Eva and Ruth are at the pool, and I don't know where Dom and Henry went," Helen said.

"So they've all left you, the star of the hour, here with this guy?"

"We were waiting for you!"

"I love you," said Neil. "Syl, you haven't met these people. Or actually, you met Eva and Henry at the wedding, I think. They're fun."

Though all of Elliott's friends had done well for themselves, Neil was the one who looked it the most; his habits of pleasure surrounded him in a cloud of goodwill. And today, Elliott thought, Neil seemed especially voluble, almost self-consciously hearty. He had long ago left higher education—he and Elliott had met while working together at Henniker College—for finance.

"What a lucky man I am," Neil said. "Three of the world's best-looking ladies right here on this porch. Elliott, how should we comport ourselves? We should buy them corsages."

Helen turned her head from side to side, looking at Neil and Sylvie as if she could not believe they were here. Elliott perched himself on the porch railing and lit the cigarette he'd been trying to avoid. He was glad Neil had arrived.

"I like gardenias," said Sylvie.

"Helen, how about you?"

In the face of his blustery charm, Helen giggled. "I don't know."

"Fantastic!" Neil said. "Let's have drinks."

A waiter was summoned and given instructions. Neil ordered Abby a white wine spritzer, brushing aside the protest he saw Elliott preparing to lodge. He had known Abby since she was a baby and had taught her one of her first words, which was "fuck." She was eighteen months old then, and her dutiful repetition of it used to send Neil into fits. For years he sent her presents on the important holidays.

Elliott looked over at Sylvie to find that she was watching him. Marriage had widened her a little, and her breasts seemed to strain against her demure blouse. She had freckles along her high cheekbones, and she looked young and coiffed but somehow secretly debauched. Like Ruth, she was not beautiful, but she was hard not to look at: there were those liberal breasts, those large, pale-lashed eyes, that yielding mouth. He smiled at her—a slightly overwhelmed, strained smile—that she barely returned before looking away and fiddling with the scarf she wore. And still, he thought, how strange; he hardly knew the woman, and yet he swore he'd seen in her open stare a deep and surprising sympathy.

Abby lingered by the side of the hotel, watching, without wanting to seem like it, the low white building where Alex and the other hotel employees lived. It squatted near the day-staff parking lot, its window boxes overflowing with petunias. The heavy fire door had been propped open, but she didn't dare enter it; instead she waited, half hidden behind two rosebushes, hoping that someone she knew would come out.

After she'd left her parents on the porch, she'd situated herself in obvious places and pretended to read. When that failed to result in contact, she wandered around the hotel as if she'd lost the key to her room and must look for it in every place she had been: the vast empty ballroom, the various hallways, and the bright, sunny conservatory, where two men playing chess looked up at her and wished her a good afternoon. She found Ellis working in the gift shop, but she was involved with customers. Abby waited for a while, fingering mugs with THE PRESIDENTIAL in ornate script, until she became self-conscious about lurking and left.

So she had decided to stake out Alex's living quarters. She wanted to explain herself, to defend her honor—or simply to make sure he didn't think her a complete and unredeemable baby. She knew that a bolder person would approach, but she kicked her toes in the bark dust and waited. She plucked a yellow rose from one of the bushes and slowly ripped its petals from its body: *He'll find me, he'll find me not, he'll find me.*

"You're messing up the mulch," Vic said, appearing beside her. "I just spread that last week."

She turned to see him in a green uniform, carrying a shovel. "Why are you always sneaking up on me?"

"I wasn't trying to. Sorry."

The sun was in her eyes and she squinted at him. "I thought you worked in the kitchen."

"I move around. I'm a Vic of all trades." He seemed to notice but did not mention the petals strewn about her feet.

"Do you live over there with the others?" she asked.

He shook his head. "Townie," he said. "I stay at my grandpa's." He leaned the shovel against a pillar. "What are you doing standing there? Are you feeling left out?"

She bristled at the accuracy—not that it was so very perceptive of him. "No. You?"

"I didn't come here to hang out with a bunch of preppy shitbags."

"That's a mean thing to say."

"You're not all that nice yourself," he said.

"What makes you say that?"

"I don't know—guilt by association, maybe. But I think you've always been a little stuck up."

He was teasing her, but she was still offended. "You barely knew me."

"I remember you."

Behind him, beneath the overhanging porch, a small brown bird darted into a nest snuggled between water pipes and then poked its head out to observe them.

"No," Abby said. "I don't think you do."

He shrugged. "Do you want to see something?"

"I'm not stuck up."

He laughed at the indignation in her voice. "Sure you are. But I like it. Anyway do you want to?"

Because it seemed easier than saying no or working up the bravery to walk into the employees' residence, she followed him into the cool lower story of the hotel. Vic stopped before a metal door next to the empty game room, glancing up and down the hallway and motioning for Abby to wait until an old man in a golf cap passed them.

"I'm just shy," she said.

"If that's what you want to call it."

When the hall was empty, Vic put a key in the lock and then leaned hard on the door with his shoulder until it jerked open. "After you," he said.

She slipped past him and he followed, stepping on the back of her heel. The room was completely black. Abby paused, uncertain; she was still a little afraid of the dark, and of things that might be hiding in it. "Where are we?" For some reason she whispered it.

"Just a minute . . . I have to find the lights."

She could hear his hand moving along the wall, and then a few bluish fluorescents sputtered to life, and in the humming, irregular light she saw that he had brought them into a low-ceilinged room full of glass diorama cases. In the small case by Abby's elbow, two stuffed songbirds clung to a branch. One bird's head had fallen off, and it lay in the moss below, gray as a dustball. On shelves along the wall were empty old birds' nests and the dark hollow shells of turtles.

Vic rested his palm on a case in which a muskrat, rearing up on its haunches, paused for eternity at the lip of a plastic pond. "Hardly anyone even knows this is here," he said.

The air was still and dry, and the animals' eyes were dead, flat glass. In another case stood a moose calf with a morose, almost canine face. A coat of dust covered his shaggy fur like ash. On the wall behind the calf, someone had painted other moose in the distance, grazing against a setting sun.

"It used to be the hotel museum," Vic said. "From the twenties to seventy-something, and then they just closed it up. I found the key in one of the garden sheds." He moved to another case and peered in, pressing his forehead against the glass. "Check out this badger. Some of his stuffing is leaking out."

Abby walked a few steps into the room, stopping before a carefully composed woodland diorama: chipmunks caught mid-scamper, a squirrel posed on its hind legs near a tree stump. In the far corner, two rabbits crouched beside each other while a yellow-eyed hawk gazed down at them from its perch.

Though the air was warm, she shivered. "All dark and forgotten like this—it's so morbid."

"You and your fancy words," Vic said. He walked around the other side of the case and peered at her from beneath the hawk. He opened his mouth wide, and his eyes, too, and made a stupid face. "It's all so *macabre.*"

"It's not funny," she said.

Vic knocked his fingers on the glass. "That"—tap—"is the kind of fox"—tap—"that I see"—tap—"out behind my grandparents' place. A red fox. I've seen mink, too, and a fisher cat, and about a hundred raccoons."

In the back corner of the room, someone had positioned three bears on a small hill of artificial grass. There were pine trees painted behind them, and mountains, and a blue sky dotted with the billowy white clouds of August. A pheasant, its feathers sooty and broken, shared their hill, and a moldering weasel peered at Abby from behind a rock.

"The second owner of the hotel was an amateur naturalist," Vic said. "He shot most of these himself."

Abby couldn't look at Vic, knowing that he was pleased, expectant, ready for her to appreciate the secrecy and strangeness of it. She didn't want to hurt his feelings, but she found the room sad and awful. "I'm sorry," she said. "I think I have to get out of here."

"What's the matter?"

"I really can't breathe." She meant it as an excuse but then realized it was true: she was taking deeper and deeper breaths, and still they weren't enough. A little ball of panic formed inside her.

"Really? Okay. I mean, weird. Just hang on one second . . ." He opened the door and stuck his head out. "All clear," he said.

Abby rushed past him into the stone passageway and all the way outside. She took deep, grateful breaths in the sudden brightness, and then she began to run. She heard Vic coming after her.

"I thought you would like it?" he called.

She ran faster and he took up the chase, and they raced down the hill and swerved alongside the golf course until they came to a stone wall and a wide green field. In the middle of the meadow, Abby stopped and collapsed on the ground. A moment later, Vic was standing above her, his shadow angling across her body. He held a hand over his face.

"Help," he said. "A bug flew into my eye." He bent down so she could see into the eye he held open, that blue blue thing, now watering and pink with a maze of tiny blood vessels. "Do you see anything?"

She saw the pores on the side of his nose, the stiff dark hair of his eyebrows, and his wet, clumped lashes. Tiny white petals had blown into his hair. "I don't know," she said. "I don't think so."

"Look harder," he said. He pulled his lower lid down farther and rolled his pupil up. She'd never looked this closely at an eye before, and the glistening, aqueous curve of it, so fragile and alive, seemed incomparably strange.

"I see it," she said. "It's a tiny black bug."

"Can you get it out?"

"It's in too deep. I can't stick my finger that far into your eye."

"Please."

"I can't—it's too much."

He fell on his back next to her. "You're useless," he said.

She said, "Maybe if I had a Q-tip or something."

"Whatever," he said, knuckling into his eyeball. "Why didn't you like the museum?"

"I wanted to like it, but it was a roomful of carcasses. It was creepy." She felt childish saying so.

"That's what a natural history museum is," he said. "Like how an art museum is portraits of dead people." He looked at her through the grass with only one eye.

"That wasn't a natural history museum—that was amateur taxidermy." Abby wondered if she should explain to Vic about abstract expressionism, which she had learned about her first semester. She thought it might make her feel like she had the upper hand. "And art isn't always figurative. Like, take Franz Kline or somebody—"

"You look a lot like your mom."

Through the straight trunks of the trees, Abby saw flashes of movement and color, and then a line of horses crossed the corner of meadow, nose to tail, carrying hotel guests along the trails. She didn't answer.

"I bet people tell you that all the time." Vic stripped the wheatlike heads from a handful of grasses. "I liked going to see her, you know. I actually looked forward to it."

She didn't want to listen to him talk about her mother, but she'd hated his museum and then run away from him, and now she felt like she owed him something. "Did it help you?" she asked.

"Help me what?"

"I don't know—be less of a delinquent."

"I wasn't *that* bad."

"What did you talk about?"

Vic waved a piece of grass at her. "Isn't that client-shrink privilege?"

"It's the counselor who isn't supposed to say anything. I think you can say whatever you want."

"I don't know," he said. "What does anyone talk about?"

"I have no idea," Abby said.

"Maybe I complained about my uncle. Maybe we compared the sad stories of our childhood."

Abby knew what was sad about her mother's, though she'd never heard her speak of it. "What's so sad about yours?"

"Nothing worth going into," Vic said. A ladybug landed on his arm, and he watched it crawl toward his wrist. "What's with the bugs today?" Then he leaned in close to her again and pointed to his eye. "Is it gone now?"

Through the grasses she looked into Vic's bloodshot eye and felt the urge to put her hand on his cheek and hold it there. The earth radiated warmth and the sharp mineral smell of grass and dirt and granite, and the whole meadow seemed to sigh in the heat of the afternoon. "I don't see anything," she said.

Now they were lying side by side, facing each other. He said, "Do you want to know how Pig got her name?"

Abby didn't like to be reminded of the banished cat, but she nodded because she could see that he was going to tell her regardless.

"There was this friend of my uncle's," Vic said. "He was a drunk. He lived on a couple of acres out west of town on Home Road, and he had a pet pig that someone had given him."

"One of those Vietnamese potbellied ones?"

"No, just a regular pig. Anyway, this guy loved it. It was really smart—it used to follow him around and come when he called it. He even taught it to fetch. One day he goes out to his garage and finds the pig dead on the floor. The guy is devastated. He goes to pet the pig and it's still warm, so he knows that it just happened. He thinks it had a heart attack or something, and he doesn't want his pig to be gone. So he decides he's going to shock it back to life like they do on TV, because he's had about a case of Milwaukee's Best and it seems like a good idea. So he takes his jumper cables, and he hooks them up, one to his pig's right ear, and one to his tail, and he guns the engine of his car. And the pig jumps off the floor from the shock."

"Alive?"

"No, still dead. And now the whole garage smells like pork chops."

Abby threw a handful of grass at him. "You're lying."

"I'm not. Ask my uncle."

"That's a horrible story. I thought it was going to be funny."

"Come on, it is sort of funny."

"What does it have to do with the cat?"

"The guy's cat had kittens, and he named every one of them Pig. Pig was the pig's name, too. I guess he had a limited imagination."

"Did you tell my mom that story?"

"I don't think I ever did. I should have."

"No you shouldn't."

A dragonfly, its body a blue-green glory of iridescence, hovered in the air between them. "We gave Pig away," Abby said, surprising herself—she hadn't thought she'd tell him.

"What?"

"My dad did. I didn't want him to."

"Why?" Vic sat up and looked at her in a way that made her uncomfortable. She shifted away from him slightly.

"She started freaking out. When my mom got sick." Abby spun an Indian paintbrush around in her fingers. "She threw up all over the house."

"Why didn't you call me?" Vic said. "You should have called me, I would have taken her."

Vic was angry, and his anger roused hers. "Called you? Don't you think there was enough to think about? My dad did what he had to." She had thought she'd never forgive her father, and maybe that was true, but it turned out that she would defend him.

"That kitten was the best one. I picked her out."

"I'm sorry," she said again, and she was—she'd loved the cat, too. "But no one could take care of her."

"You couldn't?"

"I'm going back to school."

"With your mom sick like she is?"

Abby didn't want to talk or think about it. Vic plucked up grasses by the handful, and Abby lay still, feeling angry and full of regret. Yes, they should have called Vic—or they never should have given the cat away in the first place. She should have said that she would stay home from college and take care of her mother and Pig both. She could comfort them and clean up after them. She would learn how to cook, so they could eat something besides casseroles, and she would do all the laundry and rake all the leaves and vacuum the house and go to the grocery store. She could figure out how to take care of everything.

Vic rubbed at his eye again. There was dirt on his elbow, and there were petals in his hair. He'd sat with her mother every week for two years, hadn't he? And she and Vic had both had Mr. Lopez for chemistry and Mr. Shepard for gym; they'd gone to the same movie theater, the same driver's ed classes, and the same swimming pool when they were kids. His life had run parallel to hers without ever being familiar or known, and now here they were, in a field in New Hampshire, and somehow they had disappointed each other.

"I should get to work," he said.

She said, "I'll go back too."

And so they walked toward the hotel without speaking, as grasshoppers flung themselves out of their way in great, frightened arcs.

Helen is trying to get some sun on her legs. The Schmidts and the Callahans have returned from town with packages, and Eva shows off a new sweater in soft yellow wool; she wants to copy the pattern to make one for Helen. Ruth wasn't able to find any spirulina, but she did buy a set of brown bowls with small curved handles. They're bean bowls, she says defensively, because Henry tells her they look like chamber pots. Dom and Henry have a T-shirt for Elliott, wrapped badly in a paper bag. It's tie-dyed in blue and purple and green, and Elliott reads out loud what it says: OLD HIPPIES NEVER DIE, THEY JUST SMELL THAT WAY. He laughs—appalled, Helen can tell—and tucks it right back in the bag. He wouldn't be caught dead in such a thing.

"It was Dom's idea," Henry says.

"We know you're not a hippie, but they didn't have anything about old golfers," Dom says. "Also that one was the ugliest."

They all circle up under the big gay umbrellas by the pool, and Neil and Sylvie come down from their room, freshly showered and ready to make themselves part of the gang. It's been six years since Neil moved to Massachusetts, and Ruth and Dom have never met Sylvie, who is smiling in an eager but forced way, as if someone is pulling strings attached to her mouth.

Everyone is getting along very well, except Ruth is giving Sylvie the cold shoulder because she loved Neil's first wife, Elizabeth, who moved to Kenya to work in orphanages. "Aren't you gorgeous," Ruth said, offering Sylvie a slim brown hand and managing to make the compliment sound not very complimentary.

Abby wanders away to the shade with her book. When Helen worries that this vacation isn't entertaining enough for her, Elliott shakes his head and says something about their daughter's inner resources.

Dom brings Helen a smoothie from the pool bar and sits beside her, not saying anything, just keeping his hand on her ankle, reminding her that he is there. *I used to love you,* his hand tells her. Such a silly old loyalty, she thinks, though she isn't going to discourage him now, either. She liked the attention, and she didn't think there was anything wrong with that. She was young then, and the young need such affirmation. She liked the poems he sent, appreciated his small, fastidious cursive and his monogrammed stationery.

The first boy who loved her was the son of her parents' best friends, the McDermotts, the ones who took Helen and Susan in when their mother died three years to the day after their father's funeral. Eric was tall and serious and shy, and both Helen and Susan teased him mercilessly. He was so confused, what with the linen closet cleaned out to store their school uniforms, and all the new female underthings drying on the shower rods—the long translucent stockings, the smooth silk slips—and the scents of baby powder and lily of the valley wafting out of their bedroom. They summoned him to the porch, where they lounged, and then imperiously sent him away. They borrowed his money for the movies and never paid it back. They hung around the pharmacy when he was working and tossed their curls over their shoulders. Helen was prettier, but Susan was bolder; he was compelled to give them free drinks. He wore a name tag, but they always called him by another name. *Carl,* they would say, *we need another vanilla Coke. Timmy Tim Tim, give us an extra maraschino cherry.* Poor Eric! He fell in love with Helen, who was fifteen years old and spurned him, and then he went off to engineering school in Baltimore, where, a few years later, he married a girl with only one arm.

There were other boys, too, including Denny Bristol, the one she thought she'd marry until she met Elliott. She sometimes wondered what had happened to Denny, with his letterman's jacket and his earnest, urgent way of talking about Plato. Elliott swore he'd read in the class notes that Denny sold refrigerators in Sioux City, but Helen didn't believe him. Denny had always planned to move to California, and there'd been a time when Helen thought she'd go with him. He wanted to be a poet and live on the cliffs of Big Sur.

Dom tightens his hand on her ankle and says, "I wanted to get you a papaya smoothie, but they don't have them here."

"I like this one," she says, taking a sip to prove it. She's never had a papaya—she's not even sure what one looks like.

"Or guava," Dom says. "I might have gotten guava with mango. But we'd have to be in Hawaii."

Helen smiles. "Next year."

Dom clinks his water glass against her smoothie. "Next year."

She feels him give her ankle another squeeze—*remember, I used to love you.* In the shade, Abby naps with her book on her chest. Seeing her daughter now, Helen thinks: *How beautiful I must have been.*

So we were stuck between salmon and filet," Elliott explained to Eva, glancing at Sheila for confirmation. In the clean light of the outdoors—they'd met this time at a cluster of chairs on the south end of the veranda—he observed the fan of wrinkles around Sheila's eyes, the tweezed brows, the blush that sat bright and artificial along the plane of her cheek. She wore a hot-pink jacket and silver earrings shaped like some kind of terrier.

Eva looked over the menu in her hand. "I think the salmon, don't you?"

See, Sheila's eyes said to him, *I told you—women always like the fish.*

"I don't have any idea. That's why I begged you to come with me," Elliott said to Eva.

"We can do a very nice preparation," Sheila offered. "We'll have it baked with baby vegetables—leeks, chanterelles, peas, asparagus . . . a little butter, a little white wine . . . It's very sophisticated."

"You don't want to give them time to grow up?"

The two women turned to him, mystified.

"The baby vegetables," he said. "A joke. Never mind."

"What about a salad with goat cheese and walnuts and beets?" Eva asked.

"Capital!" Sheila said.

He let them talk between themselves. He figured it didn't really matter what they ate, and besides, he trusted Eva's taste. He couldn't think about the hotel food anymore. By now all he wanted was a simple spaghetti with red sauce, a salad of iceberg lettuce with Select Seasonings Italian dressing, and a big soft piece of supermarket garlic bread. He wanted to go home. He missed defrosting the casseroles, he missed the laundry, he missed the women at Kroger's. *The idle are the only wretched*—was it Jefferson who'd said that? Elliott's labors had kept his mind occupied, and they had given him the illusion of control. But here there was nothing to do but eat and drink and talk and wait for it all to be over.

"What do you think, Elliott?" a voice said, and he turned to find the women gazing at him with wide, solicitous eyes.

He didn't know what they'd been talking about. "I don't think we should have beets," he said, purely to express an opinion. As an aside to Eva, he said, "They make your pee pink."

Sheila nodded and ran through a list on her clipboard. Did they need ice buckets for the white wine? Did he want the string quartet? If so, they would need to set up in the southwest corner of the room or risk being in the way of the servers. The Hansen party could have a fire, but they would not be able to open the windows if the room became too warm, as the frames were nailed to the sills and had been since 1943, the year the Presidential had closed because of the war. The tip would be included in the price, but if they found any server to be exceptionally helpful, they should feel free to offer him or her an additional sum.

Elliott and Eva kept nodding: yes to buckets, quartet, fire. Yes to roses, candles, champagne with the appetizers. Sheila looked pleased with their decisions; she told Eva that she had a gorgeous smile, and then she readied herself to leave. "This will be just wonderful. Here, take a pen," Sheila said, holding out two.

Elliott took them and handed one to Eva. "A souvenir."

"Goody," she said.

When Sheila clicked away, Eva and Elliott sat there for a while beneath the swaying potted geraniums.

"Thanks," he said. "I needed your help."

Eva leaned back and crossed her sandaled feet. "God knows I've planned enough dinners. Every night after we're done eating, I say to myself, 'There's one more meal I'll never have to cook again.' I think I've got around seven thousand down and about fourteen to go."

"Fourteen thousand?"

"That's if I cook every night until I'm eighty. I'm sort of hoping I can get out of it somehow."

Well, Elliott thought, *you could always get cancer.* He lit a cigarette.

Eva twisted the gold rings on her fingers. "I keep thinking about what I said about Ruth, and how horrible it was. Ruth and I have been friends for ages, and I adore her. Beneath all the showing off, she's very generous—you know that. And her posturing is a kind of self-defense. She's actually a very private person, I think."

"Maybe I could buy that," Elliott said. The pack of Merits settled back into his shirt pocket with a rustle of cellophane.

"Did you know that I used to be a singer, too? Back when I was in high school and college, I sang at weddings and funerals and birthday parties. I played guitar and piano. Then when I was twenty-one, I got chronic laryngitis. My voice dropped an octave, and I had to give it up.

"Ruth never even dreamed of singing until she heard that I had done it a thousand years ago. For some reason the story fascinated her, and a week later she bought a guitar and started taking lessons. Lo and behold, she had this undiscovered talent, and she got really good." Eva paused and plucked at the hem of her dress, snapping off a loose thread. "I couldn't help feeling like she got her idea for this life of hers out of what was supposed to be mine. It's strange to have a friend like that. She's like the me that I couldn't, in the end, become. Though I never would have gotten so deep into the mysticism and the feminism. Especially if, like Ruth Peel Callahan, I was completely and secretly skeptical of it all."

Elliott processed this information with surprise. "I never knew that."

"What part? That I sang, or that Ruth is practically a Phyllis Schlafly Republican? Not that it matters. I don't even know if I would have ever done anything wonderful with music. Maybe I would have quit. But I didn't have the choice. And now Ruth acts as if she didn't either. She makes it sound like God knocked her on the head when she was thirty-five and showed her the true path. She *is* good, and she became more successful than I would have been. She has the flamboyance and the self-regard that sort of thing requires. And what I thought I wanted to do when I was twenty is very different from what I wanted to do later. Still, there's a tiny part of me that hates Ruth more than anyone in the world." Eva's hand rested lightly on Elliott's arm.

He exhaled a puff of smoke and said, "That makes sense to me."

"You'd never feel that way. You're incapable of it."

Elliott thought about that; he wasn't sure if she was right. "I have worse flaws," he said.

"Name one."

He hesitated. "Dishonesty."

"What are you talking about?"

"My failure to tell Abby what's going on." He had begun to question his motives this week—perhaps he was not just protecting Abby but avoiding her potential hysteria. Perhaps what he'd thought was for her benefit was in fact for his.

"That's hardly dishonest, or a character failing of any sort. Look at everything you're dealing with."

"Still," he said.

"I haven't told anyone, either. I'm going to, though. Ruth first, then Henry and Dom."

Elliott laughed bitterly. "It's strange how we plan this. How we dole it out."

"What good is there in knowing, really? There's more freedom in ignorance. Though I think they must know in some way. I did—I just couldn't admit it to myself. I didn't want to."

He watched her familiar profile as she rocked in her chair. Mascara made her lashes long and brown, but he could see the lighter hairs where they emerged from her lids. She had a small, proper mouth, and her cheeks were covered in a fine blond down. She was solid and gentle and feminine—the kind of mother he would have wanted to have. He wanted to put his head on her shoulder.

"The instant I laid eyes on Helen, I knew we would be friends," Eva said. "Isn't that funny? I felt like I could have walked up and thrown my arms around her and she wouldn't have been surprised at all. That somehow she would have recognized me: 'Oh, hello, my long-lost friend,' she would say. That isn't how it happened, obviously, but our friendship was immediate. That never happened to me with anyone else."

He had heard Helen's version of the story, which was not so different; the women had met on a park bench, their baby daughters in their laps. He supposed it was something they recounted to each other as a reminder of their bond. "Your friendship has been precious to her," he said. It sounded stiffer than he had meant it to.

"I thought I'd never forgive you for taking her away from me," Eva said. Her palm ran along his wrist. "People think you need husbands to grow old with, but that's not true—what you really need is that one perfect friend. You can get fat and ornery and grow bunions together. We always had so much to say to each other. I just wish . . ." She stopped.

He didn't press her to finish, but sat quietly, feeling the light pass of her hand and relishing that one spot of comfort.

He felt Eva's love reaching out to Helen, and softly it enveloped him, not for his own sake but because he was the one who sat there beside her. Meant for him or not, still it soothed him.

"Don't you look pretty, all blue and white," Eva said to Abby.

"She looks like one of your Spode pitchers, Evie," Henry said. "Doesn't she?"

Ruth lifted her long neck and gave Abby a sideways glance. She said, "She sure is showing some leg."

As the maître d' led them to their table, Sylvie took Abby's elbow in her small hand and whispered, "I'm sitting by you."

Her eyes were the gray-green of agates, and there was something lush, almost swollen, about her body. Abby knew that Neil had met her in a topless bar after a round of golf in Myrtle Beach. She was their bartender, and she was wearing a minuscule T-shirt. Otherwise you get all sticky, she'd explained. Neil learned that Sylvie was fifteen years younger than he, that she had gone to Duke and was the daughter of a Ford executive. He appreciated a pedigree and a rebellion from it in equal measure. He bought his friends lap dances from homelier women, and six months later, Sylvie moved to Boston. Elliott had told Abby this, shaking his head with uncharacteristic incredulity. Abby thought he was almost proud of Neil's recklessness.

"Remember how we saw you that summer a few years ago in Cape Cod, before Neil and I were married?" Sylvie asked now. "Your mother had a yellow sundress on. I think she'd made it herself. We all went down to the beach and the water was too cold for anyone but her and you. And when we finally got you out and up to the house, neither of you knew how to eat a lobster. Oh, here, you take that chair next to Dom and I'll sit in this one. Do you remember?"

Abby could picture that day well—they'd spent hours in the ocean, and then they'd slept, salt-covered and sunburned, on Neil's couches until dinnertime. "Neil let the lobsters crawl around on the floor before he boiled them," Abby said.

"He likes them to have that last hurrah."

"But they can't breathe on land?"

Sylvie's agate eyes widened. "I'd never thought of that," she said.

"Abby's a vegetarian, you know," Helen said.

Abby winced at her mother's intrusion; she couldn't imagine how she'd overheard their conversation.

Neil raised his eyebrows theatrically. "A vegetarian?" he said. "What-ever for?"

Everyone at the table turned to her, and Abby blushed. Her first se-mester in school, she'd have welcomed the chance to preach lentils and seitan, but now she wished her mother had just kept quiet. "I don't like the idea of eating something I wouldn't kill," she said. "So I do have fish sometimes, because I've fished before."

"I think that's very admirable," Eva said.

"You know, Shelley was a vegetarian," Dom said.

"So was Hitler," said Neil.

"Well, if that's true, it obviously wasn't out of any sense of morality," Eva said. "So it's an entirely different thing."

"You're right as always, Eva. He had an outrageous farting problem, and some quack doctor of his told him that a diet of vegetables would cure it."

"Neil," Sylvie said. "Dinner table?"

"Right, right, sorry. No fart talk."

"I'll order fish tonight," Sylvie said, turning to Abby. "Though I wanted a steak."

"Is the life of a cow worth more than the life of a fish?" Neil wondered. "And if a cow's life is worth more—and I can see that my dear wife thinks it is—is it a matter of size or habitat? What about a chicken? How much is a chicken's life worth?"

"A cow's life is worth more than a chicken's life," Ruth said.

"Because it's bigger and it's supposed to live longer? A chicken is an interesting creature, you know," Neil said. "Think about it: we eat it before it's born and after it's dead."

"*Neil,*" Sylvie exclaimed.

"Did I say anything about farts?"

"Personally," Dom said, "I like to eat several animals a day. But I see Abby's point."

"Pigs are smarter than three-year-olds," Abby said.

"Impossible," Dom said. "Dogs, maybe—and a small percentage of my composition students."

"You know back in the olden days, people who didn't eat meat weren't called vegetarians, they were called poor people," Neil said.

"Ahem," Ruth said, readying everyone for what would be the final word, and Abby was grateful for her infantile attention span. "I say if Abby wants to eat lettuce all day long, then we should let her. These kids are eighteen, they're old enough to make their own decisions. They're on their own."

"Then why is it again that we're still giving ours an allowance?" Dom asked, and Ruth sighed.

"Because we can," she said.

Their waiter—Pete, Abby noted with some embarrassment—hovered near them, waiting for an opportunity to speak. When he looked at Abby and smiled over her father's head, she felt better.

"May I?" he managed to get in. "May I take your order?"

Sylvie called out that she wanted the trout and the avocado salad, and then she turned to Abby. "So, do you have a boyfriend?" As she leaned in conspiratorially, her blouse fell open to reveal deep cleavage.

"Sort of," Abby said. "A half-boyfriend, maybe."

"What do you mean?"

"We went out in high school, and I'm sort of still dating him because I haven't figured out how not to."

Sylvie giggled. "Silly girl. Have you seen how cute these waiters are? You should be flirting with them."

Abby watched the waiters smoothly circling the room, as if they never lifted their feet but slid along the floor. Was that something they were taught—that odd, fluid glide? Was it a mark of superior service? There was Pete, of course, who hated Bob Dylan, and over in the far corner she saw Josh, and she thought—as she saw a tall, straight back vanish through doors behind the stage—that Alex was working on the far side of the vast room.

"They're okay," she said.

"I'm sure they're dying for a little female attention. See our waiter? I'll bet he's having a fling with an older woman. For one thing, what else is there around here besides you and me? For another, it's an important component of every young man's sexual résumé." Sylvie tapped her nails on her knife, thinking. "Her name is Greta, and she's rich. Not nearly as rich as she used to be, but still rich enough to be interesting. The waiter's name is . . ."

"Pete," Abby said. He was coming toward them with their wine.

"No, he's called Justin, and he's studying art history in college, and he's always been shy around women, so the fact that Greta propositioned him suits him very well. He's quite taken with her." Sylvie peered into her champagne flute. "He's promised to write her when he goes back to Penn State. She keeps a special P.O. box for all her lovers, which is in a different town from where she lives. She thinks this helps keep away the lovesick ones—and there have been more of them than you might imagine. She's told Justin that in the fall she'll send him a book she knows he'll appreciate—some Man Ray photos, or a Magritte *catalogue raisonné,* or something equally compelling to the undergraduate mind."

Dom, who was on Abby's other side, nudged her and held up a bottle of wine. "May I?" he asked Elliott, and when Elliott nodded, Dom poured her half a glass.

"For starters," Dom said. "We don't want you jitterbugging on the tables, though no doubt you are an excellent dancer."

"I don't know how to jitterbug," Abby said.

"We can teach you," Eva said. "We took lessons. We got especially good at the fox-trot."

"Don't give Helen any wine, she's sure to start jitterbugging!" Ruth cried. "Or discoing or whatever. Remember how you used to dance? All over the back porch like you had John Travolta himself to impress. Remember that time you got up on the roof?"

"That was you, Ruth," Eva said. "That was you plus a pitcher of margaritas."

"It was not, it was Helen!" Ruth looked to Helen for confirmation.

"I don't think it was me," Helen said.

"Fine! It was me. It was me, and I loved it. You all should have done it, too. From up there you could really see the stars."

"She fascinates herself, doesn't she?" Sylvie whispered. "Anyway, Greta won't send Justin the book after all, because only mothers send care packages. But she'll write him notes in little scented envelopes until she gets bored of him, by which time he will also be bored of her, and so they will part company forever, with fading fond thoughts, each enriched by the experience. Though it will occur to Greta, lying one night beside her balding, snoring husband, that each new lover carves another piece out of her heart's muscle, and that one of these days there will be only gristle left—gristle and fat, like the remnants of an old steak."

Abby was taken aback. "Did you just make that up now?"

"Oh, no, I didn't make it up at all. It's one of the oldest stories in the world." Color had risen in Sylvie's cheeks and along the expanse of her freckled chest. "Pass me that champagne bottle, will you? Poor thing, it's over there all by itself."

"What about that waiter?" Abby pointed to Alex—it *was* him—standing with his hands crossed behind his back and his head bowed slightly, as if he were penitent. She imagined him telling the people about the wines they should select: this one was oaky, that one was zesty, this one was deep and important.

"Oh him?" Sylvie said. "Let me think about him. It's possible he's gay."

Then Elliott, who had brought his camera to dinner, made everyone pose in groups. Abby leaned her head toward Sylvie, and Dom put his arm around her, and they fixed smiles on their faces as Elliott took three shots in rapid succession. He turned to the other side of the table and posed them for a few pictures.

Abby watched Alex all through the salad course. He moved in and out of range, always on the other side of the room, never looking in her direction. Surely he'd seen her come in?

They were given their appetizers, and then a midmeal ice to cleanse the palate; the conversation was about vacations, and then exercise, and then real estate. Sylvie paid more attention to her wineglass than she did to her supper, though when her entrée came—a whole cooked fish on her plate, which gazed up at her with a dull black eye—she seemed affronted.

"I can take it back in," Pete said, "miss." Abby thought he almost winked at her.

"Yes, I think my wife wants it to look more like food and less like a carcass," Neil said.

"I understand completely," Pete said. He slipped away toward the kitchen and someone else leaned over to fill their water glasses.

"I love it when they call me 'miss,'" Sylvie said. "It doesn't happen so much anymore. It must be because I'm sitting next to you. They think we're the kids hanging out with the old people."

Abby, who didn't think Sylvie looked *that* young, nodded. Beside her, Dom sliced into a pork shoulder with a sigh of pleasure.

"Honestly," he said, "I think if you're at the top of the food chain, you ought to eat like it."

"Enough already," Ruth said.

Pete returned with Sylvie's fish, now laid out on a plate in an innocuous white strip, and Sylvie looked pleased. "This I can eat," she said to Abby, "but I don't want you to think that you haven't made a certain impression with your pro-vegetable high-mindedness."

"She'll grow out of it," Neil said. "Abandoning one's ideals is one of the pleasures of aging. Unless you're Elliott, in which case you protect them like you'd protect your own limbs. Though it's possible he had so many fantastic ideals as a kid that he was able to grow out of most of them and still remain the upright and admirable citizen he is today."

Abby's father laughed and told Neil to shut up and eat his dinner.

"I love your dad," Sylvie said to Abby. "My husband could use more of his influence." She'd had only a few bites of her fish, but she took out a mirror and painted a bright new mouth over her old one. "What shall we do tonight?" she asked the table. "Is there a place to dance around here?"

"Actually, there might be music in the ballroom tonight," Dom said.

"Oh, fun," Sylvie said. She asked Neil to take her dancing, and he said he would consider it.

In the darkening window, Abby watched as their faces were reflected, faint and wavering in the old glass, raising wine, buttered rolls, and meat to their lips. Above them the chandeliers glittered like suspended fires, and there were dancers on the parquet floor, just a few, and none of them very graceful. The bass player's face was a shifting, grimacing mask of effort, and the drummer's brow was shiny with sweat. Abby wanted a boy to dance with. Someone would put a spotlight on her, and everyone, even Sylvie, would seem clumsy and plain in comparison.

She didn't notice Alex sliding by behind her chair. But when she looked down, there was a note in her lap. *Field trip*, it said. *Meet in the parking lot at 12.*

So she had been given another chance. As she listened at her parents' door for the guttural, reassuring sound of her father snoring, Abby vowed that this time she would not make a fool of herself. She slipped out of her room and tiptoed down the hallway, though she told herself that such secrecy wasn't necessary—she was in college, after all, and old enough to be able to go where and when she chose, wasn't she?

She was creeping through the lobby when Sylvie emerged from a doorway and asked her where she was going. Sylvie's cheeks were flushed, her lips were purpled from wine, and her posture was confiding, insistent.

"I was going to take a walk," Abby answered, the lie so obvious she was ashamed to deliver it.

"It's too late for that," Sylvie said, narrowing her eyes. "I don't buy it. You're meeting someone, aren't you? You're *meeting* someone, you sneak! I want to come." She gave Abby a pinch on the arm. Her eyes had a bright, wet gleam.

Abby experienced a moment of semi-panic. Was everyone still up? Hadn't she just heard her father snoring? Or were he and all his friends wandering around the hotel corridors, ready to catch her sneaking out? She was too old to be grounded, and yet . . .

"Well?" Sylvie said.

"Where's everybody else?"

"Bed. Every single one of them. I told Neil I was going to find young people with stamina. And I did, didn't I? Here you are, off to an assignation."

"It's not like that," Abby said. She ran her fingers along the leaves of a miniature orange tree and realized that the tree was real but the oranges were balls of hollow plastic.

Sylvie leaned in to her suddenly, affectionately, her grapey breath on Abby's shoulder. "You're so pretty," she said. "I don't remember you being so pretty. Let me come."

Abby was trying to figure out how to dissuade her when Alex walked into the lobby. He hesitated, as if he might pretend that he didn't know Abby, but then he drew himself up and, though he was not in uniform, said in his best waiter voice, "Good evening, ladies. Is there anything I can help you with?"

Sylvie raised her head and smiled at him. "You can tell us where the fun is," she said. "You look like someone in the know."

His eyes flicked to Abby's. She shook her head, shrugged, tried to mime helplessness. She said, "Alex, this is Sylvie. She's a friend of my parents'. Sylvie, this is my friend Alex."

"The waiter! I can't believe you didn't tell me," Sylvie said. "Were you going on a date?"

"A field trip," Abby said.

"That sounds educational," said Sylvie.

"After a fashion," Alex said. "It's a pleasure to meet you."

"Where are you taking my Abby?"

"It was going to be a surprise."

"I love surprises." Sylvie blinked expectantly, happily, ready to be entertained.

Abby looked at Alex—what was she supposed to do with Sylvie there, holding her hand?—and Alex looked at Sylvie, at her large breasts, her wide eyes, her eager, boozy carnality.

"I think you need a chaperone," Sylvie said. "Someone mature and responsible." She bumped Abby with her hip and giggled.

Alex said, "You can come if you can keep a secret."

Abby shook her head, *no no no,* but it was too late.

Sylvie said, "I do only a few things better," and followed as he began to walk down the hall.

In the parking lot, Trey and Ellis waited for them in an idling car. Alex made the introductions, and Abby sat red-faced and embarrassed between him and Sylvie in the backseat.

"Not gay," Sylvie whispered into Abby's ear. "He's precious. But don't worry, I only like older men with thick wallets."

Their headlights scraped along the rocks that lined the driveway, while behind them the hotel grew smaller and smaller until it looked like a castle made of sugar cubes.

"Where are we going?" Abby asked Trey.

"You'll see. Watch for moose," Trey said.

The trees curved inward overhead and the pearly half-crescent of the moon appeared in bright pinpricks through their leafy fingers. Trey turned on the radio, flipping through the stations until he heard Neil Young. Sylvie put her head on Abby's shoulder again. "Really, I won't tell," she whispered.

"There's nothing to tell," Abby told her. On her other side, Alex pressed his leg against hers, and Abby wondered why he'd let Sylvie come. Politeness? Sexual interest? Did she look like a more fun time than Abby? Abby shifted her weight so that she leaned against him as much as she dared—she would show him that she was fun, too.

After a few minutes Trey turned down a dirt road, and they bumped along through the woods until the road dead-ended at a wide clearing. Trey cut the engine, and they all followed him through a rocky field. Ellis carried a backpack full of clinking glass and stumbled, cursing. The crickets were singing frantically in the grass, and here and there fireflies turned on their tiny lamps. After a few hundred yards they came to a fence, which they climbed—Sylvie had some trouble in her tight skirt—and on the other side they found themselves standing on the edge of a white cliff. Ten feet below them lay a deep bowl of water, black and utterly still, with the moon floating in the center of it. To their left, a hand-painted sign told them they shouldn't swim.

"It's the old marble quarry," Alex said. He kicked off his shoes. "The hotel sinks came from here."

Sylvie said, "I thought we were going to a bar."

Ellis reached into her backpack and pulled out a bottle of vodka, which she passed to Sylvie. "It's not very cold," she said, watching Sylvie take a swig of it. "I was going to give you a cup with ice and some grapefruit juice."

"Oh, sorry," Sylvie said. "I thought we were passing it around. Like hoboes." She handed it back and looked around uncertainly.

Alex seated himself on a rock, his legs dangling down over the water, and Abby, summoning her bravery, sat down next to him.

"I can't believe you let her come," she whispered.

"It would have been rude not to invite her."

"She probably wouldn't even remember."

"She's not that far gone. She's better off than you were last night."

Abby still felt sick even thinking about it. "That's not fair."

"She's just having a good time. Did you like my poem, by the way? I thought it was very clever."

"What if she tells my parents? What if she tells her husband and gets you fired?" Abby knew that neither of those things would happen, but she didn't think Sylvie should have been accepted so easily; it upset the balance of things.

"Don't worry about it," Alex said. "Everything's going to be fine."

Abby fell silent, unconvinced. The woods that ringed the quarry were vast and black, and the marble glinted dully in the darkness. Ellis leaned against Trey, and then the two of them lay back against the rocks, her hand on his stomach under his shirt. Trey turned a flashlight on and off, on and off, on and off.

"So what do we do now?" Sylvie asked. "Do we go skinny-dipping or something?"

Abby laughed—leave it to the lady from the topless bar to have an idea like that.

"Yes," Alex said. "After we have a cocktail or two."

"Are you serious?" Abby said.

He didn't answer, just brushed a piece of hair from her face, and even. that slight touch made her shiver.

The last time Abby skinny-dipped was at the Callahans' lake house, right before the Hansens moved to Ohio, and it was only because her mother made her do it. Abby and Rachel Schmidt had tried to refuse, but their mothers half goaded them, half stripped them naked by force. Eva paced the length of the dock, laughing, while Helen loomed over them with a camera. Rachel and Abby protested, whining and splashing, until the shame of their mothers' disbelief—*Do you really think we haven't seen your bottoms before?*—won out over the humiliation of being pho-tographed balanced on their black inner tubes, naked and defenseless as little seals.

These days she wanted to be a good sport. She wanted to be able to say that she'd done it. But she was shy with her body—so few people had seen it before. Would it count if she swam in her bra and underwear? She weighed natural modesty against potential ridicule for being a prude. Also, her bra was white and her underwear was purple, and somehow this seemed wrong.

But no one moved to get undressed. Trey sat up and lit a pile of sticks into a small flickering fire, and Sylvie skipped along the rocks above the water, oblivious to the awkwardness of her presence. Alex knocked his heels against the marble as shadows from the fitful fire played along his back. They passed the vodka around, making exaggerated swallowing noises. Trey told an unfunny joke, and then another, as they sat there waiting for something to happen. *Now?* the wind hissed. *Now?* The night felt huge, like a great, dim ballroom.

Helen had put the skinny-dipping pictures in the photo album right alongside the Hansen family camping trips, so anyone flipping through could see Abby's bare backside. Abby didn't look miserable in them, though that was how she remembered the occasion; she looked cold and earnest. In the one picture Eva had taken, Helen stood above her on the dock in her pedal pushers, smiling, delighted at the violet evening, the clear lake, the long, beautiful summer.

Abby got up and walked a little ways away from Alex. If all these people took off their clothes, it would be a chance for her to redeem herself by joining them. But she was too chicken; she knew she would fail this, too. Her mother wasn't here to goad her, and anyway, Helen wouldn't in such circumstances; she would tell Abby to keep her dress zipped up. Confidence and bravery, after all, would come to Abby with time, but innocence certainly wouldn't.

Abby balanced on one of the rocks and eyed the short leap to its neighbor. It was easy enough to bet on, she thought, and so she did: *If I make that, my mother who would not want me to be here will be okay.*

She jumped then, and as her right foot landed on the marble, the rock shifted and she slid off to the side. She didn't fall—she caught herself—but she let out a surprised cry. *That one didn't count,* she told herself, *it only counts when you're totally sober.*

"What are you doing?" Alex called. "Are you all right?"

She walked back toward him, trying to shake off her apprehension. It was a game, she thought—it didn't mean anything bad. And really, with whom was she bargaining? Who was supposed to accept her if-then proposition?

"Don't go running off," Alex said, patting the plane of marble beside him. "Just come here and relax."

She obeyed him and sat. In the quiet moments that followed, she wanted to ask him what he was thinking, but that seemed too familiar a question because it presumed a right to know. She clasped and unclasped her hands, waiting for something to happen. A kiss, maybe, or some whispered affections. When neither was forthcoming, she spoke. "Are you really writing a novel?" It was the only thing she could think of to ask.

"Yes."

"Can you tell me what it's about?"

He picked up a hunk of rock and tossed it into the water. "Like I said, if I told you, you'd think I'm a jackass. It sounds too pretentious."

"Is it?"

"Probably," he said, managing to sound both embarrassed and self-satisfied.

"Try me."

"Imagine if Borges rewrote Balzac's *Perè Goriot*," he said, lobbing another rock.

She nodded as if she had read these people. She hadn't, but at least she knew who they were. At least she knew enough to agree that it sounded like the most pretentious book she'd ever heard of. "It sounds . . . sophisticated," she said.

"It is so far one long, failed experiment. Though there are worse ways to waste one's youth." He glanced over at Trey. "One could be addicted to watching motocross and trying to brew alcohol in canning jars in one's bedroom."

"All right, everyone," Sylvie called out. She rubbed her arms; she hadn't brought a sweater. "This is boring. It could be warmer, but I'm game."

And then, without any hesitation, without the slightest tremor of modesty, she unbuttoned her blouse and flung it away. "Obviously it's up to the old lady to show you people how it's done," she said. Her bra followed, and the dark nipples on her high white breasts looked at them like another set of eyes. Then she stepped out of her skirt and panties and walked toward the edge.

They watched as she stood there, flawless as a statue, as if she herself had been carved from marble, and then she raised her arms above her head and dove into the water. Abby was appalled—and also jealous.

A moment later, Sylvie came up to the sound of clapping.

"Ten," Alex said.

"Jesus Christ, you didn't tell me it'd be so cold!"

"She was a stripper," Abby said, because it sounded more daring than "bartender," and because she wanted some of Sylvie's boldness to reflect on her.

Sylvie swam into the middle of the quarry saying, "Jesus, Jesus, Jesus." Stars rippled on the water's surface, and the moon floated in little broken pieces.

"If you just move around, you get warm," she yelled. "Come on, let's get this party started."

Ellis lifted her head from Trey's shoulder. "Want to?" she said to Abby.

Abby shook her head, and Ellis crawled over and passed her the vodka again. "One more sip and then take it all off."

Abby watched, trying to seem as if she weren't, as Ellis and Trey slipped out of their clothes, dropping them onto the rocks. Then Alex rose and held out his hand to Abby.

Abby shook her head. "Not yet," she said. "Give me a minute."

But she knew she wouldn't go in at all. Without Sylvie, she might have been brave enough, but she couldn't get naked with her parents' friend, no matter how much vodka they gave her. She turned and stared into the fire, and she heard them splash in, one by one, then cry out, shocked and happy.

"Come in," they called, "come in," but Abby ignored them. Their laughter drifted back to her, and she imagined them in that dark water, so slick, so everywhere. She imagined Trey and Ellis reaching for each other under the surface. She pictured the water that touched Sylvie swirling around Alex.

She walked over to the edge. Below her were dark heads and white arms and legs, barer than bare, surrounded by high, sepulchral walls of marble. Trey flung his head back and spat water skyward like a fountain. Sylvie's giggle carried like chimes. Abby watched Trey kiss Ellis in the water while the moon splintered over their shoulders. She drank, and the vodka was warm in her throat.

She knew that if she followed them, the moment would come when everyone got too cold and they would climb shivering out of the water onto the chilly rocks, and she would feel confused and deflated and her naked body would embarrass her. She would wish she'd never done it, but had chosen to remain in the moments before doing it, dry and nervous, full of a sense of giddy possibility. She sat down in front of the thin, doddering flames of the fire. She wasn't sorry to be still in her clothes, she wasn't sorry at all.

In the water, the others hollered and laughed. The boys dared each other to feats of bravery: Trey wanted Alex to try to touch the bottom, while Alex thought Trey should do a gainer off a higher ledge. They stayed in longer than she'd thought they would. When they came out, and the water stilled, it looked as thick and black as oil.

On the drive back everyone was subdued, but Abby could feel the low pulse of their exhilaration. By virtue of her bravery, Sylvie was now one of them, whereas Abby had once again failed to be the sort of person they had wanted her to be.

"People have died in that quarry," Ellis said. "That's why you're not supposed to swim there."

"Are you making that up?" Sylvie asked.

Trey shook his head. "Three kids drowned."

"Sad," Sylvie said, snuggling against Abby. Her hair smelled cold and vaguely algal. "It was so nice, though. You really should have come in. At your party tomorrow night, I'm going to pour wine down your throat until you do something naughty."

"Please do," Alex said.

When they got to the hotel, Sylvie asked Abby to walk her to her room, and Abby was relieved that duty would keep her from a kind of reckoning with Alex. What sort of girl was she—a good sport? A dick tease? He would want to know.

"Really, did people die in there?" Sylvie asked, blinking up at Alex.

"Yes, but they were very stupid people," he told her. "And besides, people die everywhere."

Abby tipped Sylvie into the elevator and leaned her against the wall.

Sylvie told her she loved her, really loved her, she was the best kid, she understood why people had kids now, maybe she and Neil ought to have a kid, or maybe they should adopt a ten-year-old so it wouldn't take so long to be grown up and fun like Abby. She'd heard there were orphanages full of preteen girls in India—maybe she and Neil could go there and get one. She didn't need something to be her flesh and blood, she thought it was important just to have that love. Africa, China, Ecuador—they could have a kid from anywhere in the world. Wouldn't that be nice? Wouldn't it? And Abby could come and babysit . . .

Sylvie had a hard time fitting her key into the lock. She kissed Abby on the mouth, and her lips were soft and wet. "Good night, sweetie," she said. "Thank you for including me."

In Abby's maid's room, she kept the lights off. She removed her clothes and took a shower in the dark. When she came into the bedroom, she was startled to see her mother standing in the doorway, spectral and small in a white nightgown.

"Oh, Abby, I've been looking all over for you," Helen said. Her face was creased from the pillow, and in her right hand she carried a single slipper.

"Hush," Abby said, "hush." She folded her mother into her arms, and realized how long it had been since she'd held her. "You were dreaming. I've always been right here."

FRIDAY

Neil had joined Elliott on his morning circuit of the veranda, and as they passed by the porte cochere, Neil saluted the valets, who were tossing a set of keys back and forth.

"Punks," he said to Elliott. "I swear they took my car for a drive. Hey, did I tell you the one about the old man in the nudist colony?"

"Nudist colony," Elliott repeated, trying to remember if Neil had or not.

"'Lady, I'm seventy-six years old! I fart fifty times a day, and I get an erection once a month!'"

Elliott laughed, the sound harsh and abrupt as if it had been shoved through him. "Right," he said, not actually recalling it. "That one."

Neil dunked the cigarette Elliott had given him, only halfway smoked, into a cup of coffee abandoned on a windowsill. "Well," he said. The wooden slats of the porch railing reflected in his shiny shoes.

"What did the fish say when he ran into the wall?" Elliott asked.

"I don't know."

"'Dam!'"

Neil grinned and lobbed a mock punch at Elliott's shoulder. They rounded the north corner of the hotel, and then they could see their group in a cluster of chairs. Henry and Eva were looking at a birding book while Ruth and Dom read magazines. By the way Ruth had grabbed Elliott at the breakfast buffet—a hard, tight hug that hurt a little—he knew that Eva had told her. He'd hugged her back with a plate of eggs in his hand.

Sylvie was painting a picture of Helen with a set of gouaches and a portable easel. When she moved, Elliott could see her breasts sliding around under her thin shirt; she wasn't wearing a bra. Her arms were lightly freckled, and her small hand dipped a brush into what had been his water glass. Brown pigment swirled down and settled. Elliott admired the engineering of her easel and her tight white pants.

"I couldn't have married her if she'd been topless," Neil had confided. "But there she was, in the middle of all those breasts, sexy and smart and wearing a Celtics T-shirt. My team!"

Elliott wondered if he would ever find himself in a titty bar. He'd always been repulsed by the idea, but he would not prejudge his future self. Who knew what changes death would work upon him, and where he would take solace?

"I'm going to call it *Helen After Breakfast*," Sylvie called out to them.

"She's certainly showing up our poor efforts," Ruth said, looking up from her *Vogue*. "We thought we were so good with those postcards!"

"Those were *lovely* cards," said Eva. "Anyway, you didn't make any."

"Mmmm," Ruth said.

Rinsing her brush, Sylvie looked up at Elliott as he passed, and their eyes met, again with that startling frankness, as if some particular affinity existed between them. What a strange person she was! He patted his chest pocket for his Merits, though he was already smoking one.

"Let's go round again," Neil said. "I don't want to sit."

Elliott nodded; he didn't want to, either.

When they were out of earshot from the others, Neil said, "So, did Chase call yet?"

Elliott turned to him, surprised, and a waiter carrying tea and pastries passed between them. Neil had put on mirrored Ray-Bans, so his eyes were invisible.

"The dean is a buddy of mine. I told him you were the one."

What was it in Elliott that made him want to tackle his friend, to pin him beneath his knees there on the wide, gracious porch?

Neil reached out and knocked one of the hanging planters so it swung like a pendulum. "You've slaved away for long enough, Hansen. You know you'll never make real money, not in your line of work, but at least you can go to a school that has a goddamn sports team. You don't feel entitled, and that's great, it's good to be a fighter and not some smug, lazy bastard. But think of what you could do if you didn't have to fight so hard. You're fucking dignified, Elliott, and it's about time you were in a place that deserved you. You'd be amazing. Chase! It was founded in 1790, for Chrissakes. And you'd be back on the East Coast, with us."

Elliott took a deep breath and then another inhale on his cigarette. He imagined the regal Georgian redbrick buildings, the landscaped grounds; he saw soccer fields glittering with frost and the orange leaves of stately elms sifting down; he saw students walking along the paths, ambitious and eager; he imagined a sane and stable faculty.

He didn't mind he'd been wrong, thinking he'd earned Barney Russell's notice through his presentations at educational conferences and his articles in *The Gold Standard.* He understood now how unlikely it was that Carlisle's progress had registered with or mattered to anyone but its small population of students and alumni. And he knew that his friend had meant only to be helpful. But at a time like this—what was Neil thinking? Chase was a taunt: a glimpse of something Elliott wanted terribly and was wholly unable to have.

Maybe he still should have been grateful. But he wasn't. He said, "Helen is dying, Neil." *You fucking asshole,* he thought. "I can't—"

Neil raised his hand, stopping him. "Don't say that, Elliott. You don't know."

"I do know."

Beside him, Neil staggered a little, and Elliott reached out for him, and for a moment, just the quickest moment, they walked, holding hands.

Helen is cross-legged on the ballroom floor, tucked between Ruth and a woman in a purple caftan. Ruth says the woman's name is Francesca and that she is a healer and an energy worker. *Whatever that means,* Helen thinks. Not that she's not intrigued. This person has the grounding influences of unmistakable serenity and ample girth. Francesca wears heavy ropes of beads around her neck, and the bottoms of her bare feet look as hard and dark as leather. Her eyes are closed.

"I found her in the spa," Ruth whispers. "She's studied medicinal potions in Africa and communicated with Nez Perce spirits in Idaho."

Sylvie and Abby and Eva are also there, waiting for whatever is going to happen. Helen smiles across the circle at her daughter, who smiles back and then sticks out her tongue. Helen giggles. Ruth sighs and settles into lotus position, and for a while they are all quiet.

Francesca breaks the silence by hitting a small brass chime. "This," she says, "is a healing circle." Her voice is mellifluous, soothing. "We are gathered here to pray for the healing energies of the universe to flow down and renew us. Let us close our eyes and feel the power that surrounds us."

Helen obeys. Really, she has no use for skepticism. She concentrates on Francesca's warm, dry hand and Ruth's cool thin one holding hers. She feels the breeze coming in the open ballroom windows and hears the birds calling to one another. *Yes,* she thinks, *there is life everywhere around me.*

"Now," Francesca says, "let's concentrate on the breath, the way it flows in and out like a tide. Feel it coming from the top of the head, sliding down into the lungs and filling them, and then push it down through the navel and out through the pelvic floor. Imagine you are breathing in a perfect, holy circle." She begins to hum, sliding between two notes, *do-mi, do-mi, do-mi!* It echoes in the vast empty room and it sounds like a summons.

Helen breathes in a circle, keeping her thoughts reverent, until Francesca begins to chant. Francesca calls upon the Three Holy Energies of Light and Love and Healing to bless them, to flow through them, to renew them, to heal them. She repeats her prayer over and over again, and the words gain meaning and then lose it and then gain it again. Helen can hear Eva's low raspy whisper and her daughter's soft hesitation. The words rise up along the pilasters and float among the molded plaster acanthus, lingering in the chandeliers, finding new spaces, slipping out through cracks, and then spiraling up into the sky.

Francesca says they will now call the Three Holy Energies to flow through and heal Helen, and Helen can feel herself believing.

"Imagine the healing light, feel the healing light," Francesca says. "See all the colors of a rainbow, and imagine them washing over you, red for energy and courage, orange for warmth of heart, yellow for joy and liberation . . ."

Helen wills herself to glow, to become all the colors of the rainbow. She hears the whisper of movement, and suddenly, they are all touching her, pressing their warm palms to her, and she can feel their energy flowing through her as she feels herself bathed in multicolored light.

Dear God, make this real, Helen thinks. *Dear God, please please please.*

———

She wants to rest after that, so they plop her back on the porch, where the white wicker chairs with their floral cushions are clustered together like old maids in church dresses.

She really does feel better. How much nicer the healing circle was than the pills that make her guts twist and the machines that point their hot rays at her until she can almost smell herself burning. When her head was cradled in Francesca's ample lap, Helen could feel the healing light coursing through her veins, flowing into the dark places of her body, filling everything with warmth.

"Hello?" says a voice. "Mrs. Hansen?"

She starts, twists around in her chair, and sees him a few yards off, a bouquet of daisies clutched in his hand. Vic Libby.

"Oh!" she cries, and stands up, a bit unsteadily, but she hopes he won't notice, and she quickly checks her bandanna to make sure it's covering everything it needs to. "Look at you!"

She doesn't know whether she should hug him, but he comes toward her with his arms out, and so then they are holding each other. Her ear is tight against his chest, and she can feel the daisy petals on her neck. Vic bends down so that his cheek presses on the top of her head.

When he steps back, they face each other, seeing what the years have done. Vic is not as skinny as he used to be, and he takes better care of his hair. Still she can find her young father in his face, though maybe not as much as she remembered. As for what has changed with her, she doesn't want to think about it.

"Sit," she says, "please sit. Are you hungry? I . . . Oh . . . Do you want a Coke?"

"Do you?" he asks. He lays the daisies on the table. "Here, let me order us a few things. I get an employee discount."

Seeing Vic brings back the courthouse: the smell of paper and old wood in the hallways; the walls' drab, uniform paint, neither white nor cream nor tan but some kind of cheerless anti-color; the syncopation of the secretaries' typewriters; the faded posters lining the offices; her old plastic couch with the pillows she'd made; the years of kids who'd sat on its slick black cushions, willingly or unwillingly listening to her try to help them get straightened out. All of it seems like so long ago, when it's just a matter of months.

She'd had burglars and arsonists and fighters and huffers and drunk drivers and curfew breakers. She'd had good kids and bad seeds, boys and girls, eleven to seventeen years old, and she had tried her best with all of them. Some of her kids—the grateful ones—had kept in touch with her, and she'd always thought that Vic would, too. But he hadn't; she'd lost him.

"How *are* you?" she asks. She's embarrassed and excited. She wants to tell him how glad she is to see him. She wants to apologize for how different things are now. She opens her mouth and then closes it again.

"I'm doing all right," he says. "How are you?"

Helen waves this question away. It's better not to talk about herself. "Tell me about you," she insists.

He looks around the porch as if it offers clues about what he should say. "I have one more year at OSU," he says. "It's been good there. I've got an apartment off High Street, over by Benny's Bagels, and I'm playing in a band."

"What . . ." She waves her hand around before the word comes to her. "Instrument?"

"Drums mostly, but we all sort of rotate around. It keeps things interesting, but probably we'd be better if we'd all pick instruments and stick with them."

"What kind of music?"

"Loud music. We're sort of like, I don't know, Hüsker Dü or Mudhoney."

"Oh!" Helen exclaims, as if this means anything to her. "And your uncle? How's he?" She can't remember his name, but she remembers his small, wiry body, his pinched and anxious face.

"He's all right. He's working for the county now, in the parks department, and he's gotten into fixing up the yard. I go up and see him about once a month or so. He just got a dog."

Helen remembers how Vic used to lie back on her couch and pluck at the trailing ends of the spider plant while he talked to her. She'd just *hoped* for her kids, for her own daughter and for everyone else's children, too. She'd tried to give them the tools they would need to survive. Sometimes it worked and sometimes it didn't: on the one hand, there was Shelly Hunter, a sixteen-year-old kleptomaniac who fixed herself up and went to law school; on the other, there was Trevor Rizzo, seventeen, who kept driving drunk until it killed him.

In no way, Helen thought, could she ensure that the outcome she sought for her kids would be the outcome achieved—she simply had to trust them. Vic had turned eighteen, and Abby had gone off to college, and what was left for her to do? They had gone beyond her influence. And still she hoped for them. She hoped for them and she hoped for herself.

"I've seen Abby around," Vic says.

"She's doing good, isn't she?"

"Seems so. But what about you? How are you?"

He says it with such gravity, with such tenderness, that this time she doesn't dismiss it. He trusted her, and she, in turn, trusts him.

She says, "I'm scared."

The women wanted Abby to come to the spa with them, but Abby, who had begun to feel oppressed by their company, said she was going to take a trail ride, which seemed to satisfy them; they waved and gave themselves over to attendants wearing uniforms like nurses. Francesca disappeared, too, after pocketing three hundred of Ruth's dollars.

Barring the expense, the ceremony wasn't so different from certain ones Abby had attended in college, where Wiccans sang Mother Earth songs in the meadow and environmentalists celebrated solstices or connected with their totem animals. She'd gone to these her first semester because she was curious and because she had no idea what college was going to make of her. She was young, wholesome, malleable, and she could have become anyone: party girl, nerd, activist, hippie. But what she became was the girl with the sick mother. There was a finality to that, as well as a kind of dreadful celebrity.

Abby bought a candy bar from the vending machine and then walked out to the back veranda, intending to be dutiful and sit with her dozing mother. But Helen was not half asleep in her usual chair; she was smiling that sad new smile of hers, and Vic was beside her, holding her hand. Instead of a uniform, he wore jeans, a green shirt, and scuffed old tennis shoes. Abby could see the movement of her mother's mouth and the steady nodding of Vic's head. They looked like old friends—like confidants.

A waiter set a plate of cookies in front of them, and Vic handed him a bill and waved away the change.

"Honey," Helen cried as Abby approached. "Look who's here!"

Her mother looked happily at her, and Vic, who made as if to get out of his chair, smiled in greeting, too. He had combed his hair flat and it didn't suit him. Abby sat down across from them and reached for one of the cookies. She kept her expression neutral.

"I finally found her," Vic said.

Abby understood then that she had hoped he wouldn't—that somehow the week would end without Vic ever speaking to her mother. It wasn't that she wanted him to herself, though that had been her first thought. It was that she wanted him to keep thinking of her mother as she had been before the cancer. The Schmidts, the Wrights, the Callahans—all of them were here to meet the new Helen. Was it so much to ask for one person to know her only as she'd been? However Vic had remembered her mother, whether he had loved her or respected her or merely tolerated her, his old image of her would be replaced by this one: bald, in an unflattering knit dress, unable to find the words she needed to have a conversation.

He opened Abby's book. "I've read this," he said.

"You have not," she said.

"I have," he said. "I had to. It was for a class."

Then he reached out and took her mother's hand again, and Abby felt a swelling of possessiveness. That was *her* mother—it was *her* hand to hold.

"He can tell you what happens," her mother said.

"That's a ridiculous idea," Abby snapped.

Immediately she was sorry. She closed her eyes, collecting herself. She wasn't angry at her mother, was she? Because if she was, she was a monster.

Vic handed Helen a cookie on a napkin. He made it look easy, sitting there with her, enjoying her company, when for Abby it was nearly impossible.

One of the bird-watchers wandered by with his notebook, frowning, and Abby could almost hear his thoughts. *A stranger—a male—has approached the nest. His behavior suggests courtship, and yet his focus is on the older female with the peculiar head markings.*

"I didn't mean that, I'm sorry," Abby said.

Helen only smiled. She said, "I asked Vic to dinner."

"Tonight? Your anniversary dinner? With everyone?"

"Yes, yes. It's a party. The more the merrier."

Abby thought this was a terrible idea but was now afraid to say so. "Did you talk to Dad? Isn't the menu set, and the number of people?"

"What's one more?"

"He won't have any fun," Abby said. She turned to Vic. "It'll be my parents' friends dressed up and reminiscing. And there's a string quartet. You'd have to wear a tie. You don't have a tie, do you? Or dress shoes?"

"A tie's not that hard to find."

"It can't be a knitted one. No knits, and no leather, either." Abby didn't know why she was saying that. And she was about to harangue him about his shoes—

"You know they die in the end, don't you?" Vic said.

"Who?"

He gestured toward her book. "The heroine and her brother."

"Jesus," Abby said, "thanks."

"Vic's building a boat," her mother said. "Did he tell you about that?"

"In a flood," Vic said. "They drown."

"Oh stop!" Abby said.

"With his grandpa. It's a . . . What kind is it?"

"Canoe," Abby and Vic both said. Abby looked at Vic. "Do you really want to come?"

"Yes," he said. His manner was suddenly gentle, and this, too, confused her.

"Don't you think Vic looks like my father?" Helen asked. "In that picture?"

Abby reached for her book and tucked it under her arm, as if that would prevent Vic from revealing any more of its contents. She knew the picture her mother was talking about. It was the one where the grandfather she'd never met was perched on a picnic table with his boots in his hand, while Helen and Susan sat on the bench on either side of his bare feet, their arms wrapped around his shins. Her grandmother was behind the camera, as always; her shadow darkened a corner of Susan's dress. Vic didn't look anything like Sean Murphy, Abby thought.

"He wasn't as tall as you," Helen said to Vic, "but he had your . . . your colors. Black Irish."

From the way Vic nodded, it seemed to Abby that he had heard this before, and she wondered if it had been five minutes or five years ago.

"Maybe," Abby said, and stared off into the distance. Above the postcard panorama of the mountains, the sky was the dull gray of old socks. She knew she was ruining their moment, but she would not get up and leave.

And then, after all those days, it was time for the reason they were here: the anniversary dinner. Though perhaps "ruse" was a more accurate label than "reason," Elliott thought, escorting his wife down the hallway. He steered her around a maid's cart and told himself that the distinction didn't matter, because the ends justified the means. *Exitus acta probat.*

"Slow down a little," Helen whispered. She wore a belted navy dress he'd given her for her birthday, the belt on its last notch and still too big for her.

"Sorry," he whispered back. He fingered the speech in his pocket—duty and propriety had insisted he write it—and wondered how far he'd get into it before he'd have to sit down, overcome.

A cheer went up when he and Helen entered the Gold Room arm in arm, and they were rushed by the newcomers: Alice Fellows, who had been Abby's honorary grandmother and occasional babysitter; Gregory Klein, their former neighbor, whose wife had died after Elliott and Helen moved away; and Lila Schipp, who was a potter and an old friend of Helen's.

Helen was beaming by Elliott's side as he kissed Alice and Lila and shook Gregory's hand. "Oh, it's so good to see you," Alice was saying to Helen. She reached up and patted her hair, which was dyed a soft powdery blue. "Don't mind me at all—I cry at everything."

Behind them the carved double doors opened, and in came waiters bearing appetizers and champagne flutes. Neil took two glasses and toasted Elliott. "You've come up a bit since the Schlitz-in-a-bathtub days," Neil said.

"Not as far as it looks," Elliott said.

Neil moved in closer, looking furtive. "Look, Hansen," he said, and then paused. "Listen, Elliott, I hope this won't sound too crass, but I wonder if you could use a little influx?"

Elliott allowed Alice to lead Helen toward a silk bench in the corner, and then he reached out for the sleeve of a passing waiter and ordered a Tanqueray.

"I have my checkbook," Neil went on. "Don't shake your head yet. You've got a lot of expenses."

He was wearing a truly beautiful tie, a thick silk foulard in burgundy and blue. It was English, Elliott was sure, and a hundred dollars if it was a dime. He helped himself to a pale boat of endive—on-deev? whatever it was—with a clump of apple-walnut salad on it. Something Eva had requested, obviously.

"I don't want to presume anything, buddy," Neil said, "I just want to be practical. If it's money you need, then it's money you'll have."

A forced smile stretched itself across Elliott's mouth. He'd never take Neil's money. But he *was* grateful, and he said so as he tried to maneuver himself away.

Neil put a big warm hand on his arm. "I have to be able to help," he said. "Really, Hansen, don't be stubborn. You have to let me do this."

His look was pleading, and Elliott felt a wave of love for him. Neil was trying so hard in his benevolent, ham-fisted way. A job, a blank check— what next? Maybe he would offer them a new car, or perhaps a kidney, and neither would be any more useful or easier to accept.

Lila wandered past with a dazed expression, and Elliott pulled her toward them, nearly shoving her toward his friend. "Neil, you remember Lila, don't you? She's got the ceramics studio out near where you used to live."

"How could I not," Neil exclaimed, scooping her up into a bear hug. Lila laughed with surprise into Neil's prodigious chest. "I mean it, Hansen," he said over the top of her head. "Please don't be such a stubborn ass. I need a figure—or hell, I just need a nod. I just need to know you won't rip it up."

Elliott put his hand to his ear as if he couldn't hear what Neil was saying while he backed away.

"I'm not giving up," Neil called.

"It's extraordinary, isn't it?" Eva said, appearing at Elliott's elbow. "Everything is so nice. Have you seen Henry?"

Elliott looked around the room, at the long table set with a white lace cloth and white napkins rolled up in gold rings, at the yellow roses in low vases along the mantel, at his friends in their party clothes. He hadn't realized that Henry wasn't among them.

Eva reached out and brushed a crumb from his lapel. "He was gone all afternoon, and then he came back and took a shower, and then he vanished again."

"I'm sure he'll turn up any minute. Maybe he's at the driving range. I humiliated him yesterday on the links, you know. Unexpectedly, of course."

"Elliott, I told him about Helen, and I don't think he took it well. I mean, it's not like he wasn't expecting it to some degree, but still, when faced with a time line . . ."

"Does Dom know, too?"

"Yes."

"Henry'll come around," Elliott said. He realized that almost everyone knew the truth now, everyone except for the two people to whom it mattered most.

"I could just kill him," Eva said. "He disappeared when his mother had a stroke last year, and Dom found him hours later in their pool. Henry was drunk and wearing his clothes. His shoes, even."

"Don't worry, he'll be here any minute," Elliott said, detaching himself from her. He had enough to worry about. "Everything's going to be fine."

Moving through the room, he saw how the flickering light of the candles made everyone seem softer and slightly abstracted. The husbands were decorous and sober in dark suits, and the wives had put on their jewels. As he watched them laugh and talk, he had the feeling that he was walking not among his friends but among replicas of people he knew.

"The lady violist has a mustache," Dom whispered as he passed by.

Elliott had met them all when he was twenty-four, left them when he was thirty-three, and now, ten years later, he'd brought them together again, as if doing so would help.

"You know the song about hors d'oeuvres?" he heard Neil ask Gregory. Gregory shook his head, and Neil leaned in and sang, "'Oh, look at them whore durves / Ain't they neat? / A little piece of cheese / And a little piece of meat!'"

"Ha!" Gregory said.

Perhaps, Elliott reflected, the problem was his: *he* was the replica. They were just as they had always been. Or maybe this party was all too much—maybe there was only so much playacting his friends could do well. He'd thought they had it easy, but it was no small thing to pretend that a brain tumor was something Helen would get over, like a case of mono. They loved her, too; this was easy for no one.

He spotted his daughter near the door, Vic beside her in an old but carefully pressed sport jacket. *At least he cleans up well enough,* Elliott thought.

In the corner, Helen was listening, seemingly fascinated, as Lila told her about her new bassett hound puppy. "He eats radishes," Lila was saying. "Isn't that incredible?" She turned to Elliott. "His name is August." Then she seemed to be at a loss.

"Our neighbors used to have a bassett, didn't they, Helen?" he asked, his voice encouraging.

She nodded. "The Whithakers had Liddy. She was fat."

"Right!" Elliott said, crinkling his eyes. "That Liddy . . ." As he, too, faltered, he was aware of a new hush in the room and turned to see a waiter indicating that they should all find their seats.

He helped Helen into her chair next to him at the head of the table and watched as Vic attempted the same courtesy toward his daughter. As Vic unfolded his napkin and spread it in his lap, Elliott had a sudden memory of sitting near him during a Carlisle lunch and listening to him talk about some book he was reading. He'd been failing English at the time, but he went on and on about that book; whatever it was, he'd loved it. Vic had never really been one of the incorrigibles. It occurred to Elliott that he might owe Vic some kind of apology—not for getting rid of his Pig, or even for expelling him (rules were rules), but for some larger doubt Elliott had always harbored about him, a thinly veiled mistrust, that, he realized now, had perhaps stemmed not from Vic himself but from Helen's regard for him. Maybe Elliott had felt a kind of possessiveness—a desire not to give Vic the chances that would allow him to rise higher in Helen's esteem. Could that be true? He worried that it was.

"Lookee who's here," Ruth said as Eva's husband came in on the heels of one of the waiters. Red-cheeked and grinning, Henry moved jerkily into the room as if propelled by some lurching inner force he couldn't control. Eva rushed to him and they whispered in the corner, Henry nodding, Eva holding tight to his arm. Elliott watched Ruth watching them and trying desperately to read their lips.

They were served what a waiter said was an amuse-bouche—Elliott definitely hadn't ordered that—a tiny cup of golden soup with a single flower petal floating in it, and then the salad Eva had picked out. He looked among the prickly, complicated leaves: no beets.

He saw Sheila hovering outside the door, proudly eavesdropping as her daughter played Beethoven. Elliott raised his hand in greeting, and she smiled her bright, lonely smile and then vanished.

"This must have been expensive," Helen whispered.

Elliott shook his head. "It was nothing." He supposed it had cost nearly as much as their wedding twenty years ago.

When the salad plates had been taken away, Elliott stood up, his knees cracking in protest, and cleared his throat. The string quartet left off at the end of a phrase, letting the final note fade away in a shimmering vibrato. His guests turned their faces to him.

Down the line of candles and roses, the unseasonable fire burned a deep yellow. When Abby was little, he'd given her a tube of powder to sprinkle into the fireplace; it made the flames burn in rainbow colors. It was just treated sawdust, but she'd thought it was magic. And outside, there had been the perfect New England snow, blue in the dusk that began at four in the afternoon, and the chickadees balanced on the feeder he'd made them, and the two birches he had planted in the corner of the yard leaning toward each other, ghostly and bare, and he remembered standing in his warm kitchen and knowing that he had never felt so secure. He was proud: he had made that life for them. In those days sometimes his heart would seize up in gratitude.

He took a drink of wine, and his friends watched him expectantly, ready to be moved, and he was struck again by the gulf between his experience and theirs. Standing before them, he felt almost as he imagined his childhood priest might have, looking out over the pews of fidgeting toddlers, dozing fathers, and worried mothers on a Sunday morning—how he must have loved them all as God's children but also pitied them for their ignorance of His power, perhaps even despised them a little for their inability to comprehend it. Elliott was aware of similar swirling currents of feeling in himself, though they were not so Christian; perhaps great faith and mortal illness taught a person comparable things.

All he needed was to say the words he'd already decided upon. They were in his pocket, printed in large, careful letters, in case the room's light was dim. *I think I knew the very first time I saw Helen walking across campus that I was going to ask her to marry me. I just didn't think she'd say yes.* It was important to start off with a laugh—he'd learned that a long time ago. *It's hard to believe that we were so young and so certain. I know how Neil likes to say that we shed our ideals as we age, but I think it's our certainty. To promise to share a lifetime with a person takes a certain amount of hubris, which perhaps only the young have in an appropriately abundant supply.* Here he would look at Abby and hope she would smile at him. *We are so glad you could be here to share this special day with us, a celebration of two decades of life together . . .* That was where he always faltered. He wanted to say: *And may we enjoy at least two decades more.* But he couldn't, because there was nothing left to ask for. Or fine, okay, Christ, he could ask for another month, couldn't he? *Let's make it to Christmas:*

he could plead for that. A tiny, miserable wish, and still it would not be granted him.

Here he was, at the head of a table full of all his friends, and this wasn't an anniversary party—it was a goddamn *wake,* but the body they were all mourning was still sitting with them, smiling up at him, chewing salmon. And everyone else would get to say goodbye to her in the guise of a temporary parting—vacations, after all, must end—while he would say nothing of the kind. And then when she was gone, he would be alone, and he would not be part of this circle of friends anymore, not the way he had been; it was inevitable. So he, too, was saying goodbye in a way, because they were out of time, he and his wife and all of them.

An arm reached out and touched his sleeve. "Elliott?" Helen whispered.

He looked down at her expectant face. "Hi, Helen," he whispered back.

He put his left hand on his wife's shoulder, and with his right, he raised his glass. He thought he wouldn't bother pulling out the speech. He was pretty sure he wouldn't be able to get far in it; already the room seemed to blur at its edges and something was caught in his throat. "I am so grateful to you all," he managed, "for coming here to be with us. This is a toast to you, and to my wife of twenty years."

Everyone sent their glasses aloft, where they caught the light of the fire and the candles and the chandeliers and became cups of rubies.

"To Helen," Eva said.

"To Helen!" Henry cried, and then everyone was saying her name.

And crazy as it was, he couldn't help thinking: *But what if Helen were to get well?* All of this would be just an extravagant vacation—a reunion, the first, perhaps, of many. The days would lose their culminatory quality, and time would open up again: there would be enough hours for everything. He imagined the two of them going camping, as they had when they were first married. He'd take the tent down from the attic and air it out in the backyard beside their old flannel-lined sleeping bags, and he'd gas up the Coleman stove and bleach the cooler. He'd find the coffee percolator and the gas lantern and the flashlights and the bug repellent. They could drive to West Virginia, Kentucky, even, and make their camp in hills or by a river . . .

He sat down and leaned in to kiss the soft, slack skin of his wife's cheek. "I love you," he told her, and she smiled at him, and in the warm candlelight, it was almost as if she were her old self again—not the girl he'd loved all those years ago on a college campus but his middle-aged Helen, the mother of his child, the keeper of his house, the woman who still had years of life left to go.

Stay, he thought. *Please stay.*

"Did I use the wrong fork?" Vic asked.

Abby, who had finished her second glass of champagne, signaled the nearest waiter for a refill. At the other end of the room, Alex poured wine into Lila's glass and then moved smoothly on to Gregory's. Abby could feel Alex's attention on her, though he never met her eye. Vic was looking at her, too, waiting for her to answer him.

"No," she said. "That's the one."

"Your parents throw a nice party."

She glanced over at them. Thanks to Abby, her mother was wearing eye shadow, blush, and lipstick. It had been her father's idea—"Help her get ready, spend a little time together," he'd said. So he'd gone down to Hancock's for a fortifying gin while Abby had stepped into her parents' bathroom and found her mother waiting, a razor in her hand, wanting Abby to shave her legs.

"They got that preppy shitbag of yours to serve the crudités," Vic said.

"*Appetizers,*" she said. "Crudités are sliced raw vegetables."

"I told you you were stuck up."

"I'm not stuck up," she said. "I'm just right."

There'd been hardly any hair on her mother's legs—Abby supposed that was because of the chemotherapy—but still it had been awkward; as her mother sat on the edge of the tub, Abby had stood behind her in the draining bathwater and leaned over her shoulder, her breasts pressing against her mother's back, so she could hold the razor at the right angle. "Will that work?" she'd asked. "Is that okay?"

"What's his name again?" Vic said.

"It doesn't matter."

"Do you like him?"

"Maybe." Alex was openly looking at her now, clearly wondering who was sitting beside her. She smiled at him but he didn't smile back, and she felt terrible until it occurred to her to be indignant. There was a certain justice in Vic's intrusion; after all, Alex had let Sylvie ruin everything the night before.

"I don't think he's the right kind of guy for you," Vic said.

"First of all," Abby said, "I'm leaving on Sunday, so there isn't really a question of him being a guy for me, and second of all, why not?"

"Well, there's that whole preppy-shitbag thing we talked about," he said, and grinned.

She turned away and took a sip of champagne; she did not want to be amused.

She'd held her breath as she placed the blade against her mother's shin and drew the razor up, watching as a stripe of smooth leg appeared. She'd shifted around, trying not to push against her mother so much. She was right there next to Helen's naked ear, next to the lavender-scented skin of her neck, feeling the rise and fall of her mother's breathing. She'd done both her legs—the fronts of them anyway—and then her mother had turned to her and said, "Now will you do my makeup?"

Abby had always loved to watch a person at his or her toilette: her father shaving, her mother getting ready for a party. The ritual of it and the private face they showed themselves in the mirror—this fascinated her. It was an operation of judgment and concentration, an act of pure self. She had observed the way her mother pursed her lips and sucked in her cheeks, the way her father never looked into his own eyes. Abby had watched her friends at their houses, too, and the girls in the bathrooms at school, the way they painted their eyelids bright blue and their lips an icy pink and then sprayed their hair with AquaNet until their bangs wouldn't move in a gale.

Helen never spent more than five minutes on her makeup, all of which came in yearly gift sets from her mother-in-law. She did not gaze into the mirror hopefully, as Abby did, seeking to learn some essential truth about her character, but made a quick assessment of basic presentability and bared her teeth to make sure there was no food caught between her canines.

Once, when they stood side by side in front of the bathroom mirror, Abby had looked at her mother—harried, sleepy, in her fifth decade—and at herself—dewy, vain, sixteen—and said cruelly, "I don't think we look so much alike after all." What she meant (and what Helen knew she meant) was: *I am so much prettier than you.* Her mother was still beautiful then, but Abby didn't notice.

"Dinner is served," her father now said to no one in particular, watching as a kitchen runner brought in a tray of plates and set them on a stand by the door.

Alex swept over and took up two plates, which he gave to Helen and Elliott with an exaggerated bow. He served the rest of the table next, coming last to Abby and Vic. Still he gave no sign that he knew her—there was no subtle tap on her chair, no quick brush against her shoulder—and though she would have liked to ascribe it to professionalism, she knew it was more likely pique.

From the head of the table, her mother winked at her. Helen did look better with a bit of gold eye shadow on her lids and a swipe of blush along her cheekbones. She'd sat patiently, trustingly, while Abby fiddled with the brushes and compacts, and Abby had marveled at how Helen had become accustomed to having things like this—private things—done for her.

Vic elbowed her. "You know, I think that shitbag of yours put my dinner in the freezer before he brought it in," he said. "Feel my plate." He reached for her hand and put against the rim—it was icy cold. "The food's like that, too."

Abby was surprised and amused. "You should say something."

But Vic refused. "It doesn't matter," he said. "If it makes him feel better about the fact that I'm the one eating dinner with you, and he's the one serving it, that's cool."

"I'm sure it's not about me," Abby said. But she rather hoped it was, and she wondered if it was poor form to be flattered by it.

"Of course it's about you."

"Eat the rest of my dinner," Abby said, knowing that it was a strange offer; it was intimate and possibly gross. When Vic didn't say anything, she reached out and switched plates with him as Alex watched with an unreadable expression.

Abby had once followed Vic for a mile along the railroad tracks that ran past the high school. Though he'd been too far away for her to see his features, she knew his shape, his posture, the way he moved through space. He'd been smoking a cigarette. She'd picked up a piece of gravel and thrown it as hard as she could, hoping he would hear it land and turn around to discover her walking behind him on the tracks, with the blackberry vines climbing the slope on either side and the white butterflies drifting poetically above her, lazy in the late-May heat. She'd thrown another rock, and then another, but Vic had never looked back.

Now, though, Vic ate one of her artichokes, and for some reason this made her feel better.

"May I have your attention, please?"

Ruth stood before the fireplace, the flames making the edges of her skirt glow. She held the neck of a guitar in her hand.

In the corner, the string quartet exchanged glances. One of the violinists switched bows, loosening the horsehair on one and tightening it on the other. Ruth lifted the guitar, looped a purple strap over her shoulder, and plucked a few strings.

"Okay," she said. "I'm a little rusty, but here we go."

Abby leaned toward Vic. "She's sort of famous," she said. "Ruth Peel.

Have you ever heard of her?" It would have pleased her if he had, but she wasn't surprised when he shook his head. "She's a feminist singer-songwriter," she added.

"That's not exactly my thing," Vic said.

"I thought she didn't bring a guitar?" Abby heard her father whisper.

"This is for Helen and Elliott, or Ellen and Helliott, as some clever people used to call them. Twenty years of marriage. Oh, how we adore you both."

Ruth noodled on the guitar while she talked, and Abby wondered what they were in for—a song about something mystical, she guessed, something earnest and pro-woman. But when she opened her mouth, out came Elvis. "Love Me Tender."

Singing, Ruth became someone different—greater—than the Ruth they knew, the Ruth of the monologues, the attention-mongering, the half-comedic petulance. The song was full of yearning, and everyone in the room felt it. Ruth's pure, clear voice curled around the room like a ribbon drawing them all together.

I'll be yours through all the years till the end of time.

The song rose up to the cove ceiling and floated out the door; it swept down the hall and swirled into the darkened ballroom where a valet and a maid had met on their break to practice their kisses. It floated softly in the air above all the guests, taking them back to childhoods when older sisters played that song over and over again on big RCA record players. One of the waiters stopped at the door of the Gold Room, a pot of coffee in each hand. Before Henry ducked his face into his napkin, Abby thought she saw the glint of a tear on his cheek.

When the song was over and only a sweet warm echo of it lingered and then faded, they all sat still in their chairs. Ruth took off the guitar and leaned it by the window behind the drapes. No one said anything, and Abby could see Ruth begin to wonder if she'd done something wrong.

"God," Ruth said. "Was it bad or something?"

Then Helen began to clap, and immediately everyone followed.

"Nineteen fifty-six. Elvis Presley, Richard Egan, and Debra Paget," said Alice. "I remember that one for sure. It was not a very good movie."

"But what a brilliant song!" Henry said. He reached clumsily across the table for Eva's hand, looking flushed and uncertain.

The string quartet resumed their competent playing as everyone finished dessert and coffee, and then they all walked toward the dining room like a parade. The men took their wives' hands and led them to the dance floor, pairing off beneath the sparkling chandelier. Gregory put his arm around Lila's waist. Abby's mother and father were there, too, right in the center of everything.

Abby felt loose, almost pleased—it was the champagne. She found an empty table by the door, and Alice sat down next to her. She wore a piece of horrifying old fur around her neck, with eyes and feet and a mouth; its tail swayed when she moved. Vic lowered himself into the seat on Abby's other side.

"Who's your friend?" Alice asked. "I didn't meet him."

Vic stuck out his hand, and Alice looked at it before shaking it. "Vic," he said. "I'm a friend of the family."

"Me, too. I've known Abby since she was a teeny-tiny baby." Alice glanced around the ornate pink room. "Fancy place, isn't it? And dinner was delicious. I put a roll in my purse." She opened her handbag and showed it to them, nestled in a tissue. "Breakfast!" she said.

A handful of other hotel guests had gathered on the dance floor, encouraged by the example of the Hansen party. The Schmidts and the Callahans had taken ballroom-dance lessons for Maeve Callahan's wedding, and they performed an elaborate array of steps involving dips and twirls and kicks—though Dom, Abby thought, looked joyless, as if he were merely tasked with counting over and over to four. Sylvie danced in front of Neil with her hips and breasts; everything else was immaterial.

Abby's mother and father stood in the midst of all of them, hardly moving—her father in his dark suit, her mother in her Talbots dress. He held her right hand in his, and she kept her left on his shoulder. Slowly, gently, they rocked back and forth. Their small motions and lack of skill made their dancing seem private, as if they were simply in an embrace for which someone had written an exquisitely tender score. They had such gravity—such sorrow—that the other dancers around them blurred into insignificant, unstable shapes. It was her own mother and her father who seemed largest then, who seemed earthbound, substantial, eternal.

"Do you want to dance?" Vic asked Abby.

Abby turned toward him—maybe she was even going to say yes, though the song was ending—but right then, out of the corner of her eye, she saw Henry's spectacular, climactic leap, and his one-footed landing on the slick floor, and then his headlong tumble into the corner of the bass drum.

Alice said, "Oh dear God. Now you see why I don't dance."

One of the other guests, a man named Kemp, was a doctor, and he took Henry to his room, where he bandaged him up with gauze and tape and guessed that a hangover would be the thing to cause Henry the real pain in the morning.

"I'm sorry, Eva, I'm sorry," Henry kept saying. He'd ruined his shirt and his summer suit jacket, but he was drunk enough to think it was all a big joke: what a brilliant finale to the evening, and how lucky that the gash was far back on his forehead, camouflaged beneath what remained of his hair.

Henry hadn't looked at Elliott, not once the whole evening. Each time their gaze almost met, Henry's eyes slithered guiltily away, as if Elliott were a one-legged panhandler whose suffering it was important not to look upon directly. Not that Elliott took offense. The hotel, the anniversary party, the coming goodbyes—everything was just too much.

"It's not me you ought to apologize to," Eva said to her husband, speaking to him as if he were one of her children. "How about Dr. Kemp for interrupting his dessert, and everyone else for being such a phenomenal idiot?"

"Yes, yes, to all of that," Henry said. He wobbled on the edge of Dr. Kemp's bed. For some reason he had taken off his shoes.

Dr. Kemp gave Henry four Advils and a mug of water to take them with. "We'll launch a preemptive strike on the inevitable headache," he said, tucking his scissors and tape back into what looked like a shaving kit.

"All right, then," Eva said, reaching for Henry's arm. "Let's leave Dr. Kemp in peace. I really can't thank you enough."

Dr. Kemp inclined his head modestly: it was nothing, he told them. He was glad to help. Frankly, he was bored stiff at the hotel—how much golf did his wife expect him to play?

As they all filed out of the room, Dr. Kemp stopped Elliott with a brotherly hand on the shoulder. "What kind is it?" he asked.

Elliott saw the cool, deep sympathy in the man's eyes—born of habit, maybe, but sincere nonetheless. There was curiosity as well, which did not feel prurient. "Brain," he said.

Dr. Kemp nodded. "Let me give you something." He turned and went back into his bathroom. As Elliott waited for him in the doorway, the three gins in him rose up, bearing on their crest a wild, unreasonable hope. He had needed a miracle, and here, he imagined, his miracle was: this Dr. Kemp, who'd continued to sip his Tom Collins while applying gauze to Henry's forehead, was not some aging, half-soused country GP—he was a Harvard-educated oncologist whose research work included targeted radiation and alchemical drug interactions. He'd nuked anaplastic astrocytomas into oblivion, shrunk Stage IV glioblastomas into encapsulated nodes of operable malignancies . . .

Then Elliott saw Dr. Kemp coming toward him in his mortician's suit, his golfer's tie, and his patent-leather wing tips, and the wave crashed upon the shore as suddenly as it had risen.

The doctor held out a plastic bag of small blue pills. "Take them at night," he said. "One—two if necessary."

Elliott didn't reach for them. "Me?"

"Yes, you. They'll help you sleep," Dr. Kemp said.

Elliott shook his head. "That's not necessary, but thank you for your generosity."

"I'm sorry I don't have anything else," Dr. Kemp said. "But please, you must take these. You have to sleep."

Elliott held out his hand because it seemed easier than refusing, and the doctor placed the bag in his palm. *Sleep,* Elliott thought bitterly. *I'll sleep when she's dead.*

"The best of luck to you," Kemp said. "Good night."

Helen takes off her earrings, her necklace, her gold bangle bracelets; she removes her pumps and slip and panty hose; she pulls her dress over her head. In the old days she would have hung it up, but tonight she tosses it onto the damask chair, where it briefly lands, still warm from her body, before sliding down to the floor.

Elliott approaches with her pills, and she has a momentary urge to fling them in his face. She doesn't need his constant attention—she needs her life back the way it was. Can he bring her that? Can he order her sight back from one of these waiters? Her coordination? She's so tired of everything being hard. *Shit piss fuck damn,* she thinks.

But why is she upset? It was such a nice evening—all her friends were there, and there was the good food, and the fancy silver, and the string quartet playing Pachelbel's Canon, her favorite. There was Vic and Abby sitting next to each other, dressed up like they were on a date, Ruth singing, the waltz with Elliott, her dear old Elliott . . . Really, it was lovely.

She takes the pills; there are only two. Next Elliott hands her a nightgown, and she puts it beside her on the bed. They used to have *sex,* and now he is telling her to cover up her body, which is sitting there on the soft hotel bed in a pretty bra and pretty panties, the prettiest ones she has ever owned, which she never would have bought for herself but which came, like all her other new clothes, from Elliott's sisters. The satin is ivory, the lace periwinkle blue.

She had a dress that blue once, an Easter dress, and she remembers wearing it one night to a party at the McDermotts' when she was ten, and how, on the way home, in the backseat, she stared into the lit windows of all the houses in their neighborhood, seeing the silhouettes of furniture, of people moving through the rooms, and she was aware of a queer but profound ache in her chest, which made her feel much older than ten. It was a sense of recognition and alienation simultaneously, the strange lonely thrill of a life utterly similar to hers and yet wholly beyond her ken. What if she lived in that pink bungalow? What if that fat man in the driveway were her father? Beside her, Susan begged to go to Dairy Queen, and their mother told her to hush. But Helen gazed out the window, rapt, silent, knowing that her life was separated from another's by a thread, by luck, by some decision nature had made before she even existed. She wondered how her consciousness became hers, and what would have to change to make it someone else's.

Sometimes she feels as if it's someone else's now. Her body certainly isn't hers anymore, and whoever it is, she wishes that person would take it back because it's defective. She takes off the pretty bra and slips the nightgown over her head.

"Happy anniversary," she says to her husband's back. He's untying his tie but she knows he's not staying. He can't go to bed this early—he'll lie awake for hours, anticipating sleep long before it comes to him.

He turns, smiling. "Happy anniversary to you, too."

She gets under the covers and he comes to kiss her forehead. "The lips," she says, "the lips." He obeys, and then he's at the door.

"I'm going to go check on our guests. Do you need anything?" he says.

She shakes her head and closes her eyes. For her, sleep comes quickly, and then she is dreaming. And when she turns over, she whispers, without knowing she does so, "Holy Mary Mother of God pray for us sinners now and at the hour of our death. Amen."

The valet surged up the road in the old MG and left it running; it seemed to tremble beneath the porte cochere. Sylvie had wrapped a pink scarf around her neck and was shrugging a jacket onto her shoulders.

"We're going to take a spin," Neil said. "Going to look for moose. Syl wants to catch bats in her hair."

"Can I go, too?" Ruth asked.

"It's a two-seater, Ruth," said her husband.

"But I love moose—mooses?—they're so regal." Ruth leaned toward Neil and batted her eyes playfully.

Neil put his hand on his wife's shoulder, unable to abandon chivalry now. "Well, Syl, why don't you stay here and let Ruth have a ride?"

"I don't mind," Sylvie said. She was already unwinding her scarf. "I've been in that car before."

Elliott hoped Neil had not drunk as much as Elliott thought he had. On the other hand, if there was anyone who'd had years of practice keeping a car between the ditches, it was his old friend Neil, a man who never let practicality slow him down.

Ruth climbed into the car and Neil gunned the engine. "Back soon," he called, and Ruth waved like a movie star. Elliott's gaze followed the red taillights down the curving drive. The throaty putter of the engine faded until there was just the sound of the crickets.

"Should we say good night to the mountains?" Dom asked, and though no one answered him, they all turned and walked through the yellow lobby, empty but for a man polishing glasses at the little bar.

The Presidential mountains were a dark line against a dark sky. Sylvie sat next to Elliott on the love seat, and he could feel the heat she gave off, smell the subtle perfume of her body.

"You shouldn't smoke so much," she said.

"So they tell me."

"I've heard good things about hypnosis for quitting. You could try that."

Elliott nodded as if considering this. But he never wanted to quit. He'd done it once and wasn't going to do it again. "I could go to hypnosis to learn how to smoke one or two a day for the rest of my life," he said. "Or maybe four or five. How bad could five be?"

Sylvie leaned against him. "Bad enough."

Dom did not sit down or face them but turned his gaze to the mountains, his posture pensive, nostalgic; maybe, Elliott thought, he was recalling some line of poetry suitable for the occasion, which he would enjoy privately. They all felt the diminishment of their numbers, and it made them shy with one another.

"I want to thank you all for coming," Elliott said.

"No, no," they said, "thank you, thank *you*."

"You are the kindest man in the world," Eva said.

"If there's anything we can do—" Dom said.

Elliott thanked them again with sincerity, so they would understand that the futility of their offers did not lessen the value.

After a moment Dom straightened up and clapped his hands together lightly. "I think I'm going to hit the hay."

"I'll come, too," Eva said. "I ought to see how Henry's doing."

Dom headed for the stairs, and Eva lingered, looking at Elliott and

Sylvie together on the couch. She took Elliott's face between her hands and kissed him once on each cheek. "I love you," she said. "See you in the morning. Good night, Sylvie."

And so healthy Eva went to lie beside healthy Henry, the way they had done for decades. Eva would wear a flannel nightgown, Elliott thought, and Henry dark blue pajamas with white piping. They would sleep soundly and when they awoke, there would be no unpleasant dreams to remember.

Sylvie sat soft and warm along his right side. "Just us now," she said, putting her feet up on the table.

He supposed he should make it clear that he was grateful to her, too. He reached around for the right sentence in the dull, mechanical part of his brain trained to sift through equally hackneyed options. In times of trouble, one just had to keep thanking everyone. One had to take into account the comfort of others and not disturb them with extravagant expressions of sorrow. One ought to apologize, too, for the inconvenience, for the bad news, for bringing the awareness of mortality into the room, the way Helen had apologized to him, heartbreakingly, after her chemotherapy, when she was vomiting into the bathroom sink, weeping: "I'm sorry, Elliott, I'm so so so sorry."

He said to Sylvie, "I know it must have been hard to come here, not knowing us all very well, but I'm glad you came, and I want you to know that your presence means something to both me and Helen."

She drew away from him the slightest bit; he'd been too formal. "Please—I hardly deserve gratitude," she said.

He decided to be honest with her. "I thank everyone whether I mean it or not."

She turned to him, smiling, and put her hand on his bicep. He met her bold green-eyed gaze. Somehow through all the wine, she was still there with him, experiencing this stillness, the darkness, the end of the night and the months of planning being over.

"I think you're a very good man," she said. "I think everyone here is lucky to know you."

He waved this away with another cigarette, though this one he didn't light.

"Don't," she said. "It's true. Do you want to go inside? For a quick drink? A bit more champagne? Neil won't be back for ages."

"Remember who he's with. He knows Ruth is best taken in small doses."

"Still. Let's sit in the lobby by the fire."

She got up and held out her hand, and he let himself take it, and she led him inside where they sat on a couch in front of the fire like a married couple. He wondered what things were like between Sylvie and Neil. What did they do in the evenings? What did they have to say to each other? What did they have in common? He couldn't imagine.

"Talk to me," Sylvie said.

She had lovely round arms and her hair was swept back into a twist with loosened tendrils hanging delicately around her face. He appreciated her attention, and he could feel how her presence enlivened him. But he didn't know what to say to her beyond "Thank you" and "I'm sorry." He said, "I could read you my speech. It's still in my pocket."

"If you want to," she said. She folded her hands in her lap, ready to pay attention.

She was, he realized, fundamentally imperturbable. Maybe it was her relative youth—she was younger than two of his nieces—and maybe it was her money (or her father's and Neil's money, to be more accurate) that softened the unpleasant edges of things. But either way, she was content to drink a cocktail with him at an hour when they should have been asleep. This relaxed him somehow, as did her unfamiliarity. *Sometimes,* he thought, *you just want to sit with a stranger, someone to whom your grief can't truly matter.*

"It was a good party, wasn't it?" he asked.

"It was excellent," she said. "Start to finish."

He didn't say anything more, and she picked up a newspaper that someone had left on the coffee table, and opened it across their laps. "All this week there's been a comet in the sky and we've never seen it," she said. Her finger stabbed at a picture of a fuzzy white dot. "Doesn't look like much, does it?"

"Not really," he said. He shifted in his seat; he had a bit of indigestion.

"I took a lot of science classes in college because that was where the boys were. But I never learned anything. Astronomy, biology, chemistry—nothing. It's as if I was never there." She swirled her Kir royale and watched the liqueur settle into the champagne. "Not that I needed to know any of it—I was an art major. Who cared about the rings of Jupiter or the moons of Saturn? Actually, it's the other way around. I do know *something*. But the point is that I didn't need to. I was painting my friends naked, like all the other art majors."

"I'm sure that was more fun," Elliott said.

"I suppose it was. I still have all those paintings in the basement."

"Blackmail," he said.

"That never occurred to me," Sylvie said. "I like the way you think."

Elliott let his eyes close, and he heard Sylvie turn the page of the newspaper.

"Oh, the police blotter," she exclaimed. "I love this section, don't you?"

Elliott didn't answer. Maybe if his stomach stopped hurting, he'd sleep tonight. He had those pills from Dr. Kemp—he could try one of those. And then he wondered if there was anything besides exhaustion for which he might need a pill. What, he thought, had begun to go wrong with him? He had the bum knee, the iffy digestion, the loosening flesh. These were small losses, sure, and they were only a few. But when would they begin in earnest? When would they start to add up?

"We could try to find it," Sylvie said.

"Find what?"

"The comet."

He opened his eyes and smiled at her. "Or we could just sit here."

She looked at him over the rim of her champagne glass, and beneath the open newspaper, she put her hand very carefully on his leg.

Suddenly the Tanqueray, the fatigue, Sylvie, everything overwhelmed him. He wanted to take another sip of his drink but he couldn't even lift his arm.

Sylvie slowly moved her hand up his thigh. Immobile, he felt its insistent warmth. He looked down the paper and saw a picture of a couple on a tandem bicycle. Sylvie squeezed his leg. Peeking out from the newsprint was her bare knee, and he marveled at the perfect engineering of bone, tendon, golden skin. Her beauty made him feel like crying.

He knew what could happen next. It wouldn't take anything at all. But desire was a stop on a different road entirely.

After a while, Sylvie took her hand away and stared into the fire. "Everyone else—they can just be here and it's enough," she said. "I don't know either of you. I only met Helen twice. I can't knit you a sweater or write you a check or sing you a goddamn Elvis song. I'm just here, and it's hard, and I don't know what I'm supposed to do."

"You can have another drink," he said.

"The last thing I need is another drink."

"A similar awareness is not going to stop me," he said, though it seemed to him that he was as sober as he ever had been. He began to stand. "You won't leave?"

"You don't want me to?"

"No," he said.

At the bar he ordered a Tanqueray and another Kir royale and ate a handful of cashews. He looked at the back of Sylvie's head, bowed now, revealing her slender neck. What if she really were waiting for him? What would it be like to have a wife like that? An emissary from another generation.

He wondered if it was possible to truly understand someone else, or if there was always an essential mystery inside everyone, no matter the small range of things they did, no matter how average they were. They slept, they ate, they worked, they made love, simple as animals. And still they were unknowable.

The bartender placed the drinks on white cocktail napkins. Elliott signed the tab with his name and room number. Twenty-five dollars for two drinks, not including tip. He was going to owe thousands.

Sylvie turned, ready to welcome him back, urging him to hurry. He didn't want to sleep with her—he wanted only to sit with her, to have her long thigh against his. He thought that would be good enough. She smiled at him, and he sat down, and it was.

"He likes you, it couldn't be more obvious," Alex said.

Abby stood in the center of his room while he watched her from a rocking chair. There was a single bed, an open book lying facedown on the dresser—something called *Carpenter's Gothic*—and red and white gingham curtains that fluttered lightly in the open window.

"I've known him since high school," she said. She knew this wasn't the denial Alex was looking for, but she was loath to bring Vic further into what had been, until the dinner, an essentially uncomplicated flirtation. She liked Alex, didn't she? He was handsome in a delicate, well-cared-for way, and he had tried so hard to entertain her. But she felt very tired, and it was strange to be in his room, that impersonal yet private space where she could see the socks he had been wearing balled up by his chair and his waiter uniform rumpled in a hamper. His novel was in this room some-place, and his silly play, and his toothbrush and his underwear and all the intimate objects of his unknown life. He rocked back and forth, back and forth.

"I put his dinner in the freezer," Alex said.

"I know. That was really mature of you."

He shrugged. "One works with the tools at one's disposal."

"I didn't even invite him," she said. "It was my mother's idea. She's the one who thinks he's so great." But she was conscious of her dishonesty even as she spoke, that in fact there was still something left of the fourteen-year-old who had kissed Vic in a hallway and fallen halfway into love. Not that it mattered! After Henry hit his head, everyone had scattered, confused; she'd taken her mother upstairs, and when she'd come back down, Vic was gone.

Alex gestured to his bed, and Abby sat down on the edge of it. "Your mother," he said.

"She's very sick, in case you hadn't noticed."

"I noticed. I guess I thought you didn't want to talk about it. Do you want to?"

"No." She smoothed the quilt beneath her. It was faded cotton, so worn and soft it felt almost like silk.

"My grandma made that for me when I was little," he said.

Abby kept running her hand over the quilt. She was exhausted. Was it the wine? Had he mixed pot into her dinner rolls?

"Just lie back," he said, as if reading her thoughts. "Take a rest."

She did as he suggested, letting her shoes dangle over the edge. Alex's pillow smelled like a hair product of some kind, and beneath that was the warm, human smell of scalp. She heard the rocking chair rhythmically creaking. Alex struck a match and lit two candles on the table by the end of the bed. Their flames ducked and feinted in the breeze.

"Do you want to get under the covers?"

"No, I'm fine."

He got up and pulled a blanket from the closet and spread it over her. "There," he said. "That's something." He eased her hair away from her face with a gentle hand. "It was a good party, don't you think? I asked them not to be sloppy in the kitchen. I told Arthur that there were VIPs in the Gold Room and that he should make sure everything was as fault-less as his mediocre skills could make it. And I think he listened, don't you?"

She watched the shadows pulsing on the wall in front of her. His hand moved down her shoulder to her arm and then to her hip. Already the party seemed like a long time ago, and her arrival at the hotel seemed a thing of the very distant past.

"Is she going to be all right?" he asked after a while.

"Yes," she said. "I don't know. I really have no idea."

In the hotel her mother was also lying down, her body still digesting food, her lungs still expanding and contracting, her blood still coursing, all the pumps and valves inside her working as they always had, and yet nothing was right anymore. Alex sat down next to Abby, and his hand continued its reassuring pass across her forehead, then up and down her side.

When he lay down next to her, she didn't move. She registered the weight on the bed, the way the mattress sloped down, pushing her toward him, his minute rearrangements to make himself comfortable. She would not acknowledge any of it. He scooted close and kept rubbing her arm, her hair, her hip. "Everything's going to be fine," he said.

She took a deep breath and sighed. "How would you know?"

"Sweet Abby, sweet, sweet Abby," he said.

That wasn't an answer. But the way his arm arched over her protec-tively, the way his breath fluttered her hair—she felt almost loved. She was surrounded by the overwhelming sense of him: his scent on the pil-low, his hand on her waist, his voice saying its meaningless things. There was the heat of his arm, the rise and fall of his chest, the muscles shifting lightly beneath his sweater, and yet she was hardly present; none of it meant anything.

When his hand went under the covers and slipped between her shirt and her skin, it seemed no great leap from where it had been before.

"You're so lovely," he whispered.

She felt his fingers slide beneath her bra and cup her new breasts, and she shivered but did not move away. His hands were cool, tracing lines down her stomach, and his breathing was steady and deliberate. But his touch could not bring her back from where she had gone. The hands were in the other world and she was in her mother's. She was remembering the way her mother would climb into bed next to her and run her fingers through Abby's hair, and how she had loved this when she was little. And how her mother had kept doing this even when Abby got older, even when such physical contact had embarrassed her. And how Abby, who understood her mother's wordless love and need, had let her lie there in bed because she adored her mother and would never hurt her feelings.

Her poor, poor mother!

Alex's hands were light and soft and insistent. In the world she wasn't in, they carried themselves around her chest and shoulders and stomach and paused at the waistband of her skirt. She didn't care, she didn't care. Gently he rolled her over so that she faced him. The candlelight was flickering on the side of his face, and his right eye seemed to glow orange while his left was in shadow. He was pressing himself against her, and he was going to kiss her while his hands made their way around her body. She watched his pretty face come nearer.

"Stop." The voice was her mother's.

"What?" Alex whispered. "Why?"

When Abby said it again, he pushed himself up and moved away. Scooting to the end of the bed, Abby knocked over a candle and it fell, still burning, on the cement floor. She stood up, and though he reached for her arm, he didn't take it.

"What are you doing?" he said. "Abby? Come here—come lie down with me."

There was tenderness in his voice, she heard it. But she grabbed her purse from the dresser and, without saying anything, went to the door.

"Please," he said to her back.

She paused, just for a second, only to seem less rude, and then she left him. In the hall she passed Trey and Pete carrying six-packs, and they called out for her to stop but she ignored them.

Tumbling out into the night air was like waking from a dream. The chill breeze and the wet grass on her legs shocked her senses back into alertness. She took the stairs up to the hotel veranda two at a time. Its empty benches, their pillows straightened, made a line into the deepen-

ing gloom. Below lay the illuminated sinuous paths and the pool glowing aquamarine.

She would have let Alex do whatever he wanted, she thought, she really would have, as long as he didn't ask her to acknowledge it. He could
have removed every last stitch of her clothing and then taken off his own,
and she would have stayed there, nearly unconscious, in another place
entirely. If he'd let her keep her eyes closed, anything could have happened, and maybe that would have been all right; maybe it would have
been tender. But he'd wanted to kiss her—he'd wanted her to be there
with him. And now he was alone in his room, bewildered, and she was
sitting on a dew-dampened couch, her hands shaking with nerves.

"It's you!" The voice came from behind her.

Startled, Abby turned in the half-light to see Dom with his white
dress shirt untucked and wrinkled about his waist and a drink in his
hand.

"Kiddo," he said warmly. "What are you still doing up?"

"I wasn't tired," she said. "So I've just been sitting here." She could see
that he believed her.

"I'm not tired, either." He walked over. "So can I buy you a drink?"

"Everything's closed," she told him. Stubble made a faint shadow
along his cheek, and his hair flopped over his left eye. She had known
him since she was a baby.

"I believe my minibar's still open."

"That's okay. But thanks."

"Baileys? Girls like Baileys. I know there's some of that in there. That
or Kahlúa." He ran his hand through his hair, pushing it away from his
face.

"No, really."

"Maybe it's Godiva. It's in a brownish bottle, I know that much."

"It's okay," she said.

"I'm not trying to corrupt you. Alcohol is a sleep aid." He sat down
beside her on the flowered couch, gave her a sluggish, gentle smile, and
then gazed skyward. "Ah," he said. "Much better to be sitting. So here we
are, two people who ought to be in bed. 'Bright star, would I were stead-
fast as thou art— / Not in lone splendour hung aloft the night . . . ' Are

you an insomniac? I always believed insomnia was the sign of an interesting mind."

"No," she said.

He stretched his long legs out. He was barefoot, and the dark hair on
his toes seemed foreign and private.

"Me, either. But I left all my academic reading at home, which is what
I usually rely on to knock me out. That or one of my wife's interminable
stories." Dom sipped his drink meditatively. "'Coleridge's Night Life'!"
he exclaimed. "That was the title of my paper on Coleridge's dreams. I finally remembered it. 'Sleep, the wide blessing, seemed to me / Distem-
per's worst calamity . . .'" Dom turned to her, and she could hear his
voice become earnest and professorial. "Did you know that the whole
landscape of Kubla Khan came to him in a dream? 'Twice five miles of
fertile ground / With walls and towers were girdled round / And there
were gardens bright with sinuous rills . . .'" He stopped. "Well, I don't
know how much that matters to you."

"No, really, it's nice."

"I've memorized a lot of the Romantics over the years."

"Do you know any Neruda?"

"He's not my specialty, I'm sorry," he said. "Do you like him?"

"I don't know—I guess so."

"He's a sensualist, isn't he? All those odes. I suppose that appeals to
the young. Experiences slight, but passions strong, or something like
that . . ."

"I don't feel very young."

"But you most emphatically are. You're not even twenty, are you? You
have decades and decades ahead of you."

Abby found a paper napkin tucked between the cushion and the
wicker armrest, and she brought it out and began to tear it into pieces.
She couldn't imagine being so old. Even a decade took forever—she'd be
a hundred by the time she was twenty-eight.

Dom said, "We can talk frankly, can't we? It seems like the hour for it.
I'm sure we're the only two still awake."

"Probably."

He coughed into his fist and then stared into the dark on the other side of the railing. "The truth is that I loved your mother. I really did. I used to write her letters."

Abby sat up straighter. When he didn't go on, she said, "Love letters?"

"Of a sort. Never explicit. But they were written out of love. This was a long time ago, when you were little."

Abby couldn't believe that he'd done so, and that he was telling her. "What did she do?"

Dom didn't seem to hear her. "I keep thinking about this day I drove over to your house. I was returning something, I don't remember what it was. A pan Ruth had borrowed, a pan or a bowl or something. I could have waited—it wasn't urgent—but I wanted to deliver it. I figured your mother would be at home, and your dad would be at work because he always was. It was summer, fifteen years ago at least, in that house you had on Penacook Road. Your mom's car was in the driveway, but when I rang the doorbell, no one answered. I waited for a few minutes and then I rang it again. Still nothing. And as I waited there on your porch, I realized that there was nothing in the world I wanted more than for Helen to be home and for her to open the door to me. I had the pan or the bowl or whatever in my hand, and I could have put it on the stoop. But I was in agony—I mean it. I stood there like it was the only place in the world to be and I waited. It seemed to me then that my life depended on her answering the door."

"Did she?"

"Fully half an hour later. She'd been in the backyard because you'd found a sick baby rabbit in the grass and she'd put it in a box and she was going to take it to the vet. By then I was nearly in tears."

Abby watched his profile as he stared into the darkness. His mustache sat like a small brown pelt on his lip. She watched it move when he spoke.

"She invited me in, and we sat in the kitchen, and she made me a peanut-butter-and-jelly sandwich because that's what you were having. You ate in your room, with the rabbit all wrapped up in a washcloth, crouched in your doll crib. Then she and I had a beer, sitting there in the kitchen. I kept looking at the place mat on the table—it was a plastic *Sesame Street* one, with a picture of Oscar the Grouch—because I could hardly bear to look at her. She was wearing a green dress, and her hair was in two pigtails. *I'm going to kiss her,* I said to Oscar, and Oscar said, *Don't you dare.* Oscar and I stared each other down, and he told me not to fuck with anything or I was going to be sorry. I'd written her all those letters already, and that was more than enough. So I decided it was time to go, and when I was taking my plate over to the sink, I bumped into her and then I did what I promised I wouldn't do—I set the plate down and I took her in my arms and I kissed her. For one minute I held her like that, and then she ducked away. She called goodbye from your bedroom. She was standing over you, like she was going to protect you, or like you were going to protect her. I was miserable. What had I done? But then she smiled at me, and I knew that it would be all right."

He swirled his drink, and the ice clicked against the glass. "We didn't talk about it, ever. But it was never awkward between us. I don't know. It was something that seemed, then and now, to be special."

Abby watched him take a sip of his drink with a mouth that had kissed her mother's. It had never occurred to her that her mother might be the object of some other man's desire. And had her mother desired back? Had she wanted to kiss Dom, too? Was it possible that she had loved him, even just a little? And though this mattered less, she couldn't help wondering—what had happened to the rabbit?

Beside her, Dom sighed. "A mistake of incomparable sweetness," he said.

Back then he had been young and unlined, and he had been handsome—more handsome, maybe, than her father. She wondered what Dom's body was like beneath his clothes: if it had gone wrinkled, or if it would look like a young body, only softer and hairier. She imagined the cavern of his skull with his brain inside it all gray and rippled, and she wondered what it was that made him healthy. What was the secret to not dying?

Almost without thinking, Abby leaned toward him and kissed him on the side of his mouth. She felt the shock of the warmth and the brush of mustache against her lip. His breath smelled like whiskey and like something else, too, something strange and mysterious, like his very insides. She held herself close to him for as long as she could stand it—as if, by staying there, she could learn something, about him or her mother or her own self, she didn't know—and then she pulled away and looked down at her hands, which were twisted in her lap.

"Well," Dom said. He reached up and touched her hair, then tucked a piece behind her ear. He blinked slowly; the look he gave her was tender and paternal. "I don't think it will be weird between us, either," he said.

She realized that he was in his pajama bottoms. They were thin, striped cotton things that ended high above his tanned, bony ankles, frail as an old man's. He reached for her hand, and she let him hold it. She thought she should be appalled at herself, but she was not. The rules for everything were different now.

"I'm sorry," she said.

Dom shook his head—there was nothing to be sorry about—and spoke:

"Therefore all seasons shall be sweet to thee,
Whether the summer clothe the general earth
With greenness, or the redbreast sit and sing
Betwixt the tufts of snow on the bare branch
Of mossy apple-tree, while the night hatch
Smokes in the sun-thaw; whether the eave-drops fall

Heard only in the trances of the blast,
Or if the secret ministry of frost
Shall hang them up in silent icicles,
Quietly shining to the quiet Moon.

"Let's just sit here for a while," he said. "Let's just sit and think about her for a while."

Behind them, the yellow light of the conservatory seemed to promise warmth and pleasure, though the fire had been put out and the room was empty. It was as if the great hotel slumbered behind them, and the whole world was also asleep, and they were two people who would never sit beside each other in the night again, and they were there together knowing that, yet remaining inside the fleeting bubble of their companionship.

Abby listened to Dom's breathing, the long inhale and the swifter, fuller exhale. She wondered if he was deliberately feeling the air in his lungs, calming himself. Knowing that his breaths were not yet measurable toward their end.

"I should—" she said. She meant to say "go," but for some reason she stopped herself.

"I should, too," he said, but he didn't move, not even when she got up.

She saw on the top of his dark head a tiny, tender spot where the hair had begun to thin. She watched Dom's shoulders push themselves up and then fall heavily down as he began to cry. Pity and embarrassment rooted her for a moment. Then she reached down and put her hand on his wrist. His pulse beat a light, insistent tapping, like something trying to get out. Her own grief was outside her, floating somewhere in the night.

Dom cried quietly. It was good, or almost good, to be there with him. Even after what she'd done, he still reminded her of being little again, of those nights she spent running in the field with the other daughters between the Schmidts' and the Callahans' houses. They wrote their names in the air with sparklers and watched how the letters existed and disappeared all in the same moment. They were allowed to stay up past their bedtimes, catching fireflies in Eva's pickle jars. They played tag and freeze tag and capture the flag, the sky a starry dome above them and their parents silhouetted on the porch, their voices reassuring, content. And when Abby collapsed at her mother's feet, Helen would scoop her up and put her to bed on a couch, and Abby would fall asleep with a feeling of almost unbearable happiness.

"Oh, Abby," Dom said, "I don't know . . ."

She didn't know, either, and it was very late, so she gave his arm a gentle squeeze and then she let go.

SATURDAY

After breakfast, the Callahans and the Schmidts packed their bags and had them sent down to the lobby, where they sat in a clump like presents beneath one of the orange trees. The bird-watchers were also preparing to go; they clustered on the porch in their utilitarian clothes, having filled up their notebooks and marked off the species they'd seen. "It wasn't a red-eyed vireo," one was saying, "it was a Philadelphia vireo . . ." And there again was valet Dave in his ill-fitting uniform, waiting to sling the suitcases into the trunk. Dave's compatriot had been dispatched to get the Volvo, leaving Elliott and his friends to stand around in that awkward stage of goodbye, with the farewells begun but not yet near completion.

"Did I mention how many bugs I caught last night? In my mouth?" Ruth asked.

Neil snorted. "You shouldn't have screamed so much on the turns."

"Oh please," she said. "The way you drive—"

"Ruth, your song last night was perfect," Elliott said, hoping that a compliment would help her keep her mouth closed now.

"It was a little nothing. I should have gotten you china—isn't that what you get for your twentieth? I should have gotten you some really fantastic gravy boat or something."

Dom said, "You know, I forgot to tell you this whole time—Tom Abel sends his best. I ran into him at Armond's. He's getting his pilot's license, flying prop planes out of Nashua."

"No kidding," Elliott said.

"No," said Dom.

"Well," Elliott said.

"Well," Ruth repeated.

On a bench by the front door, Helen was sitting with Eva, who had put her arms around her. Elliott felt the female emotion in the air as palpable as humidity.

The next time Elliott saw these people together in the same room he would be serving them cold cuts and Helen would be gone. He would put her picture on the mantel, and that would stand in for her. That and the clothes still in her closet, her bandannas folded in a drawer, the plants she'd watered, the pieces of paper she'd stuck to the refrigerator—a few odds and ends left in the physical world. For the first time in his life, Elliott wished he'd gotten filthy rich and correspondingly acquisitive so that there might be thousands of things for her to leave behind.

"We had a terrific time, didn't we? All that food we ate, the pool, the party . . ." he heard Eva say to Helen. "You be good. I'll come visit you in the fall."

Henry shifted from foot to foot. "Really sorry about the falling business," he said to Elliott. "A thousand dollars' worth of ballroom lessons and I can't even stay on my feet. I'm never going to hear the end of it."

"As long as you don't have to get stitches," Elliott said.

"Right. As long as I keep this bit of hair so you can't see the scar."

Neil put his arm around Henry. "Sylvie is waving goodbye to you all from her bed," he said. "She never gets up before eleven on weekends. But I know she wants to see you again. Maybe we should visit in a few weeks—fire up the old barbecue. You can't be more than three or four hours away."

"Three max," Henry said. "Come whenever."

Abby lingered on the periphery of their group, looking sleepy and uncomfortable. Elliott pulled her toward him in a gesture motivated less by affection than by possession. As his guests left, he wanted to present a united front: here they were, Abby and Elliott, allies; they would be fine.

Dom knelt at Helen's feet. "Thank you," he said. "I don't know what else to say. I can't even think of a poem."

"Oh, Dom," Helen said, wiping her eyes.

He said, "I'll miss you."

Helen put her hand on his shoulder, as if blessing him. "I'll miss you, too."

Then the Volvo was ready, its trunk open, and Dave was packing in their bags. Elliott let go of Abby, and Henry grabbed him in a fierce hug. Elliott kissed Eva and Ruth and shook hands with Dom, and then Helen and Abby joined him on the steps, and the three of them waved goodbye, goodbye, as the Volvo pulled away, everyone waving out the windows, Eva weeping softly in the backseat, a bit of exhaust from the muffler for a moment obscuring that idiotic license plate, and the bumper sticker Elliott had coaxed Henry into buying and affixing: OLD PROFESSORS NEVER DIE, THEY JUST LOSE THEIR FACULTIES. It was so stupid, but nevertheless, it gave Elliott a kick of pleasure. They curved down the long drive and then vanished behind a stand of trees.

Neil came to stand beside Elliott, well rested, untroubled, his body scented with soap and aftershave. "They're good eggs," he said. "I forgot how much I missed them."

"Good eggs," Elliott repeated.

"Hey, gorgeous," Neil said, grabbing Helen, "do you think Syl's ever going to get up? She can't have had a rougher night than me, driving in the mountains with Ruth. Did you see her, Elliott? Was she walking around with a bottle of vodka under her arm?"

"We sat by the fire in the lobby. She had a couple Kir royales." Elliott took out his cigarettes and offered one to Neil, who shook his head.

"Too early for me today."

Soon Neil would be following the snaking highway in an MG with the top down and a woman fifteen years his junior in the passenger seat, back to his Boston brownstone where two spaniels paced the halls, waiting for him. Maybe that would be enough, Elliott thought, to make Neil feel as if he could outrun death for as long as he chose.

"About that money," Neil said, pulling Elliott aside.

"No," Elliott said.

"What are you going to do?"

"What do you mean?"

Neil flapped his hands around, uncharacteristically at a loss. "I want to do something."

Elliott remembered Neil when he didn't have a single line on his brow, how the two of them walked across the Henniker College campus, surrounded by the young, themselves impossibly young—Elliott, especially, could have passed for a student then, though he'd listened to Simon & Garfunkel instead of David Bowie and Iggy Pop. Neil's first wife was plucked from the graduating class of 1974, a fact that didn't strike them as unseemly then; she was only a few years younger than he was. After Henniker, their lives had gone in opposite directions, but they had never lost touch.

"Smoke one," Elliott said, extending the pack again. "That's something."

Neil nodded and took a cigarette. "I don't know how you do it," he said.

The Duke watched as Neil and Sylvie prepared to leave. Neil was wearing a sweater with the hotel insignia on it, and Sylvie teased him that he looked like one of the Presidential employees. "It's Egyptian cotton," he said, unperturbed. "Extremely high-quality." He had also bought Elliott a heavy gold lighter with a silhouette of Mount Washington etched into it.

Sylvie had her purse slung over her arm and wore a pair of red driving moccasins. It seemed impossible that her three suitcases could fit in the tiny trunk, but Neil waved away the stumped valet; he was an expert packer, as men with fashionable women must be.

Elliott and Helen held hands in the driveway beneath the porte cochere.

"Hey," Elliott said, and then paused, unsure what to say next. The week, the ceremony, everything had used up his script of grateful phrases, even in moments when he meant them to be more than rote.

"Hey hey hey hey," Neil said.

"Thanks," Elliott said.

"For what, I don't know." Neil turned to Helen. "The most beautiful woman in New England, I love you."

Sylvie stood in front of Elliott and took his hands, squeezing them. "I'm sorry," she said softly.

"Not a word," he said. He kissed her fragrant cheek. Their night had been a gift, in a way. He was glad to have it to remember.

Neil got in his convertible and gunned the engine for his old friend's benefit, while the first woman to proposition Elliott in years waved goodbye to them. "So long, you two!" Neil called. "It was a fantastic party!" And with a final press on the gas pedal, they hurtled away, Sylvie's scarf picturesquely trailing behind.

Elliott and Helen had begun to mount the steps when they heard the shriek of brakes and turned to see the MG stopped in the road, two puffs of smoke rising up from the tires. Elliott motioned for Helen to wait and ran toward the car.

"Fuck!" Neil was saying, "fuck!" He climbed out of the car with his hands up in the air.

"What's wrong?" Elliott called as he ran.

"That bird! Christ, that fucking, motherfucking bird!"

The Duke lay on his side, a blue heap in the freshly mown grass by the side of the road. As Elliott approached, the bird lifted his head and looked wildly around. His eyes were like tiny black stones ringed in white.

"Fuck," Neil said again. "Fuck fuck fuck." Sylvie had begun to cry.

Elliott knelt on the ground beside the Duke, and he could feel the bird's confusion and fear. *I'm not going to hurt you,* he thought, *not going to hurt you.* Without touching him, Elliott inspected his body; he saw no blood, no loose feathers fluttering down the road. There was nothing to suggest that the peacock was not simply stunned.

Sylvie had opened her door and was halfway out of the car, looking not at the bird but at Neil. "He always drives too fast," she cried. "It's this stupid convertible of his—I always tell him to slow down, he's going to kill something. Look, Neil, look what you've done!"

"I can see, Sylvie," Neil said.

"Sylvie, can you go tell someone at the hotel?" Elliott asked.

She clearly wanted to keep on yelling at her husband, but for Elliott, for that good man who would never tell Neil what had or had not happened between them, she would obey. As she climbed the hill, Elliott watched the congenital swish in her hips—even halfway into a panic attack, she walked like a vamp—and remembered her breast soft and hot against his arm.

The bird let his head drop back down and his dark eye gazed up toward the clouds; the lid slid closed, paused, and then opened again. The Duke's neck was shimmering, and he wore a delicate crown on top of his head like the flourish in a woman's hat. His breath came in light but audible pants. Elliott put his hand on the bird's wing.

"Christ," Neil said.

Beneath Elliott's palm, the stiff wing quivered. Then the peacock tried to right himself: his legs scrambled for purchase on the grass and his body shook with effort, but it didn't work; he couldn't lift himself up. It was terrible to watch him struggle, and Elliott was relieved when he stopped and lay there, his rib cage rising and falling from his shallow quick breaths.

"Go after your wife, Neil," Elliott said, and Neil did as he was told.

When the Duke strained again, Elliott reached out and tucked his hand beneath the bird's body. He knew he shouldn't move him—he could hurt him more, couldn't he?—but it seemed kinder to get the Duke where he wanted to be. He lifted; the bird lifted; and then he was up. His legs were folded beneath him and he listed at an angle, but he was vertical.

"It's going to be okay," Elliott said softly. He withdrew his hand. "Everything's going to be fine."

The bird looked around, taking in everything—the sloping lawn, the darting yellow butterflies, Elliott beside him, the vast hotel in the distance, the lilies swaying in the breeze. The sun emerged from a cloud and shone down on them all with a ray of the most incredible golden intensity. Elliott could feel it touch his shoulders, then slip down his back like liquid heat. The light shone into the bird's eyes, which opened and closed and opened again in bewilderment.

Then the bird seemed to take a deep breath, and like an immense fan, his feathers slid open in a clicking glissade. Some of them brushed, sibilant, against Elliott's knee as they rose. The peacock opened his beak, but instead of crying out, he seemed to tremble deep in his body, and then this tremor rippled outward, traveling from the base of his train to the tip of his spectacular feathers, blue and green and black, all iridescent in the sunlight, and in the last moment of his life, every yearning part of him shimmered.

Then the bird convulsed and sank into the grass, and slowly, the great fan settled back down.

Elliott ran his hand along the bird's side, touching the glossy spike of his feathers. He hoped it had not hurt too much. He realized that the MG was still running, and he had a moment's desire to release the emergency brake.

In a few minutes one of the groundskeepers appeared with a wheelbarrow, and Elliott watched while the man wrapped the bird's body in a hotel sheet. The groundskeeper was stocky and gruff, not a man to be moved by such a death.

"It is too bad, though," he allowed, his eyes squinting up to meet Elliott's. "He was tamer than the last one. The last one bit." He heaved up the Duke and loaded him into the wheelbarrow.

"What are you going to do with him?" Elliott asked.

"I'll dig him a hole by the stables," the man said. "There was a horse down there he was friends with."

He grabbed the wheelbarrow's handles and then straightened up and began to roll the Duke away. The bird's train, spilling over the edge, traced lacy feathers along the soft green grass.

Abby and her mother sat by the pool in a rhododendron's flickering shade. Abby leaned over and touched her mother's hand. "Do you want to swim?" she asked. "I could go in with you."

Helen shook her head. "Too tired."

"Do you want a smoothie or an iced tea? Something from the hut over there? A banana, maybe?" Abby wanted her mother to say yes to something, because the week was almost over and she was going back to school soon, and after that there would be no offering her anything.

"No thank you." Helen lay back on her chaise longue, a magazine open on her chest, her eyes hidden behind those ugly yellow sunglasses. She was wearing a blouse that she'd made years ago out of pink and blue calico, and for some reason the careful seams and hand-sewn buttons filled Abby with sadness.

She said, "Maybe I'll ask you again in a little while. You like their smoothies. You ought to have them while you still can."

Her mother didn't answer.

"Or maybe you want to take a nap."

Abby trailed a foot in the pool, drawing swirling shapes in the turquoise water. Since their friends had gone, the hotel seemed duller and less populated, even though every few minutes another car drove up with new guests. And who would greet them now that Neil had killed the peacock? No one but Dave, Abby thought, or someone like him in one of those ridiculous uniforms.

"Yes, I could take a nap," her mother said.

There was something remote in her manner, something private and disengaged. Loneliness fell over Abby like a shadow. Here they were, the two of them, and it was as if they were on either side of a chasm. Instead of a bridge, Abby could offer only a nap or a banana.

She walked over to the drink hut, which wasn't open yet. When she was younger, she'd loved leaving her mother simply for the exquisite pleasure of the return to her—for the mad dash through the house to find her and then the leap into her arms. Later, when Abby was older, they used to sit together at the kitchen table, not even talking about anything important, just taking delight in being together. It all seemed so long ago, but it wasn't: when Abby had come home for winter break after her first semester, they'd sat at that table for hours, Pig purring on her mother's lap.

She missed her mother's attention. It was as if the cancer had finally proved that she and her mother were not two complementary sides of the same person. All along Helen had been in possession of a secret self—a part unknown to Abby, a part unwelcome and incomprehensible.

Abby went back to her chair and pulled a towel over her legs. Yesterday the weather had turned. The air was cooler and carried the smell of rain. Maybe there was nothing left to talk about except what they weren't talking about; maybe the only topic was Helen's sickness and what it meant. But Abby was afraid to bring it up. This was supposed to be fun—this was vacation. And maybe her mother didn't even think things were that bad. *Hope my mistakes don't botey you too much kiddy,* she'd written to Abby in the spring. *It'l get better.*

Abby told herself that she was here to talk to her mother, about what didn't matter. She closed her eyes and wished for the words to come, but instead she only thought of her tests: *If the wind changes direction, if I can keep from blinking for two minutes, if those boys stop doing cannonballs, then my mother will be okay.* She wondered if she should start praying.

She reached for her mother's hand. "I just—" she said.

Helen didn't move.

Abby tried again. "Do you know how much—"

She wanted to ask if her mother was afraid the way she was afraid. She also wanted to apologize.

"If I've seemed distant—" Abby said, her voice already getting caught in her throat.

She touched her mother's wrist and then moved her hand up the soft skin of Helen's inner arm. She was thinking about the drive home, and then the fall, about going back to school. As she moved her fingers along her mother's arm, she had the feeling that she was telling it goodbye.

"Darling, I know you love me," her mother said.

Abby didn't want that to be the end of the conversation. She didn't want to be so easily forgiven. But she couldn't speak anymore. Then her mother moved her arm away, and Abby felt the sudden absence of warmth.

Elliott hadn't planned out what he was going to say to his daughter, but he told himself that it didn't matter; this wasn't a speech he'd write and then fail to give. Abby was sitting on the edge of her bed with her book—still unopened—in her lap, and her dresses hanging neatly in the closet, and her shoes in a careful row beneath.

"Where's Mom?" she asked. "She said after her nap she wanted to sit in the hot tub."

He sat down on the desk chair, and Abby placed her book beside her on a pillow.

"She's still asleep. I want to talk to you about something. About your mother." He leaned forward with his elbows on his knees and his hands clasped together. It was his posture for talking to his troublemakers at Carlisle, and he'd never talked to Abby this way. When he'd grounded her, he'd done it from her doorway. He'd kept that authoritative distance.

Abby scooted back on the bed and looked down at her ankles. He had delayed, yes, but in the end he was not unprepared. He felt as if everything had been pointing to this moment, as if the innumerable coincidences and choices in a life—everything from where he should live to what drink he ought to order—had all brought him to this room, with these words lined up in his throat. His distant, confusing daughter was waiting in her thrift-store blouse, her hair in two braids so she looked fourteen instead of eighteen. One side of her face was creased and slightly red; she had been lying down. Each movement forward had brought him here.

"There was that morning your mother went for a run—" he said.

"I know what happened."

"Just listen," he said. "She went for a run, and then she came back and started to make coffee. And then she had the seizure that left her unconscious. That was when I found her in the kitchen. I took her to the emergency room at Brady, where she had another seizure. They took her away to the ICU and wouldn't let me see her. After two or three hours, they came to me and said I had to be prepared to say goodbye. I thought she might have a concussion—you know, from a slip, because it was icy that day—and then they were telling me that she wasn't going to live. I'd been annoyed at her for not being careful enough and not taking off her wet shoes, and then they were asking me if I wanted a priest. I'd been wondering if she was going to have time to get to the grocery store that day, and then they were telling me that in a matter of minutes it was probably all going to be over." He had to stop saying the same thing again and again. But he'd never told Abby that part of the story, and it seemed important that she know.

She didn't look up at him, and maybe it was easier that way. He said what he'd been needing to say to the top of her head.

"I'm not sorry I didn't tell you that before. If your mother was going to die, she was going to die in that next hour or that next minute. They were either going to be able to stabilize her or they weren't. I didn't call you because I couldn't imagine telling you that I didn't know what was going to happen to her, and that whether she was going to live or not, there was no way to get you to her fast enough. What if I did call you, and you had someone drive you to the airport, and she died while you were sitting on a runway? I told myself that if she died and I called you afterward, at least you wouldn't have had the hours of hell that I did. That would be the one thing I could do for you. That was the only thing I could protect you from, the one power I had left."

He could see that Abby had begun to cry, though she wiped the tears away fiercely.

"You didn't call me until that night."

"Because your mother stayed alive. The seizures stopped. They didn't know what was wrong, but they knew she wasn't going to die. They knew she was going to hang on."

"How did they know that?"

He sat back. "I don't remember, Abby, EKGs or an MRI or something." It was a good question, though—how *had* they known? If she'd had another seizure, that would have been the end right there.

"Why are you telling me this?"

"Because I want you to know that I have always protected you, and I have always done what I thought was right by you."

"Is that why my curfew was always two hours before anyone else's?"

He thought that she knew what was coming next and was trying to deflect it. He ignored the question.

"I've tried to do what was best, which is why I thought a long time about telling you what I'm going to say next." He took a breath. His heart was beating heavy and fast in his chest, and he could feel the adrenaline ache in his limbs. Yes, he had dreaded this, and he hadn't even known how much. "Your mother is not going to get better. There was a time when I thought that she would."

"What are you saying?"

Was she going to make him spell it out? *She will experience continuing loss of motor control and cognitive function, culminating in unconsciousness and death.* "Your mother's cancer is terminal," he said, and with those few words, he felt as if he had raised a stick in the air and was beating his daughter with it.

Abby didn't say anything. She fell over on her side, then slid off the end of the bed onto the floor where he couldn't see her.

He sat in the chair, staring at the wall, feeling his own grief swirling around inside him. It made his head hurt. Then he went to where she was and reached out to her, but she scooted away until she was half under the bed.

"I'm trying to protect her like I tried to protect you. She doesn't—she can't—know this. For now she has to believe she can win." He became aware that his hands were clenched, and as he opened them, his knuckles popped one by one. "Abby," he said, but she shook her head and tried to move farther away. "Abby . . ."

She wanted to be left alone, and he understood that. When comfort is impossible, why pretend to accept the charade of it? But it broke his heart to see her like that, inconsolable on the faded carpet. He put his hand on her back; he couldn't help it. It was still, as if she weren't breathing at all.

He said, "It's not the end yet." *In cases like these, a cure should not be considered the only successful outcome of treatment.*

She made no indication that she had heard him. He ran his hand over her shirt and realized what a long time it had been since he had really touched her.

When he'd heard, he'd fallen to his knees, hadn't he? Though in most recollections of that day, he kept himself in the chair, the truth was that he'd slipped out of it and knelt before the doctor's desk as he had once knelt before an altar draped in velvet and fragrant with incense.

"Please go," Abby said after a little while. "Please, please, please."

And because he adored her and was utterly unable to help her, he did what she asked him to. That night he ate dinner with only his wife, the way it had all begun.

When Abby woke, it was dark, and there was a fleeting, blissful moment inside that darkness when she didn't know why she was lying on the floor; she was conscious only of being stiff and cold. When she remembered, the sick feeling washed over her again and propelled her to her feet, so that she stood, unsteady and sore, at her window. In the gardens below, there were kids with sparklers running between the gas lamps, trailing streaks of light. She watched them dart and dodge each other and wondered if she should jump. Whether doing so would kill her or just hurt very badly.

She had been so impossibly stupid. She'd been looking for signs to reassure her about her mother—she'd asked *rocks*, for God's sake, she'd thought *birds* held the answer—while the whole time it had been obvious what was going on. She'd just chosen not to understand. She'd told herself that her father, like her, was waiting in hopeful ignorance for things to get better. But that had never been the case, because while she was away at college, he had been taking her mother to doctor after doctor, and during one of those appointments, someone in a white coat would have looked at the data and said, *I'm sorry, this doesn't look curable.*

Quietly she opened the door to her parents' room. Though it was only ten o'clock, they were two unmoving shapes on their bed. Light from the muted TV flickered on the wall behind them. Her mother slept deeply, with her mouth open and her arm dangling off the edge. Her father was asleep, too, his back to Helen. There were postcards in a neat stack on her mother's side of the bed, a granola bar, a single white pill, a bottle of lotion. By her father's side was an empty highball glass.

Abby hadn't seen them like this since she was little and seeking solace from a bad dream, and she was surprised not by their vulnerability but by their solidity, their adultness, even in this helpless sleep: the long curve of her father's back, the slow sigh of her mother's breath. She moved carefully into the room, but she knew they wouldn't wake. From the dresser she took her mother's purse by its shabby cloth straps, and from the top of the television set she grabbed the wig in its plastic bag.

Back in her room, there was a note on her floor that she ignored. It didn't matter anymore what Alex thought of her or what he wanted from her; she would never see him again. She pulled the desk chair into the bathroom and perched herself on its edge before the sink.

She was conscious of a low, hard ache in her stomach, but it seemed as if the pain belonged to another person, a person who was living inside her. That person was shaking and weeping and maybe even dying of grief, but she, Abby, was unscrewing the cap of her mother's foundation and pouring a puddle of it into her palm and rubbing it into her face. Then she was putting on her mother's gold eye shadow, swiping it onto her lids and up toward her brow bone.

After she was done with that, Abby took Helen's eyeliner and drew careful horizontal brown lines into her forehead, and then she pressed the tip of the pencil to the corner of her nose and drew a line down to each side of her mouth, blending it in so that it looked like a shadow. She put a few dark strokes in the places where her eyes wrinkled when she smiled. Through the tears that blurred her vision, she saw a face like her mother's, maybe a bit older. A face like her mother's in ten years, ten years that she wouldn't live.

But even as she drew her mother's face onto her own, Abby could feel the theatricality of the gesture, not far beneath the surface of what she meant to be only an expression of grief. This made her ashamed but did not make her stop; she moved as if this were a ritual both familiar and meaningful. After applying her mother's lipstick and two blotches of blush, she reached for the wig. The curls gave way beneath her hands before springing back to their places. She tucked her hair into a bun and slid the wig onto her head.

Then she returned to her bed and sat on its edge as if waiting for something. She thought, *This will be a story I'll tell.* Some time passed, and she thought about her father, and she wondered if he'd assumed she would figure everything out for herself. And when she didn't—and how could she? it was beyond imagining—he'd finally had to tell her because her ignorance was starting to be ridiculous.

There was a soft knock at her hallway door, but she didn't acknowledge it. A few minutes later the knock came again, and then a voice whispered, "Abby?"

She stayed where she was. If she was very still, the person inside her would remain quiet, and she could exist like this, stuporous, anesthetized, in a kind of deep limbo. She was conscious mainly of the wig's heat, its strange itchy weight upon her head, and the waxy taste of her mother's lipstick.

"What happened to you?" Vic said.

He was in the room somehow, in his kitchen uniform, looking confused and not handsome at all.

"Abby?" Vic said. "Abby?" He put out his hand to touch her but then he turned and went into the bathroom.

She heard the sound of water running and a small soap being unwrapped. Vic came out with a washcloth in his hand and whispered, "Close your eyes," so she did, and she felt the warm wetness as he drew it across her eyes and lips and cheeks. The cloth was rougher than she'd thought it would be; it was like being licked by a giant cat's tongue. Around her face it went, wiping, wiping, and he held her chin to keep it steady. He patted her dry with a towel, and then he lifted the wig away and unclipped her barrette, sending a tickling cascade of her own hair down her back.

"There," he said. "That's better."

She opened her eyes and saw that his uniform was covered with flecks of chopped parsley and stained green near the pockets. "You don't look that good yourself," she said.

He sat down next to her on the bed and put his arms around her shoulders, and she remembered what it had been like in the hallway of that awful party. How he'd overwhelmed her then, just by being alive and male, by wearing a flannel shirt that brushed against her fingers, by breathing the same air that she did, by putting his mouth on hers. How that kiss had been a gate that she'd walked through, and after that, she had found herself in a place where, for a little while, she had loved him.

"Tell me," he said.

She shook her head, and his grip tightened.

"Please."

She managed to say, "I'm sure you know. I'm sure everyone knew but me."

"Knew what?"

She couldn't say "die," or "death," or any of those words like that. "That she isn't going to be all right."

"I thought—" he said. "I wondered— I'm so sorry."

Abby pulled away from him and lay down on the bed. Vic brought the chair in from the bathroom and sat facing her. His tears made two tracks down his cheeks. He didn't move to wipe them away, as if he wanted her to see them. And what for? So she would cry, too? And if she started again, when would she ever stop? She turned her face to the wall.

How little Dom's grief had meant to her—then again, she hadn't known why he was crying. She'd thought it was overindulged nostalgia, or maybe too much Scotch. But he'd known, hadn't he? He'd known and he hadn't told her; no one had told her, and they'd let her walk around and eat her dinner and sit by the pool in complete and utter denial of the most obvious of facts.

After a while Vic got up, and she heard him open the window. "You know you can climb out on the roof," he said. "There's a fire escape at the end of the hall, and from there you can reach a ledge. Once you're on it, you can walk all the way around the hotel, a hundred feet up. You can see everything." When she didn't answer, he went on, "That was the kind of thing I used to get in trouble for. Trespassing."

He stopped, and she heard him blow his nose quietly. She dug her face into the bed, into the pillows that smelled like bleach.

"I do remember you, you know," he said. "From school."

"No you don't," she said into the sheets.

"I do. You sat with that girl Frances at lunch, over by the door to the hall."

"I never had a conversation with you."

"No," Vic said. "You didn't."

"But you kissed me," she said.

"What?"

She could tell he'd turned to face her, but she didn't look at him. She kept staring at the wall. "There was a party at Calvin Miller's house and you kissed me in a hallway."

"You're kidding," he said.

"No, I'm not. You did."

He paused. "I'm sorry," he said. "I don't remember. I must have been really drunk."

She decided she wouldn't tell him that he hadn't known her name. It was a long time ago, and she could forgive him because it didn't matter at all anymore. "Tell me about the canoe," she said. She just wanted him to talk.

"What?"

"The canoe. I want to hear about the canoe."

"Um," he said. She could hear him tap his fingers along the windowsill. Probably he was still trying to bring back that party. "Do you really want to know?"

"Yes," she said.

"It was my grandpa's idea. It's made out of birchbark from the woods around his place. There's a cedar frame—ribs, sheathing, that kind of thing. He wanted to make it traditional, like how the Indians made theirs."

"Go on," she said, and she half listened as he told her how they stripped the bark from the birch trees and how they used boiling water and stones to fit it around the form they wanted for the canoe's bottom, and by the time he was telling her about the split spruce root that the bark was sewn together with, she felt as if she had passed through another gate and was in another place she had never been before. She looked at her hands, flat against the wallpaper, and while she knew they were hers, she did not recognize them.

Vic's voice swung into her consciousness—*We spread the spruce gum over the seams*—and then veered away again.

She could see her shadow on the flowered paper: the rise of her shoulder, the dip at her waist, another hill at her hip. She pressed her feet and her hands into the wall and pushed, and the bed slid a ways into the room.

"Should I stop talking?" he asked.

"No," she said.

She went to join him at the window. There was a dead moth on the sill and she flicked it away, watching its white body twist into the dark like a scrap of paper. They stood side by side, gazing out of the hotel onto the lit night grounds like prisoners.

"I'm so sorry," he whispered. "I loved her, too."

Outside the world was cloaked in shades of black and white, and there were people sitting on the patio and kids running around waving sparklers, and as she looked down on them, she understood that she wasn't at all like them anymore. She wasn't even the same species—she was something older and more ponderous and a thousand times more sad. She was like a rock or a tree, mute and powerless. She wondered whether Vic would understand that if she tried to tell him. It was possible that he would.

Without thinking she shrugged her dress off her shoulders, and it slipped down her body onto the floor. The cool air made goose bumps rise on her skin.

"What are you doing?" Vic said.

She didn't answer him because she didn't know. Why had she ever done anything? Below them, sparklers sputtered and dimmed, and more were lit. A single shout rose up to where they were.

She felt Vic's shyness, and her shyness met it, and for a while they were motionless inside their awkwardness. Then Abby reached back and unhooked her bra, and she let that, too, fall to the carpet. Vic took her hand, and she couldn't tell if he was trying to stop her or urging her on. Still they gazed out the window while his fingers tucked themselves between hers. Clouds slid in from the south, obscuring the stars one by one.

"Take off your shirt," she said, and without very much hesitation, he obeyed.

They turned to face each other. She reached her arm out to his waist and held it just above his belt. He brought a hand up to her cheek, and they stood together with all that space between them until she stepped forward, and her body pressed against his body, and above her head she heard him sigh. She was conscious of a heaviness lifting and of a strange calm taking its place, a dim, primal knowledge that there was something to be done now and she would know how to do it and she would not be alone inside that knowing.

She felt her breasts against his chest, his breath stirring her hair, and his hands, still uncertain, meeting each other at her shoulder blades. She took a step backward, pulling him toward the bed, and he came with her awkwardly; they fell onto the covers.

"We have to get under the blankets. They never wash the comforters," Vic whispered. He took off his pants so that he was in his boxers and his socks, and they slid under the sheets and faced each other, almost naked, and Abby wasn't sure how to do what she knew came next, but she was aware of a seriousness of purpose: she must finish the task. She felt the fear of the little person inside her, and there was another part of her up by the ceiling, looking down on herself with a gentle but clinical curiosity.

Vic touched her face with the tip of his finger, moving from her brow to her nose to her cheeks; when his finger came to her lips, she pushed it away and brought his face toward hers.

When the rest of their clothes came off, and when he positioned himself on top of her and pressed his body into hers, she felt like it was real and true and also that it was happening between two people in another universe. In the dark room he looked down at her tenderly and she held his hips and it hurt and she was not sorry, she was not sorry, she was not sorry.

But afterward, while Vic slept, she cried for what had happened, and for all the things that were still to come.

SUNDAY

Elliott felt the first glimmer of fall that day. That happened in New England sometimes—autumn seemed to arrive suddenly in mid-August. He wore his camera on a macramé strap that Helen had made years ago, and he carried water, trail mix, Ensure. He led his family down a well-groomed path, its dips and hollows smoothed and its pebbles swept away by the hotel groundskeepers.

The green crowns of the trees waved in the chilly breeze and a stream rustled along beside them. Seeing the water, Helen decided that she wanted to wade in it. Off the path, the way was steep, littered with branches and slick with leaves and ivy.

"Helen, please, no," Elliott said. "Please don't, it's not safe."

But she was already on her way. She eased one foot and then the other down the slope, grabbing the trunk of a tree to steady herself. She paused and then moved forward again, feeling for the next tree. Three feet from the water, there was nothing left for her to hold.

"*Goddammit,*" Elliott said. He was just so tired—so profoundly, irrevocably tired.

But he went to her, and she reached out to clutch his arm. Carefully, the two of them picked their way to the edge of the stream. Once there, Helen sat on a rock, removed her shoes and socks, and stuck her toes in. "It's cold!" she said happily.

A bird swooped by, scooping up bugs, and an orange newt, its tail a tiny question mark, scurried halfway up a maple sapling. A few leaves sifted down and swirled past his wife like miniature boats. She kicked her feet, flinging water droplets onto the rocks, and he thought again of their honeymoon—the musty tent, the river they'd skinny-dipped in. That was the first time he'd seen her naked in daylight. How her hair had been slick down her back and her whole body had glistened, and how he had been amazed at what stupendous gifts life could bring him.

"Are you ready to keep going?" Elliott asked after a few minutes.

"Okay," she said.

He helped her put on her shoes and socks, and then he helped her stand, and then he helped her walk up the five-foot hill back to the path, where Abby was waiting.

Emboldened by her adventure, Helen walked on faster, humming to herself. Elliott stopped his daughter when she tried to follow. Abby shrank at first from his touch, then stood quietly beside him.

"Stay with me for a bit," he said.

Her father's hand was soft on her arm. He said, "Let her go on ahead."

Abby didn't want to, but she obeyed him, waiting as her mother walked away. When Helen was a few more feet up the path, Elliott lifted his camera and took a single picture.

"All right," Abby said. "I'll get her now."

"Stay here for just a little longer," he said.

Helen stopped to pluck a black-eyed Susan, and Abby dug the heel of her sandal into the dirt. She could hear her mother's low, atonal hum, and the sound seemed to hover in the air like the scroll of smoke from her father's cigarette. As both faded—her mother too far ahead now, her father done with his Merit—she felt possessed of a new, savage clarity. A sparrow, startled from the underbrush, twittered up into the cold morning.

Her father lifted the camera again and fussed with the shutter speed.

Abby pulled her sweater tighter around her shoulders. She thought of Vic, who'd slipped from her room while she was still half asleep. How the night before, standing by the open window, he had unbuttoned his shirt, and how he had kissed each one of her fingers, and how, when they lay down, he had been careful and tender. She'd loved him then.

The stream whispered along, hidden behind the slender spines of birch and ash. She bent and picked up a rock. *If I can hit the creek . . .* It was pointless now. It had always been pointless. Still, though, she aimed and threw.

Her mother got a little farther away, a little less substantial beneath the cathedral arch of the trees. She didn't need their help, and she didn't look back. Elliott took another picture, waited for a minute, and took another. Helen got smaller and smaller in her new bright clothes. The wind stirred the leaves, and water came shivering down on them.

"Okay," Elliott said, letting the camera fall to his chest. "That's good for now."

Helen can hear the birds calling out to one another, and a line from an old Joan Baez song comes to her like a gift: "I will try to be your glad bluebird of happiness." She should ask Abby to sing it for her. Abby knows all the old songs.

The pale light is like molten silver, and each water droplet clinging to a leaf holds the entire trembling world inside it. It seems that always there has been this moment and her life moving toward it—a clean, bright morning, the people she loves nearby. Everything that happened before comes back to her in such dim traces that she can hardly tell what was in sleep and what was in life; it is like a dream inside a dream of living.

She takes a deep breath. The world is beautiful, and she is so glad she has seen it. She stretches out her arms in the cool air. She hears footsteps, and she knows that her daughter and her husband are jogging up the path to meet her—and here they come, and here they are, and now they are beside her, holding her hands.

Acknowledgments

I am grateful to Heather Abel, Rachel Graham Cody, Jennifer Gilmore, and Johnny Marciano, both for reading early drafts and their abiding friendship; to Sarah Adams, Ingrid Binswanger, Mark Chin-Shong, Holly Cundiff, Mark Hansen, Farrin Jacobs, Katharine Johnson, David Kennedy, Maud Macrory Powell, Camela Raymond, Carole and Dick Raymond, Storm Tharp, Betsy Tripi, and Laurie Volm for being there in important moments; to Daniel Menaker, Henry Dunow, Laura Ford, and Jynne Martin for being brilliant professionals and dear friends; to the KGB Sunday Night Fiction Series, my former students and colleagues at Scattergood Friends School, and my many teachers at Swarthmore and Columbia for inspiration and support; and to the extended Chenoweth and McWilliams families, as well as my parents' friends, for their kindness and generosity. Thank you to my beloved family—my dad, my brother, and my late mother—for everything. Thank you to Jon Raymond for being my companion in writing and in life. And to Eliza, for just being.

ABOUT THE AUTHOR

EMILY CHENOWETH is a former fiction editor at *Publishers Weekly.* Her work has appeared in *Tin House, Bookforum,* and *People,* among other publications. She lives in Portland, Oregon.

ABOUT THE TYPE

This book was set in Garamond, a typeface
originally designed by the Parisian typecutter
Claude Garamond (1480–1561). This version
of Garamond was modeled on a 1592 specimen
sheet from the Egenolff-Berner foundry, which
was produced from types assumed to have been
brought to Frankfurt by the punchcutter Jacques
Sabon.

Claude Garamond's distinguished romans
and italics first appeared in *Opera Ciceronis* in
1543–44. The Garamond types are clear, open,
and elegant.